Valor on the Move

Also by Keira Andrews

Valor on the Move

BY KEIRA ANDREWS

Valor on the Move

Written and published by Keira Andrews
Cover by Dar Albert
Formatting by BB eBooks

© 2015 by Keira Andrews

ISBN: 978-0-9940924-3-4
Print Edition

This is a work of fiction. Names, characters, businesses, places, events and incidents are either the products of the author's imagination or used in a fictitious manner. No persons, living or dead, were harmed by the writing of this book. Any resemblance to any actual persons, living or dead, or actual events is purely coincidental.

Dedication

Many, many thanks to Anne-Marie, Anara, Becky, Jules, Mary, and Rachel for their fantastic beta reading and friendship. And a big thank you to Annabeth Albert, who inspired me to dust off this story idea and bring it to life.

Chapter One

S OMEDAY WHEN PEOPLE ask what it was like growing up gay in the White House, Rafael Castillo will tell them it sucked donkey balls.

And not in a good way, for the record. (Not that Rafa had any desire to fellate a donkey, but he was keenly interested in going down on a guy before his own balls went so blue they shriveled up and fell off.)

"Babe, I'd better get to sleep. It's, like, ass o'clock in the morning over here." Ashleigh yawned loudly. "Glad you made it home from the bullshit seminar okay."

Home. Even after seven years, it was still weird to think of the White House that way. "Thanks. Have fun eating croissants and reading existential poetry by the Seine. Or whatever people do in Paris on their days off." Rafa twisted his foot in his sheet idly, staring at the old Kelly Slater surfing poster he'd had up since they moved in. His mother had forbade thumbtacks and insisted on framing it in tasteful red wood on the pale cream wall.

Ashleigh laughed. "I've been telling you what people do in Paris for two hours, and I did not once mention pastry or angsty poetry. But it is all rather glamorous, I admit. Even as a lowly intern, it's still *Vogue*. I got to take home a negligee from the closet. That is the legendary *Vogue* closet, by the way."

"Ohh la la." He pitched his voice low. "Are you wearing it

now?"

Her voice went husky. "Sure am. It's lacy and black and almost completely see-through." She paused. "What are you wearing, lover?"

He laughed. "The usual." With Ash, he could talk and have fun and not have to think about every word. He wished it were so easy with the rest of the world, but Ashleigh was really the only person who knew him. The *real* him.

"Hmm. Since you're in your room where no one can see you, I'm guessing you've traded your usual slacks and button-down for boxers and a Yankees T-shirt with some kind of food stain on it."

"Close. It's an old UVA tee from freshman orientation. Stain is of the pizza variety."

"*Hot.* And hey, tell your dad thanks again for pulling those strings, okay?"

"I will when he gets back from wherever." Rafa glanced at the digital clock on his bedside table. Just past eleven, so perfect timing. Downstairs should be nice and quiet.

"When was the last time you talked to him?"

"I thought you wanted to go to sleep?"

Ashleigh huffed, and he could imagine the roll of her eyes. "Answer the question."

"I dunno. A few weeks ago. He's been busy. You know—the G7, the Karelian peace talks, backslapping with the NRA. Anyway, get to sleep. Glad you met a friend who loves Renaissance art as much as you do."

"Yeah, me too. I think it's going to be a fun summer. Love you, babe."

"Love you too, Ash."

He tapped off the phone and tossed it on the bed beside him, chuckling to himself. While Ashleigh appreciated Michelangelo as much as the next person, the staff who monitored his calls must have marveled over her passion for it. While he knew the Secret

Service and White House staffers didn't care about his personal life and were only interested in protecting the president and his family, Rafa still maintained the charade at all times.

He and Ash had come up with the code not long after they'd started dating—or should he say "dating." In their secret language, motorcycles filled in for hot guys. For example, if Rafa said, "I saw a gorgeous ride today—a Ducati with red trim," that meant he'd spotted a sexy redhead he wanted to bang. Anyone who shared Ash's interest in Renaissance art was a lesbian she wanted to hook up with.

At first it had been a fun game to talk in code, but now it was just normal. Most importantly, it was effective, since it had been three years and they hadn't been outed. They'd played their roles as young lovers perfectly, and it had served them both well. Ashleigh hadn't been ready to come out to her incredibly conservative parents, and Rafa couldn't either. Not yet, anyway.

Most of the world might have come a long way on the subject of gay rights, but the neoconservatives in the States had pushed back hard. A Republican president with a gay son living in the White House? It would have been a nightmare for his father, let alone for him. Rafa had about seven months to go in DC until the new president's inauguration in January, and then he was free.

He wished Ash had been at the young leaders' summer seminar his mother had forced him to suffer through after his exams. Sitting in lectures just wasn't the same without his best friend.

While the rest of the class in Intro to American Studies at UVA in freshman year had stared and whispered furtively, splitting their attention between Rafa and the Secret Service agents in khakis and polos at the back of the lecture hall (who were *not* blending in even a little), Ashleigh had plopped next to him and started complaining about the water pressure in her dorm. She'd also inquired as to whether his "goons" could kill her snoring roommate and make it look like an accident.

Yawning, Rafa stretched out on the mattress. Before he'd moved in at fourteen, there'd been a four-poster bed in his room, complete with canopy. Fortunately they'd redecorated in tasteful earth tones of rich, reddish brown and green, and his bed was canopy-free. They'd even redone the ensuite bathroom for him in gleaming white and silver. Aside from the surfing poster, it might have been a hotel room.

He'd already unpacked, and everything was neatly tucked away in his closet and shiny mahogany dresser. His sister Adriana's room had typically looked akin to a hurricane disaster zone, but Rafa always kept his neat and tidy. Their parents had insisted they be responsible for keeping their own rooms and bathrooms clean, and the fewer things he gave them to criticize, the better.

After getting up and yanking on his jeans and sneakers, Rafa took a quick glance in the mirror, frowning at his stupid freckles, already more prominent even though summer had just begun. His thick, dark brown hair tended to curl, and after his evening shower he hadn't parted it and slicked it back with his usual extra-strength pomade.

He brushed the gentle curls off his forehead, making a mental note to ask Henry, the chief usher, to get the barber in since there were waves forming just above his ears. And the last thing Rafa needed was to be called a Chia Pet again.

His cheeks still got hot when he thought about the internet meme with his face Photoshopped on a fuzzy ceramic animal with bushy chia growing from it. He'd just started his new high school in Washington mid-year after his father's inauguration, and at fourteen he'd been gangly and pimply with a mouth full of metal.

Suddenly his new classmates would say "Ch-ch-ch-Chia!" when he came into a room, and he hadn't even gotten the joke until he'd Googled it. The kids at school had usually been nice to him, but they'd gotten a kick out of the meme. Even though Rafa had cut his hair an inch from his scalp the next day, the nickname had stuck.

He edged open the door and peeked out of his room—officially known as Bedroom 303. There was really no need for stealth since the second and third floors of the residence in the White House were the only place in the world he had freedom from his Secret Service detail, but it was a habit.

His eldest brother Christian's room was across the center hall, but Chris was twenty-seven and hadn't ever really lived at the White House full time. Now he was in New York, and Rafa was alone up on the third floor as usual. To his left were the Music Room and Workout Room.

As he headed to the stairs he passed the Cedar Room, a little space paneled entirely of cedar that had been used for winter storage back in the day, and the Linen Room, which was exactly what it sounded like. The Game Room sat on the other side of the hall, and a few bedrooms dotted the rest of the level.

Behind the Linen Room was his favorite place in the whole world—the Diet Kitchen. The dictionary said a diet kitchen was used to prepare special meals for invalids in a hospital. FDR had the Diet Kitchen built because he'd hated the housekeeper's food and wanted his own meals made there.

Rafa went down the little passageway. The small rectangular kitchen was right over the north portico, and the moon shone through the skylights in the sloped roof. Along with a stove, fridge, and sink, a counter and cupboards wrapped around the space. Rafa didn't need to turn on the light to navigate it, and he ran his hand over the smooth counters.

It was a basic kitchen, and he had no special or fancy equipment. But it was *his*. At least for the time being. Most of the year he was stuck in his dorm, and he itched for the sizzle of butter in the pan and freshly ground spices in the air. He'd make the pasta tomorrow and roll it out in sheets to create ravioli, but he could start on the filling tonight.

Rafa went back to the center hall and tiptoed down to the ground floor, using the back stairs next to the family elevator. These stairs went almost right to the kitchen, but one of his agents still appeared, straightening his suit jacket.

"Heading out?" Brent asked. He was tall and a little paunchy, and his dark hair was graying.

"Just getting a snack. I won't be long."

Brent nodded. "Thanks for letting me know, Rafa."

Rafa continued into the darkened kitchen. It was blissfully empty, and he exhaled. If he'd been Adriana or their brother Matthew, Brent would have probably followed in a minute to double check that they weren't trying to sneak out. Not that they'd be able to get past the gate, but just being outside on the grounds without their detail was a big no-no. But Rafa had never tried to give his agents the slip. They were only doing their jobs, and there was no sense in being a pain.

Low lights under cabinets cast shadows over the counters and huge island, and he could see well enough to keep the overhead lights off. As he opened the door to the walk-in fridge, his pulse raced. Goosebumps immediately spread over his bare arms, and the light automatically came on over his head. He surveyed the shelves quickly, scanning the containers for what he needed. He was sure Magda would keep prosciutto on hand, and hoped he'd luck out on the goat cheese. She never minded if he borrowed a few ingredients.

Okay, it was technically stealing, not *borrowing*. His parents paid for all the food the family ate that wasn't for an official state function or party, and he knew the ingredients he snuck out were added to their tab. In the early days, Chris had had his college friends over for a party while their parents were out of town, one of his rare displays of rebellion. He'd ordered a ton of snacks from the kitchen, and their parents had made him pay back every penny.

Rafa would happily buy the prosciutto and cheese himself, but then there would be the inevitable questions. He couldn't just drop into the ShopRite. His detail would know, and if his mom asked them, he didn't want them to have to lie. Besides, it was a dumb thing to even ask them to lie about. It was easier to just make do.

He grabbed a log of goat cheese and moved to the walk-in freezer. He kept the door open, shivering as he surveyed the shelves for prosciutto. "Come on, come on…" He went through what little meat there was, hoping Magda kept some emergency ham on hand. Most ingredients were fresh, and it looked like he was shit out of luck.

Over the hum of the industrial fan, heels clacked a moment before he heard, "Darling, shouldn't you be in bed?"

He jumped despite himself, blinking into the blank darkness of the kitchen as he tucked the goat cheese onto the shelf by his hand. His mother's tall silhouette moved into the freezer doorway, and Rafa forced a smile. "Just getting a snack." He reached for the nearest carton of ice cream. Had she bribed Brent to narc on him? Not that First Lady Camila Castillo needed to grease the wheels— she only need ask, and most people were too terrified not to comply immediately.

"Good idea. Still need to put some meat on those bones." She said it with a smile, but a hot rush of embarrassment washed over him. He'd grown to almost six feet during college, and though he'd put on muscle over the years, he still felt like he had knobby knees and elbows. He hunched his shoulders as he closed the freezer door.

Rafa went to one of the many cutlery drawers for a spoon, feeling his mother's eyes on him. When he glanced up, she raised her hand to the string of pearls around her neck. Even in the low light, they shone. She wore an unwrinkled pencil skirt and white blouse, and her black hair was sculpted into an up-do. Sometimes he suspected she slept in a hermetically sealed tube especially designed not to muss her hair.

"Still working, Mom? Shouldn't you be in bed too?" Camila Castillo had many rules, one of which was to always dress appropriately for the task at hand. If she was working, she was dressed for success, no matter how late or early it might be.

"Touché. But yes, I have quite a bit of foundation business to take care of before my next trip."

"Why don't you let your staff do it? Isn't that what they get paid for?"

She smiled, her lipstick shimmering. "Sometimes to have a task done right, one must do it oneself."

Since he'd likely done plenty of things wrong lately, Rafa changed the subject and asked, "How's Aunt Gabby?"

"She's well. Visiting her cousins."

His mother had a habit of talking about her extended family as relations of her sister and brother, but not her own. "In Mexico City? How long is she there?" Rafa twirled his spoon. His grandparents had all passed away by the time he was old enough to really know them, and he hadn't seen his Aunt Gabriella since Christmas. Granted, he didn't see her much. She'd never gotten along with his father, and he felt like his mother thought her family was simply far too...*ethnic*. "Maybe I could—"

"Darling. You know how dangerous it can be there. It's not a good idea."

"But I've still never been. It can't be *that* dangerous. I mean, you lived there when you were little."

His mother's full name was Camila Castillo de Saucedo, but after his father had quit his law firm and gone into politics full time to make a run at the Jersey governorship, she'd dropped the traditional Mexican naming convention. Rafa and his siblings had always just been Castillo, his father's name. His parents had worked hard to make them into the whitest, most non-threatening

Hispanics Republican money could buy while still courting the Latino vote with great success. He still wasn't sure how they'd pulled it off, but here they were.

"Besides, I'd have my detail, Mom."

She tilted her head, looking at him with clear exasperation. "We've discussed this before. My parents left the old world behind to make a new life for us here in America." For a moment he was afraid she might launch into her full American dream speech. "Why would I ever want to go back? Or want my children to go back? This is your home. The greatest country in the world."

Before she could really get going, Rafa nodded. "Yeah, okay. You're right. As always." He smiled.

"Of course I am." She laughed softly and then was silent for a moment. "Well, I wanted to tell you I had a chat with your detail leader today."

Rafa's heart skipped a beat even though he hadn't done anything wrong. "Okay." He dug his spoon into the carton and stuffed his mouth with mint chocolate chip so he didn't have to say anything else.

She grimaced. "A bowl, Rafael, please. Let's be civilized, shall we?"

He mumbled, "Sorry," through his ice cream and pulled down a bowl from one of the cupboards. "You want some?"

"No, dear." She patted her trim waist. "As I was saying, there's going to be a change to your detail starting tomorrow."

Rafa paused with his spoon hovering over the carton. "What kind of change?"

"Five of the agents are being reassigned, and you'll only have two agents total at a time with you."

"Who's being reassigned?" His twenty-four-hour detail had three rotating shifts with two primary agents who stayed close to him when he was outside the White House, and at least one or two secondary agents on point, depending on where he was going and the threat level.

"I'm not sure." She waved her hand dismissively, her polished nails catching the light. "It doesn't matter, does it?"

He scooped a few blobs of ice cream into the bowl. "It matters to me. I get to say goodbye, right? I want to say goodbye."

She sighed. "Darling, you know this is why they change our details every year. We can't get too attached. The agents are less effective when we do. We're all being switched."

With his mother on one side of the island, Rafa stood across from her. He filled his mouth before he could snort derisively. The Secret Service changed their detail teams every year so the agents wouldn't get too attached to *them*, but no one was under any illusions that would happen with Camila. The only time she remembered any of their names was to order them to perform some menial task not in their job description.

He could only imagine how eager her agents were to be reassigned. But Rafa's agents had always seemed to like him. Not that they'd show it if they didn't.

"But it's June now, and the election's in November. We'll be gone in January. Why change now? We're almost done."

"The more experienced agents are needed with the candidates' families, especially as the election draws nearer. Livingston has six children, and all those grandchildren. Apparently they need to beef up security. We all know he's going to win, whether we like it or not."

Camila Castillo most decidedly did not like it. Rafa ate another spoonful so he wouldn't smile. His mother would clutch her pearls if she knew he was totally going to vote for Democrat Stephen Livingston instead of his father's Republican successor, Tom Margulies. The country was ready for a regime change, even though nothing would really change at all with Congress and the Senate so partisan. Having been at the heart of the American government half his life, Rafa found it all rather depressing how little ever changed for the better.

"I still want to say goodbye to my agents." With a pang, he hoped Joanna and Stuart weren't going. "I guess it makes sense, though."

She sighed, and her voice was unusually sad. "Yes, I suppose. Soon we'll be out on our ear." If she could, Rafa's mother would surely hang on to the White House until they pried it from her cold, dead hands. Abe Lincoln's ghost was definitely going to end up with some company down the road. Rafa could already imagine his mother floating around the sedate hallways, passing judgment on future First Ladies' choice of china patterns.

"Mom, we had two terms. Not too shabby. Won't it be nice to get back to regular life?" It was beyond weird to think of his parents moving back to New Jersey. "You must miss it, right? Even a little?" he asked hopefully. He didn't like to think of her unhappy.

She smiled. "A little."

Leaning across the island, he held out a spoonful of ice cream. "Come on. One bite won't hurt."

"I suppose not." She met him halfway and gracefully took the spoon. After she swallowed, she stared at the curved metal. "It'll all just seem so…small. I…" She stopped.

Rafa barely whispered, holding his breath. "What?" He couldn't remember the last time he'd seen his mother anything but perfectly poised and on message.

"It's a strange feeling, to know the most important days of your life have gone by." She kept her eyes on the spoon. "That you'll never do anything else that could possibly compare."

"Mom…" Rafa wanted to reach out to her, but as he moved, her gaze snapped up and she smiled, her mask back in place.

"Never mind that silliness. Have you talked to Ashleigh? How's she enjoying Paris?" She held the spoon back over the island.

He took it and played with the melting ice cream in his bowl. "It's good. She loves it."

"Won't you be lonely all summer?"

"It's fine. We still talk all the time."

"Rafa, just be sure you stay connected. This is a crucial time in your relationship as you go into your last semester of university. You have to plan for the future. We need to talk about where you'd like to start your career in the new year. Your father and I have some ideas. Why don't you tell me more about what you learned at the seminar? We haven't discussed it properly."

"I told you it was good."

She raised a delicately penciled eyebrow. "That's all you have to say about it?"

What he wanted to say was: *Actually, I hated every minute. I don't want to be a young leader, or make connections and smile and pretend to be interested in goddamned politics or the Republican Party. But it counted as an extra half credit, and I've worked my butt off to be able to graduate early.*

He shrugged. "It was interesting, I guess. Helped me think about the future." In that it cemented his determination to stay far, far away from politics or the corporate world.

"Did you make any promising connections? You know you can't just ride your father's coattails. You have to make a name for yourself the way Christian has."

"Uh-huh." He chewed on a minty sweet mouthful, and his stomach clenched. He knew he'd have to tell his parents the truth before too much longer, but he still had a little time.

"And a lovely young lady like Ashleigh isn't going to wait around forever to settle down. Don't take her for granted, sweetheart."

"I won't. I promise." He and Ash had already planned their breakup for after the new president's inauguration. They'd taken summer school and every extra credit they could to be able to finish classes in December.

In January, they'd both come out to their parents, and with any luck Rafa would be heading to the other side of the world—without Secret Service agents tailing his every move. His parents would have protection for life, but he would finally be free. The thought of the secret plan quickened his pulse. Not long now.

"She's a keeper, Rafael. Don't let her go. Don't do anything you'll regret."

Rafa stared at his bowl, and his mother's gaze across the island felt unbearably heavy. He'd always been so diligent in hiding any hints of who he really was. *Hadn't he?* Here in the shadows, he felt certain his mother could peer right into his heart. And was she telling him to stay hidden? Or was he letting his imagination run away on him?

"All right, we should get to bed, don't you think?" Her soft laughter was lilting. "I know, I know, you're not a baby anymore."

Rafa rinsed the bowl and spoon in one of the sinks. "I'll be right up, Mom." He needed to get the goat cheese out of the freezer.

As if she could read his mind like a news ticker, she said, "Darling, you're not planning on using the Diet Kitchen again for your little…experiments, are you?"

He shrugged as he continued rinsing the now-clean bowl. "I was maybe going to make a few things. It's just for fun."

"We talked about this. You really should be devoting your time to more substantial activities. I'd like you to take a bigger role this summer at the foundation."

"Uh-huh." His mother's foundation did good work, and as long as he didn't have to do any public speaking, he was happy to help. "I will." He finally put down the bowl and turned off the tap, plastering a smile on his face as he turned. "It's only a hobby."

"I wish your sister was as interested in cooking. Her poor future husband!" His mother laughed throatily. "But really, it's not fair to go dirtying up the other kitchen, dear. The staff have so much to do already."

As if you give a shit about the staff's workload. "I always clean up after myself."

His mother's smile faded. "You know that your father and I don't think it's an appropriate use of your time. Tomorrow we'll go over your expanded foundation duties. I think you'll be very excited with what we have planned. All right?" She didn't wait for a response. "Excellent. Now let's get to bed."

There was no point in arguing. Even though Camila Castillo had eaten the food of hundreds of male chefs, cooking wasn't a suitable interest for her son. Period. Rafa regretfully abandoned the cheese to the freezer and followed her out of the kitchen and down the hall, the only sound her high heels echoing on the polished floor. As she swept up the stairs, Brent grimaced sympathetically, and Rafa shot him a fleeting smile.

At the second floor landing, Rafa's mother pressed a kiss to his cheek, undoubtedly leaving a red stain from her glossy lipstick.

"Get some sleep. This is your last summer in Washington, and we're going to make it memorable. Be up early, all right? Wonderful."

Head high and her back as straight as a ballerina's, she was already walking toward the master bedroom as he answered, "Okay."

His last summer in Washington.

After more than seven years, freedom was so close he could almost feel it like sunshine on his face. Next year he'd be a million miles away in Australia, learning to cook and finally dating men. The thought of actually being able to have sex sent a thrill zipping down his spine, followed by a sticky pang of longing that filled every pore.

Rafa took a deep breath. *Soon.* In the meantime, he just had to keep his head down. Seven years done, and only seven more months as the president's son.

Piece of cake.

Chapter Two

"**O**HHH, IS IT the hot one?"

Shane ignored Darnell as he stepped into his boxer-briefs and switched on his electric razor. Of course Darnell was nothing if not a persistent son of a bitch. Naked, he bounded off the bed and leaned against the bathroom doorway.

At six-four, he filled it with muscles, and could put on a scowl that had intimidated more than one confession out of suspects in the box at MPDC. He'd been the youngest African-American detective on the force, and had crafted a rigid and effective professional persona. But right now, in Shane's tiny bathroom at five a.m., he was in full gossip mode.

"Okay, I'll take your silence as a no. Oh, oh, is it the athletic one? The swimmer at Berkeley? Matthew? He's scrumptious. Did you see his abs at the Olympic trials last year? Yum." Darnell frowned at the razor. "Too bad there's no scruff allowed. It's a good look on you." He grinned. "Can still feel the beard burn down where the sun don't shine. Shane Kendrick, the things you do with your mouth."

Shane smirked. "Sorry, vacation's over." He lifted his chin and shaved his neck. Thanks to his newly receding hairline, he kept his dark hair shorn at his scalp. Not completely bald, but he trimmed it very close. He'd prefer facial hair to balance it out a bit, but could only indulge on time off. It had been the best thing about the past week, which was supposed to be relaxation before his new assignment. As if he could *relax* before starting this detail. He breathed through the burst of nervous adrenaline.

"Well?"

"Well, what?"

Darnell raised his eyebrows. "Is it the swimmer or not?"

"Not."

"Oh. It's the other one." Darnell visibly deflated and waved a dismissive hand. "Whatshisname. Beanpole."

"Rafael." Shane turned his face and made sure he got all the hair from his cheek. He rattled off the briefing info. "Twenty-one years old. Just finished his junior year at UVA. Major is American Studies—whatever the hell that is. Girlfriend is Ashleigh Hastings, daughter of very wealthy South Carolina dentists. Blonde with perky tits. Currently in Paris. Rafael spends most of his time studying in his dorm room at school. This summer he's volunteering with his mother's foundation—the Castillo Healthy Children's Council."

Darnell squeezed by to piss in the toilet. "Sounds like it'll be a thrill a minute."

"Sounds like." But it was an important move up. Protecting a presidential child was a step closer to getting the POTUS detail. He'd paid his dues with field offices and a stint in rural Montana. The past year in DC he'd protected senators and visiting dignitaries. Now he was ready for the White House. If it meant trailing a boring kid, it was worth it.

Darnell nudged him over at the sink and splashed his face with water. He slapped Shane's ass lightly and reached for a towel. "Thanks for the fuck. It was just what I needed last night."

"Me too." Shane grinned at him in the mirror. "Hope you're not too sore."

"Hurts so good. Next time I'll return the favor and pound your lily-white ass for a change." Darnell grinned back and turned to go. "Hey, you coming by to watch the Orioles game this weekend?"

"I'll have to see what my schedule is. I'm going to be on call a lot more now. Also, you do realize it's not even July yet? The Orioles are on top of the league right now, but it's a little early to get excited."

"And there's that sunny, optimistic attitude that wins you so many friends and influences so many people."

"You're one to talk, Detective Hardass."

"My ass is nice and juicy, as you well know. Have a good first day, man. You know, I remember when I first met you, when you were in training? And you told me you were going to protect the president one day. I know you're not quite there yet, but you've worked damn hard for this. Try to enjoy it, yeah?"

"I guess. It's work." Shane shrugged.

Darnell rolled his eyes. "Yeah, but you busted your butt for this, so give yourself some credit. You're allowed to, you know. You might even be proud of yourself or some shit like that." He hesitated. "I know you don't like talking about it, but they'd be really proud."

Shane focused on his chin, running the razor over it. He swallowed hard. "Thanks."

Darnell squeezed Shane's shoulder, and when he spoke his tone was light again. "And damn, you've been hitting the gym harder than ever. Looking buff, my friend."

"Thanks." Shane pushed aside the thought of his parents. Didn't do him any good to get sentimental. "Cut way down on the carbs." He wasn't too bulky, but he had upped his workouts, and had to admit he was proud of the new ridges in his abs.

"I wish I could, but you know I love my pasta."

"Good thing you can eat an entire buffet and still look like a gym queen." He muttered under his breath, "*Prick.*"

Darnell's teeth gleamed. "Haters to the left. Or whatever the kids are saying these days."

"Go catch some bad guys. You should have plenty to choose from in DC."

When Darnell closed the front door behind him a few minutes later, he shouted, "Go, Orioles!" In the silence, Shane chuckled. Same old Darnell.

He was a good friend, and, once in a blue moon, a good fuck. It had never been more than that and never would, and that was exactly the way they wanted it. They were pushing forty and in the prime of their careers, and besides, making their friendship anything more would be a surefire way to fuck it up. They'd kill each other within a week.

Unbidden, Shane heard the distant echo of his mother's voice the day Darnell had driven Shane and his visiting parents out to Monticello. *"Why just friends? He's so handsome and smart. He has a good job too. What are you waiting for, Shane? Christmas?"*

It had been years now, and he'd never met anyone he wanted to wake up beside every day.

As he came into the bedroom, Shane realized Darnell had left something on the bed. He laughed out loud when he picked up the hardcover book, the release like opening a pressure valve. A yellow note was stuck to the front.

Pro tip: No farting or belching. Also, don't pick your nose.

The book was called *United States Protocol: The Guide to Diplomatic Etiquette*, and according to the blurb was "the perfect guide to any official event." Shane breathed deeply as stupid nerves skittered through him. He was actually going to work at the *White House.*

And not just on the grounds at a standing post, manning the perimeter at a state dinner. He was going to be inside Castle, as they called it. Inside Crown, even—the first family residence. Even if the Rafael Castillo detail was going to be boring as hell, it was worth it.

He checked his watch and quickly pulled his suit from the closet. After strapping on his holster, he unlocked his Sig Sauer pistol from its metal box and gave it a quick function check. Then he attached his badge to his belt, along with his handcuffs. He could smell the coffee brewing in the narrow kitchen, and went to pour a cup.

He flipped on the TV to distract himself while he quickly scrambled egg whites with turkey bacon. The furnished apartment had come with the wall-mounted flat-screen TV, which had sold him on it. The paintings framed on the walls were hotel-room style scenes of pastoral life.

It wasn't Shane's taste, but he didn't even know what his taste was. There was no point in decorating or putting down roots when he could be transferred anywhere tomorrow. Chewing a forkful of egg, his gaze flicked to the one decoration that was his, sitting on a side table beside the floral couch.

The frame was silver, and as Shane picked it up and ran his fingertips over the edges, he saw it needed polishing. In the photo, he stood between his parents at his college graduation, taller than both of them, especially his mother, who only reached his shoulder. She'd just snatched the black mortarboard off his head and put it on, the yellow tassel hanging over her face. All three of them laughed. Shane's father wore a new suit he'd bought just for the occasion, even though Shane had assured him it wasn't a big deal.

"Like heck it isn't. My only child is graduating from college. Deals don't get much bigger than this, my boy."

Breakfast tasted like sludge as he returned the frame to the table, angling it away. Six years now, and at times it felt like forever. But sometimes it hit like a ton of fresh fucking bricks, and he rubbed impatiently at the sting in his eyes. *If I'd been there…*

No. This wasn't the damn day for it. It was time for work. Time to be his best, and his best didn't include…*this.*

A red headline flashed up on CNN, screaming of a dire threat to the life and liberty of the United States due to an incoming storm front. Standing in the entry to the galley kitchen, Shane watched the early morning anchors and their pinched faces. He didn't bother turning on the sound.

The drive to the unmarked headquarters building on H Street was quick, with early dawn fortunately one of the few times traffic in DC wasn't a fucking nightmare.

After he went through a security check, he drove his silver Yukon down into the garage below the building, smiling as he spotted Alan Pearce leaning against a black Suburban. Most of the official vehicles they called G-rides were Suburbans or sedans, with some limos sprinkled in. All were black, of course.

When Shane parked and joined him, Alan held out his arms with a grin. "Ready for the big show, Agent Kendrick? Well, it's more like the pre-show, but we're close. Damn good to see you, Kenny." Pearce extended his hand, and then pulled Shane into a back-slapping hug. "Apparently you're stuck with me again. We can relive our glory days from the Albany field office."

Shane stepped back and gave him an exaggerated once-over. "How long has it been? You're looking old." Shit. As soon as the joke left his mouth, he realized the last time he'd seen Alan had been Jessica's funeral.

But Alan only laughed. "Yeah, fuck you very much too. I'm forty-one, and if I recall correctly you're not that far behind."

Pearce actually looked hot as hell with threads of gray at his temples in his dirty blond hair. His green eyes still popped, and his grin was boyish. His lanky frame filled out his dark suit nicely, and if Alan was gay, Shane would have tapped that ass years ago. "Still thirty-nine for a few more months." He paused. *Should I ask? Is it rude to not ask? Or is it rude to ask?* "How are Jules and Dylan?"

Alan's smile tightened, and he hitched a shoulder. "Okay.

We're doing our best. One day at a time and all that shit." He shoved his hands in his pockets and pressed his lips together. "It's been tough. Especially now that Dylan's been diagnosed."

Son of a bitch. Life really knew how to kick certain people in the nuts over and over. Losing his parents had been harder than Shane had ever thought possible, but it was still the natural order of things. He could only imagine what Alan felt to lose his daughter—and now possibly his son too. "God, I'm sorry. Is there anything I can do?"

"No, but thank you. It's genetic." He laughed harshly. "My genes, to be specific. I passed down this shitty disease, but I'm fine. Just going to end up killing my kids. Guess it's good Jules and I only had the two."

"God. I'm sorry. There's nothing the doctors can do?"

Alan scuffed the toe of his leather shoe over the concrete floor of the garage. "There's an experimental treatment. Swedish doctor. We're saving up."

Shane had never had kids, and never really thought much about them. But he'd met Jessica once as a baby, and she'd clutched his finger and flashed a crooked little grin, and his heart clenched to think of that smile gone now. He couldn't imagine what it would be like to have your child die. To watch them waste away.

"If I can help, just say the word." He couldn't call a clear image of Dylan to mind, but the kid had to be seven or so by now. Shane couldn't remember the name of the rare disease they were afflicted with, but he wasn't about to ask.

"Thanks. I'm trying not to think about it too much. Makes it hard to get out of bed if I do. So if you don't mind, I'd rather focus on the job. Or sports. Or even politics. Pretty much anything else."

"You got it."

Alan tossed him the keys with a smile. "Come on. Showtime."

At the southwest gate of the White House, the sun peeked over the East Wing. One of the Uniformed Division officers stepped out of the guard house. This was the gate for those who already had clearance, but of course their vehicle still had to be searched. He rolled down his window, handed over their IDs, and waited while a sniffer dog eagerly went about its business.

"You're the new suit guards on Valor's detail, huh?" the officer asked. He looked about sixteen with blotchy skin, but had to be at least twenty-one to be in the Secret Service. The uniformed officers only needed high school diplomas and tended to be younger.

Shane kept his tone even, despite the insult. "Yep." The quickest way to get under a Secret Service agent's skin was to call him or her a "guard." He'd heard there was sometimes friction with the Uniformed Division, but he couldn't blame them if they were jealous. They were the low men on the totem pole.

"Little mouse won't give you any trouble. They say he's even better behaved than Chelsea Clinton was." The officer yawned and glanced to his cohort in the gatehouse running their credentials as the guard dog went to work.

Shane watched the dog in his side mirror. It was similar to a German shepherd, but was called a… His mind spun. *Holy shit, what was it called?* He wracked his brain, which was alarmingly blank. He knew this. He *knew* this. Of course he did! He'd known it for *years*.

As it finally came to him, he resisted the urge to shout, *a-ha!* It was a Belgian Malinois, which the Service had determined to be the best sniffers and attackers.

Sheesh, the flutters in his belly were ridiculous. He hadn't been this nervous since training. Alan seemed calm beside him. He'd been on what they called the "little show" before—the VP's detail—so this was apparently old hat to him.

The dog finished his inspection, and the guard pulled a ball from his pocket. "Now he gets to play for a few minutes." He passed back their ID and patted the Suburban's hood. "Have fun in there."

The gate whirred shut behind them, and Shane parked in the numbered spot they'd been assigned. He and Alan walked around the West Wing before going inside the residence through the Palm Room. They entered the center hall of the ground floor, which used to be considered the basement since the residence was built on higher ground.

Their leather shoes were silent on the thick orange carpet as they passed under the vaulted ceiling, where simple chandeliers hung down every several feet. Marble busts stood sentinel.

Shane thrummed with eager electricity. He was working a regular detail in the *White House*. Granted, Rafael Castillo would be back at school in Virginia in September, but for the summer, Shane would get the chance to really be on the inside of the president's home.

They passed the entry to the kitchen on their left, and Shane's pulse spiked as they reached the door of the Secret Service command post.

"Come on, let's go meet our new boss." Alan led the way.

Inside the office, a small Asian woman with her hair pulled into a bun stood and extended her hand. "Kendrick—good to meet you. I'm Sandra Nguyen, SAIC. The box creatures give you any trouble? They can get uppity with new agents."

"Nah," Shane answered. "No trouble at all." As special agent in charge, Shane hoped Nguyen lived up to her reputation as fair and fierce. It had taken years for the good ol' boy network of power to finally give way to more diversity.

She introduced him to a few other agents manning the console and wall of TVs with security camera feeds. After she went over the protocols, she gave Shane and Alan their earpieces, mics, and radio transmitters to attach to their belts. A clear coiled cord connected the earpiece to the transmitter beneath their suit jackets.

When they were set, an older agent came in and introduced himself as Brent Harris. "I'm staying on as Valor's new detail leader, so if you have any questions, ask away. Good to see you back on the job, Pearce."

"Thanks," Alan said. "Anything we need to watch out for? Does Valor have any tricks up his sleeve these days?"

One of the agents at the console chuckled, and Harris answered, "No way. The kid's a mouse. Virtue and Velocity are the ones to watch out for. But they only come to DC a few times a year now, so it's not our problem."

Shane went through the list in his head. Virtue was Adriana Castillo—twenty-five years old. After college she'd traveled and had "internships" at international PR firms. She was now an associate at an LA firm that worked with movie stars. Big party girl.

Velocity was Matthew Castillo—twenty-three, star swimmer at UC Berkeley. Came close to making the last Olympic team in the freestyle and butterfly. Stayed in California to train after graduation. Member of the national swimming team.

"What about Vacation?" Shane asked. Christian Castillo— twenty-seven, a lawyer in New York, married to a leggy blonde model/actress. One of *People*'s Sexiest Men Alive the year before, and Shane couldn't argue with the declaration. "He's not around much either?"

"Nope. He never really has been, and he wasn't a problem," Nguyen answered. "He's Vagabond and Venus's golden child."

Vagabond was the president, and Venus the first lady. "What about Valor? What's their relationship with him?" Shane asked.

Nguyen and Harris shared a glance. Harris said, "He's a really nice kid. Shy. Wound pretty freakin' tight. Never puts a foot wrong, and doesn't say much. Vagabond doesn't seem to pay him much attention, and Venus has always been caught up with the other kids. But it seems now that Virtue's settled down a bit from her party days and less likely to get arrested on a coke bust, Venus is taking a closer look at her youngest."

"She sounds like a treat. Are the stories true?" Alan asked.

The agents in the room all made affirmative noises, including Nguyen, who sighed. "Frankly, she can be a demanding bitch. She'll treat you like the help, and won't thank you for jack shit. But she's fair—I'll give her that. She may not thank you, but she won't bust your balls for no reason. And if her agents tell her she can't go somewhere, she listens. She's a very smart woman, and she won't give anyone a hard time for the sake of it. But warm and fuzzy isn't in her wheelhouse."

"She's one of those people who's always *on*," Harris added. "You know what I mean? Never has her guard down. Maybe up in the family quarters, but from what her aides say, not even then."

"Got it." Shane nodded.

"The most Valor will do is sneak down to the kitchen late at night," Harris said. "But he won't dick you around. When his parents are away, he cooks up a storm in the kitchen on the third floor, but he has to poach the ingredients from the main kitchen. The staff have orders to tell Venus if he does, but they cover for him."

Shane frowned. "Why isn't he allowed to cook?"

Nguyen rolled her eyes. "Who knows? Too menial? Not macho enough? He's always had an interest, but his mother's tried to crush it since he was a little boy, apparently."

"What's she afraid of? He's not gay, is he?" Alan asked. He glanced at Shane, and Shane half expected him to add, *Not that there's anything wrong with that.* While Shane wasn't flying rainbow flags, it had never been a problem with the agents who knew, like Alan.

"Not that we know of," Harris answered. "He's a sensitive kid, and I could certainly believe it. Obviously anyone could be gay. But if he is, let me tell you he's hidden it extremely well. Never a whiff of it. No clandestine movements to meet secret lovers, and we'd know if he was sneaking off for quickies in the bathroom. He and his girlfriend are two peas in a pod."

Alan asked, "What's the deal with her? Will she give us problems?"

"Nope. As you know, she's in Paris for the summer. She'll be back for September when you guys head down with Valor to Charlottesville. She's friendly. Respectful. Sleeps over in his dorm room from time to time. No issues. They hang around with a few other students sometimes, but Valor isn't very social. Always polite, but he keeps people at arm's length. Easier that way, I imagine. He was the same in high school—he'd have kids over, and went to parties and such, but it didn't seem like any of his friends were very close to him."

"We're reducing his detail so some of the agents can go on Livingston's watch," Nguyen said. "Two of you will do just fine. He's not going to be happy that his other agents are gone already, but that was the way Venus wanted it. Thinks it's easier to rip off a Band-Aid." She checked her watch. "He should be up soon. Let's take a tour of the ground floor and make sure you've got your protocols down cold. Then you can meet Valor."

THE TAUPE AND cream checks of the floor of the White House entrance hall shone brightly, buffed to perfection. Marble columns soared almost twenty feet above, and the enormous chandeliers were turned off, the sun streaming in through tall windows topped with thick red and gold curtains.

The Red, Blue, and Green Rooms opened off an east-west hallway where former presidents in oil paint watched from gilt frames as Shane and Alan followed Nguyen to what was officially known as the Family Dining Room on the west side. There was a private dining room upstairs on the second floor of the residence, but apparently Mrs. Castillo preferred the first floor for reasons unknown.

At a shining wooden table that at the moment was set for eight—the smallest size, Shane guessed—Rafael Castillo looked up from a tablet and bowl of soggy-looking Cheerios he was half-heartedly pushing around with his spoon.

Across the table, on the other side of a low bouquet of pink tulips, sat his mother and a young female aide reading off the first lady's morning schedule. Impressionist portraits hung on warm yellow walls, and yellow velvet curtains framed the windows. The chandelier over the table was an explosion of cut crystal. Shane could only imagine how ornate the State Dining Room next door was.

A furrow appeared between Rafael's brows, but he put down his tablet and smiled politely. "Hi."

Nguyen smiled. "Good morning." To the first lady, she added, "I hope we're not too early."

"No," Camila Castillo answered. "Rafa was just finishing up. Darling, time to meet your new agents." With that, she turned back to her agenda, the aide murmuring something as she flipped the pages.

Rafael pushed back his chair and came around the table, leading them into the hallway. "Are Joanna and Stuart on the next shift? I wanted to say goodbye before they got reassigned."

Nguyen shook her head. "I'm sorry—they're already on their way to Livingston's headquarters in North Carolina. Brent will still be on your detail, along with a couple other new agents for the other shifts. This is Shane Kendrick and Alan Pearce. They'll take good care of you."

"Oh. Right. Um, hi." Rafael extended his hand.

Shane shook it firmly. As Alan did next, Shane quickly took stock of Rafael, automatically cataloguing his features. The kid usually stayed out of the press, so it had been a while since Shane had seen him.

His voice was surprisingly deep, and he was tall—had to be almost six foot, barely a couple inches shorter than Shane's six-one. Darnell had called him a "beanpole," but beneath Rafael's pressed khakis and sky-blue button-down with navy tie, it looked like he'd filled out a bit, although he was still slim.

His leather loafers just needed pennies in them to complete the perfect preppy look. Rafael's short hair was neatly parted and slicked back, and his brown eyes had long lashes. He almost looked like he was wearing eyeliner, they were so lush. Freckles dusted his nose and the tops of his tan cheeks.

Not a bad-looking kid by any means, but Shane supposed he was nothing to write home about compared to his older brothers, who got all the attention.

"Can you tell Joanna and Stuart thanks for me?" Rafael asked Nguyen. "The other agents who left too." He glanced at Shane and Alan and hastily added, "Not that you guys won't be great."

"We totally understand," Alan said. "And I know I speak for your former detail when I say we appreciate your consideration."

Rafael checked his watch. "I guess we should get going." He grimaced. "I have to give a speech. Do you guys mind driving me so I can look over my notes? Mom kind of sprung it on me."

Nguyen smiled. "Not a problem. As you know, it's always your choice to take your own vehicle or have a driver. I'll leave you all to it. Have a great day."

Shane nodded, breathing deeply. The butterflies had quieted, and confidence surged through him as they strode the White House halls.

This detail was going to be a piece of cake.

Chapter Three

"**V**ALOR ON THE move."

As the new agent—Shane, the walking wet dream—murmured into his wrist radio, Rafa resisted the urge to snort. He climbed into the back of the Suburban as the name echoed through his mind.

Valor.

If ever there was a codename that didn't fit, it was his. Courage and bravery were not exactly the first, or second (or third or fourth or fifth) attributes anyone would give him. Each family being protected had codenames starting with the same letter, and he wondered what other names they'd considered for him. Vegan. Vomit. Vagina.

Virgin.

Squirming in the backseat as they drove away from downtown, Rafa ran a hand over his hair and tried to banish the nervous energy jangling through him. He detested public speaking, a fact of which his mother was naturally well aware.

His stomach roiled with acid. He knew she thought it was good for him to get over his fear—that it would help his future career. But in a kitchen, he wouldn't have to give speeches. He exhaled slowly and reminded himself that either way, it would be over in an hour. Even if he blew it and made a fool of himself, it would be done.

He'd scribbled notes on old-fashioned note cards, and now he pulled them out of the pocket of his navy sport coat. He repeated the words in his head, not really hearing them. His mind ping-ponged from subject to subject, and he tapped his foot on the rubber mat as he whipped through the cards one by one.

He wished Ashleigh was there to tell him to chill the fuck out, as she'd surely put it. He had to focus. *Healthy kids. Community support. Leading by example.*

With a sigh, he stared out the window. Shit, he was horny. *Should have jerked off this morning in the shower.* He watched the back of Shane's head as the agents quietly discussed the advance security report for the park. Shane was scrolling through the document on his agent phone—black, of course—as Alan drove.

They were both handsome, but Rafa wondered what it would feel like to run his hand over Shane's nearly shaved head. Wondered if Shane had hair on his chest and powerful body. Rafa had fantasized about hairy men—not *too* hairy, but not too smooth either—since about the time he'd moved into the White House. Even in high school, he'd never paid much attention to the other guys. Why look at boys when he had all those men in suits around?

As they neared the site of the future playground, Rafa forced his mind back on his speech. He scanned the fake-sounding words one last time, cringing already without even having said them. Adriana and Matthew had never had to do much of this since Christian had been so good at it. Rafa had almost made it through two terms without having to do much more than smile and wave behind his parents at events.

Now he was suddenly expected to give speeches on his own? Of course he'd tried to argue with his mother, but that never got anyone anywhere, and he was no exception.

"Um, can I ask what you guys think about this?"

The agents went silent in the front of the vehicle. Alan glanced at him in the rearview. "Of course. About what in particular?"

"Oh." Rafa's cheeks got hot. "The speech. It's, um...hold on." He cleared his throat and gave his little spiel about the importance of community spaces in helping promote active lifestyles. "Does that last part sound too...I don't know. Lame?"

"No, I think it sounds good," Alan answered. "You're getting the message across clearly."

"It's not fake sounding?"

"Of course not," Alan said.

Shane opened his mouth to speak, and Rafa's heart skipped. It was dumb to care more about what Shane thought because he was hot. But Shane only directed Alan to take a right turn. They quietly began discussing tactics again, and Rafa didn't want to interrupt.

Although he was used to the agents and their constant presence, it was always weird with new people. They weren't supposed to talk to him about anything not related to protection, and they weren't allowed to ever comment on anything they overheard from their protectees. Naturally they heard a million conversations when they were driving his family around or flying with his father, but they were only supposed to respond if the protectee initiated the conversation. But even then, he didn't think they would ever actually tell him what they thought if it was negative.

When he'd first started college, some of the other kids thought the agents would narc on them for underage drinking, but the Secret Service genuinely didn't care about that. It had taken a while before his dorm mates had realized the agents weren't there to tell Rafa what to do, or to be his parents. They only cared about keeping him safe. Stuart had helped Rafa haul Ashleigh up three flights before Christmas break when she'd had one—or five—too many spiked eggnogs, and had been so nice about it.

Rafa tried to focus on his notes, but his mind wandered. He wondered how Stuart and Joanna liked the Livingstons. He wished he could at least text them to say thanks for everything they'd done to take care of him, but of course he didn't have their numbers. Not that anyone would try to kidnap him of all the presidential children, and he knew the agents were just doing their jobs. It didn't mean they *liked* him. They weren't *friends*.

He pulled out his phone, making sure his panic button that sent an alarm to his detail and Secret Service headquarters was still safely tucked in his pocket. He'd never had to use the little black rectangle yet, but his parents had drilled into him the importance of never leaving home without it. Rafa quickly typed out a message to Ashleigh, hoping he'd get a comforting response before his speech. But the message remained stubbornly delivered and not read.

Then they were arriving, and he had to put on his best smile and shake hands as the foundation director, Marissa, met him by the Suburban and shepherded him to the makeshift stage set up in the corner of the new park. Marissa was a tiny redhead with a bob cut and black rectangular glasses. She was barely thirty, but ran his mother's foundation *and* handled her demands, so Rafa reflected that Marissa must be a marvel of both effectiveness and patience.

The grass was still seeding in cordoned-off areas, and young trees dotted the space. A jungle gym gleamed by swing sets and a teeter-totter. He smiled and thought of a humid August day years ago when he and Matthew had tried to break the world record and failed miserably, giving up after only an hour that had felt like ten.

When he went up to make his little speech, the gathered community applauded like they were genuinely excited to have him there, which was sweet. Of course he'd done absolutely nothing to assist with funding for the park or building it, but he smiled and waved as he took the microphone.

Oh God, I'm so bad at this. Why isn't Chris here? Why does he have to live in New York? Why couldn't Mom do this damn speech herself? Why is this my life?

As the people waited, he blinked against the glare of the morning sun, and sweat dripped down his spine. He spotted Shane at the edge of the crowd, looking every inch the stereotypical Secret Service agent with his dark suit, ear piece, and sunglasses. Alan was likely positioned somewhere behind Rafa.

He cleared his throat, and the mic buzzed with static. "Hello. I'm Rafael Castillo, and it's my honor to be here today to celebrate the opening of this beautiful park." His note cards were in his pocket, and he realized he should have taken them out before he started talking. Heart pounding, he smiled awkwardly as he reached for them. "Um, I…" He fumbled the cards, spilling them at his feet.

Shoot me now. Well, not literally.

He scooped them up as a murmur went through the couple hundred people gathered. "Um, sorry. As I was saying…" He gripped the cards, which of course were now out of order. His eyes scanned the words, but nothing penetrated the buzzing in his head. "I…this park is great. Obviously." Nervous laughter tittered from the audience. "I know you've all worked hard, and…to make kids healthy a park helps, because they can do things here. Health things."

Oh my God. Abort, abort, abort!

His head spun, and his breath came short. "And I…uh…" Rafa blew out a long exhalation. "I am really bad at public speaking, but you already know that."

Genuine laughter rang out, and when he focused on people in the crowd, they were smiling at him. Then everyone applauded encouragingly, and his tongue became a little looser. *Screw it.*

"Um, when I arrived and I saw that awesome new playground over there, I remembered this time my brother Matthew and I tried to break the world record for teeter-tottering. Now, the world record is completely insane. Seventy-five hours." The crowd murmured. "Yeah, crazy, huh? But Matty and I were convinced we could do it. Our dad gave us a little pep talk that morning about reaching for our dreams, and I'm sure you know he gives pretty good pep talks. I was seven, and my brother was nine, and our sister Adriana came with us to supervise—which meant texting her friends and working on her tan."

The crowd laughed again, and Rafa barreled on. "Well, I'd love to tell you that we made a good run at the record, but we didn't even come close. That hour felt like forever, especially since I already had to pee." *I'm talking about urination. Mom is going to kill me.* But the crowd laughed harder. *Bring it back to the point. Get the message out.* "Even though we didn't break a record that day, we still had fun and got active. That park near our house was like our second backyard, and I know this wonderful new space will be home to countless activities and memories for your community. Hey, maybe two of you can take a run at that teeter-totter record."

Then Marissa was at his elbow, taking the mic with a smile. "What a great idea! How about it, kids?"

The rest of the event was a blur of more hand shaking and picture taking, with people lining up for their turn as Alan and Shane kept a close watch and asked people to take their hands out of their pockets. Rafa's cheeks hurt from smiling, and he was just glad it was over without *too* much humiliation.

"*Usted ha crecido mucho,*" a tiny gray-haired woman exclaimed as she shook his hand.

"*Gracias.*" He smiled and nodded. She'd said something about him being bigger or taller, but the truth was that Rafa and his siblings were the whitest Hispanics ever and could barely speak a word of Spanish. His father was born in Miami to Puerto Rican immigrant parents, and his mother in Mexico before her parents moved to Chicago, so they were both fluent. But they'd been hell-bent on assimilation and filing off their accents the way a criminal would a serial number on a gun. It had only ever been English at home.

His throat was dry by the time Marissa walked him back to the Suburban with Shane and Alan close by. She pressed a bottle of water into Rafa's hand.

"Good work. You had me worried there, but you saved it. People like genuine. It worked well. Just go with it straight away next time. As long as you still get in the talking points. Okay?"

"Next time?" Rafa's heart sank.

Marissa smiled sympathetically. "Your mother's idea. I'll try to convince her she still needs to be the primary spokesperson. It is her foundation, after all."

"Thanks." Rafa took a gulp of water.

As he suddenly smacked the concrete of the sidewalk, he registered the *bang* that filled the air. He choked, spitting water, the plastic bottle spinning out of his grasp as someone heavy landed on top of him, further pushing the air from his lungs. Hot breath hit the back of his neck, and Shane's low command filled his ear. "Stay down!" His hand pressed Rafa's head to the sidewalk, and pebbles dug into Rafa's cheek. Adrenaline and terror roared through him.

Oh my fucking God. Is this actually happening?

Shouts and a buzz of exclamations filled the air, and Rafa heard someone—Alan—call, "Clear!"

Then there were more shouts, and Shane was hauling him into the back of the Suburban, crawling on top of him as the door slammed and they zoomed away. Rafa couldn't breathe. His head was jammed into the side door, and now there was leather beneath his cheek. His long legs were scrunched up and tangled with Shane's, and Shane's hand was still palming Rafa's skull. His heart was close to exploding.

Alan was saying something, and Shane answered. But they sounded like the grown-ups on old Charlie Brown cartoons, their voices making noise with no discernible words. Rafa tried to speak. "Wha…" His throat was like sandpaper.

The vehicle slowed and came to a stop. The engine was still running. For a moment, no one moved or said a word.

Then Shane gently pulled Rafa up to sitting. Their legs were still tangled, but Shane was focused on Rafa's face, peering at him intently. "Are you all right?" He squeezed Rafa's shoulders.

"Uh…uh-huh." Rafa blinked. It was dark now, and he looked out the windows at what seemed to be an underground parking garage. Alan was on his phone, speaking quietly. Rafa focused on Shane, who was sitting so close to him and seemed to take up most of the room in the backseat. His eyes looked like they might be blue up close, and when he sighed, his breath ghosted across Rafa's face. Rafa's pulse thundered.

"Backfire?" he asked.

"Huh?" Rafa blinked.

But Alan answered. "I think so. They're on their way to the scene now to make sure."

Then Shane was letting go of Rafa, and their legs were untangled. Shane leaned back against the seat, his cheeks puffing out. "Jesus. First day too."

Alan shrugged in the driver's seat. "Better safe than sorry. We followed protocol. It was a good dry run. Escape route was effective." He turned around and smiled crookedly at Rafa. "Sorry about that, kid. Can't be too cautious."

"It's okay. I…thank you. I'm glad no one was shooting at me."

Alan chuckled. "That makes three of us." He turned and put the vehicle in drive. "Let's head back to Castle."

As they returned to the White House, Rafa stared at his left palm, poking the new cuts there. He didn't remember feeling it, but he must have scraped his hand when Shane pushed him to the sidewalk.

"Did I hurt you?"

Rafa looked up to find Shane frowning beside him. "It's nothing. Don't worry about it."

But Shane was sliding closer and reaching for his hand, taking it in his own. As he lightly brushed his fingertips over the scrapes, dislodging a few little pebbles, Rafa shivered. Shane's hands were callused and thick, but he examined Rafa's palm as if it was made of glass. As the Suburban bumped over something, their knees touched.

The adrenaline rushing through him made an abrupt left turn into arousal, and Rafa yanked his hand back. "I'm fine. Thank you." His voice was little more than a squeak, and his face blazed. His clothes had been disheveled, and he prayed the sport coat was covering his crotch. His groin was tight, and he knew an erection wasn't far behind. He didn't dare look down to check.

"Sorry if I was overzealous."

Rafa forced himself to meet Shane's gaze with a smile. "Don't be. I really appreciate everything you guys do. Honestly."

Shane nodded, and then they were at the gates, and Rafa turned to look out the window. He thought of seeing his mother any minute. There was nothing better to kill a potential hard-on.

WITH HIS HAND down his boxers that night, Rafa gazed longingly at his laptop. His left palm was bandaged, even though he'd gotten worse scrapes a million times as a kid. *At least my right hand wasn't injured. I'd probably die of blue balls.* But his mother had called for the doctor.

It was overkill, but it had still been nice to be worried about, he had to admit. Shane and Alan had apologized again, and Rafa had been relieved his mother wasn't angry at them. She said she'd rather he got a hundred cuts and bruises than one bullet.

Flexing his left hand with a twinge, he smiled as he thought of Shane examining it. He bit his lip, staring at the computer. Maybe it would be okay, just this once.

Maybe he could just watch some porn and jerk off like every other guy in America without having to worry that the White House monitoring staff would notice. Not that they *cared*, but porn was…well, it was personal. The fact that he was gay was personal. It was just better to keep it completely locked up until he had his freedom back. Besides, nowadays *nothing* online was safe.

When Adriana's accounts had been hacked a few years before, along with posting her sexts and half-naked selfies, the gossip sites had gleefully screamed that she visited sites about big black dicks. And knowing his luck, some hacker douchebag would spread the news to TMZ that the president's son liked to watch twinks get fucked in the ass by hairy daddies.

Because *damn*, did he like to watch that.

But he'd always been vigilant—it had to be on Ashleigh's computer. She'd give him alone time when he needed it, and never judged (although sometimes she teased mercilessly). And most of the time he was happy to just jerk off to his fantasies, but tonight that wasn't working. Well, it was working, but every time he closed his eyes and took his cock in hand, his mind was filled with Shane. The rumble of Shane's voice, and the weight of him pressing Rafa down. A shiver rippled through him, and he cupped his balls.

He groaned in frustration and opened his eyes.

If he was going to be around Shane for months to come, he absolutely could not use the guy for his spank bank. Not because he had a moral or ethical dilemma—fantasies didn't hurt any-one—but because he'd likely spontaneously come in his pants the next time Shane so much as brushed against him.

Despite himself, Rafa thought of how Shane's callused hand had felt on his head as he'd flattened him to the sidewalk. How his breath had been hot against the back of Rafa's neck, his big body covering him completely. Willing to die for him.

Rafa's cock twitched, and he gripped it. He knew it was stupid—Shane was willing to die for any asshole he was assigned to protect. It didn't mean Rafa was special. It didn't mean Shane *cared*. It didn't mean there was anything between them whatsoever. Rafa could have been a Labradoodle—it wouldn't make a bit of difference to Shane.

He needed to nip this crush right in the bud. Adriana had mooned over one of her first agents so obviously that the poor guy had been reassigned. Rafa could hide it the way he hid everything else, but it would be better to just not crush on the guy at all.

"Did I hurt you?"

Kicking off his boxers, Rafa gave in and spread his legs, reaching for the lube he'd brought out from the bathroom (purchased by Ash, of course). Closing his eyes, he imagined Shane's warm, comforting touch. In his mind, those rough hands were skimming all over his body now. Shane kissed him, his lips soft compared to the scratch of stubble on Rafa's skin, and murmured that he'd go slow in that gravelly voice.

But as Rafa pinched his nipples, he wanted it harder. In his mind, he got on his hands and knees. His hair wasn't tamed with pomade, and Shane ran his hands through it, pulling Rafa's head back as he bit his shoulder. His stubble sent shivers over Rafa's skin as he kissed down his spine, and Rafa shoved a slick finger inside himself, imagining it was Shane's tongue.

Whimpering, he bit back a groan as he fucked himself with another finger. The first time he'd made himself come with just his fingers, it had felt like a miracle—somehow even more intense than when he jerked his dick.

In his mind, he held his cheeks open with Shane's face buried there, and begged Shane to shove his cock inside. Of course there were no condoms in his fantasies, and when Shane rammed into him, the burn of flesh on flesh heated every pore. Panting, he jerked himself faster, his fingers pistoning in his ass. He imagined

Shane heavy behind him, Shane's hairy thighs and balls slapping against him, his cock like a hot poker.

Rolling over, Rafa went up on his knees, burying his face in his pillow to muffle his cries. It was awkward to get deep into his hole now, so he concentrated on his cock and balls with his other hand, imagining it was Shane touching him.

He pulled down the foreskin, teasing the head of his cock. All the while in his mind, Shane pounded his ass, grunting and murmuring a litany of dirty talk about how tight Rafa was, and how he was a cum slut, and Shane was going to fill him up until it gushed out.

With a groan into his pillow, Rafa came, toes curling as his orgasm vibrated through him violently. After a few gasps, Rafa lifted his hand and licked it clean, imagining it was Shane feeding him his own spunk as he filled his body—cum in his ass and in his mouth, hot inside him and salty on his tongue.

Collapsing onto his belly, he swallowed the bitter drops, knowing he was probably a total freak for eating his own jizz. But until he could eat someone else's, it was all he had. He moaned softly as he wondered what Shane's would taste like.

I'd kneel at his feet and let him fuck my mouth. Suck him until he came down my throat, his hands pulling my hair. Maybe he'd smile...

As the glow faded, Rafa hurried to the bathroom and cleaned himself, thanking God that Shane wouldn't be able to read his mind when he saw him again.

Chapter Four

"K ENDRICK." Brent Harris motioned him into the Secret Service office as he approached down the center hallway.

Inside, Shane glanced at the protectee locator, the electronic box listing the location of the president, vice-president, and their immediate families. Rafael was upstairs on the third floor. "What's up? Pearce should be here soon." Alan's text had only said he'd be late and not to wait for him. Being late wasn't acceptable, but it was their second week on the midnight shift, and they'd only seen Valor once. Odds were that Rafa was staying put upstairs.

In the three weeks since the false alarm at the park, he'd only gone out to foundation events or meetings, aside from one barbecue hosted by an old high school friend. He'd talked and laughed with his former classmates while eating hot dogs and drinking beer, but Shane had the feeling his heart wasn't in it. There seemed to be a switch he flicked on when he had to be polite and friendly. He didn't talk much otherwise and kept to himself most of the time. It made for an easy detail, at least.

"Actually, Pearce isn't coming in," Harris replied. They stood in the corner of the office, the other agents monitoring the live feeds from security cameras. This late at night there was fewer staff, but the office was of course monitored twenty-four seven. Harris went on. "He's got a family emergency."

Shane's stomach dropped. "Serious?"

"His son has an infection. He's been hospitalized."

"But Al said he's been doing okay." Just the other day he'd shown Shane a video of the boy laughing as he and Alan played catch in the yard. There was a gap between Dylan's teeth that he'd been eager to show to the camera. "Damn."

Harris nodded grimly. "I told him to stay at the hospital and I'd cover if need be. I called Nguyen, and we've discussed it. If Pearce can't come in the rest of the week, how do you feel about taking the night shift alone? Of course you'd have backup from the uniforms if need be, but Valor isn't one for taking off at three o'clock in the morning to go party. Odds are you'll barely even see him all week. Good thing it's the mouse's detail and not his sister's."

"Sounds good. It should be just fine. You can't get anyone in to cover for Pearce?"

Harris sighed and rubbed a hand over his face. "We're short-staffed. This election season is killing us. Between Livingston and Margulies and their veeps, we're stretched thin." He laughed humorlessly. "Fucking cutbacks. They keep asking us to do more with less, and who'll get blamed if something goes wrong? My buddy's on Livingston's detail, and they're constantly on the road. He's barely slept. Working eighteen hours a day, but of course he's only officially on the clock eight of those."

"I hear you. Look, head on home. I've got this. Like you said, the kid doesn't go anywhere at night. Pearce and I would just be shooting the shit anyway. I can handle this."

"Great." Harris gave Shane's back a slap. "Have a good night. Call me if there are any issues."

"You got it."

Shane grabbed his radio and headed up to the state floor. Within the executive residence on a quiet night like this with only one protectee on site, they used small walkie-talkies that clipped on their belts instead of the ear pieces connected to wrist mics and radios.

The president was still overseas, and Venus had left that morning for Los Angeles to stump for Margulies's campaign. All was quiet. He stayed near the back stairs, since they were the ones Valor was most likely to use. As he took a seat in a wooden chair left there for agents, his phone buzzed. He answered quietly. "Al?"

"Yeah. Just wanted to make sure things are okay there."

Jesus, Alan's voice was wrecked. Hoarse and wavering. "We've got it covered. Don't give it another thought, okay? How's Dylan?" He was almost afraid to ask.

"Not great. Fever's high. This wasn't supposed to happen yet. He was still supposed to have a year before he got really sick. At least."

"I'm sure he'll be okay." He wasn't sure at all, but he didn't know what else to say.

"Yeah. Thanks. Fuck, man. We just got this detail and I'm causing problems. They're going to shitcan me first chance they get. I need this job."

"Hey, don't worry about it. They understand."

He laughed bitterly. "Nguyen and Harris, sure. But the top brass couldn't give a shit. I barely made it back after…last time. My old boss fought for me to get back on a detail. They don't want agents who can't be on call constantly or work doubles or triples. They don't want agents who have a life outside the job." He paused. "Shit, I'm sorry. Listen to me—I'm a goddamn mess. I wouldn't want me on the job either."

"You're fine. Everything's covered here. Just concentrate on Dylan and your family."

"Sorry, man. This just really blindsided me. Like I got hit by an 18-wheeler."

Shane could only imagine. "Nothing to apologize for. I'll call you in the morning and check in."

"You're a good friend. Thanks, Kenny."

It was hard to sit still after hearing Alan so raw with pain, and Shane paced a little circuit to the door of the Red Room and back to the rear stairs. He thought of Dylan's gap-toothed smile. No one should have to watch their seven-year-old child die. Especially not after Alan already lost his little girl. Shane didn't believe in God, but he grimly thought that if there was one, the bastard was a sadistic fuck.

Shit, he needed to focus on something other than dying kids. He pulled out his phone and Googled the president to catch up on the latest news. Vagabond had finished up glad-handing at the G7 and was now in Vienna, the neutral location for the Karelian peace talks, which weren't going well. The Russian dictator was making things difficult, but what else was new?

Shane thumbed through some other news stories about President Castillo, then did a loop of the floor and radioed in an all-clear report to the office in the basement. He ended up in Google images, and tapped on a picture of the Castillo family from last Christmas, which led down a rabbit hole of scrolling through pages of pictures. The president was a handsome man—around six foot, with thick, dark hair accented with gray at the temples. He was a regular jogger, and according to agents on his detail he was in damn good shape for fifty-four.

His wife was a few years younger, and also in trim shape. She truly was a beautiful woman. So far he hadn't interacted with her much at all, but the other week he'd seen her bark a command to one of her agents to be careful with a garment bag as her detail schlepped her suitcases to the car. As far as working the first family went, Shane was more than happy to stay with Valor.

The whole family was damned attractive, although Shane winced as he flipped through older pictures of Rafael. Valor had certainly had his awkward years well documented. Although even in later pictures, he always seemed to fade into the background, hunching a bit as if he was trying to make himself less visible.

Shane scrolled through the shots, wondering idly what was going on in Rafael Castillo's head.

In a picture from the White House Easter egg hunt, Rafael held hands with his girlfriend, smiling as they watched children run. She was a pretty girl—blonde and flowery. They looked like the perfect young Republican couple.

Shane closed the app and radioed in another report that all was quiet. It was going to be a long night.

IT WAS ALMOST two when a distant crash and shattering of glass echoed down the stairwell.

Shane was moving, taking the stairs two at a time and reaching for his gun, while the vibration still rang in the air. He grabbed his walkie. "Breaking glass on third floor. Confirming Valor's position. Hold."

He checked his blind spots as he edged around the final flight of stairs and out onto the floor. Center hall was clear. He came around the Linen Room, listening intently. From the direction of the Diet Kitchen, he could hear angry muttering. His shoes silent on the wooden floor, he approached, gun in hand. He did a fast peek into the kitchen before exhaling and holstering his weapon.

Rafael leapt to his feet, the shards of a white casserole dish and shattered glass of its lid scattered around the floor, along with the contents, which appeared to be some kind of tomato concoction. "What are you doing up here? This is *my* place! You're not allowed! We don't need protection up here!"

Shane raised his hands. "I heard something smash. Just double checking." He pulled out his radio. "Everything's ten-four. Valor is safe and sound."

Rafael scoffed. "Of course I am. What, you think someone dove into the skylight to kidnap me?" His cheeks were flushed, and he was in bare feet and plaid boxer shorts, his white T-shirt splashed with red. His hair, usually slicked back within an inch of its life, was tousled over his forehead. "You can go now. I'm fine." He jerked his gaze to the floor.

The kid didn't seem to like looking Shane in the eye, but he'd never been hostile. Perhaps Shane had jinxed it. "I'm sorry to upset you. I'm just doing my job."

"Well, consider it done. Can you please leave?" He took a tentative step and winced.

"Don't move. Is there a broom?"

"I can clean up. It's my mess."

Shane choked down a swell of frustration. "Yes, but you don't have shoes on, and there's broken glass and crockery and tomato goop everywhere. So tell me where the broom is. And the paper towels."

With a sigh, Rafael nodded to a cupboard. "There's a dustpan and little broom in the back." He squatted and started collecting large pieces of the dish.

Crouching beside him, Shane swept up the mess, emptying the pan in the garbage more than once and using paper towels to mop up the oily tomatoes. As he went after some stubborn shards of glass, the question slipped out. "What were you making? Smells good."

"Nothing much."

Shane raised an eyebrow. "Whatever you say."

"It's none of your business," he muttered.

"You're right." Shane swept forcefully. If the kid wanted to be a snotty brat about it, it was no skin off his nose. "Don't move. I'm not sure I've got it all."

"It's fine." Rafael took two steps and then stifled a cry. "Fuck." He lifted his foot, and a drop of blood hit the checkered floor.

With effort, Shane bit back an *I told you so* and motioned to the counter. "Hop up and let me see."

This time, Rafael did as he was told. His face was beet red, darkening his freckles as he lifted his foot for Shane. Shane prodded the shard of glass embedded in the sole. "Is there a first aid kit?"

Rafael nodded to the cupboards below the sink.

Shane took off his jacket, hanging it from the handle of one of the cupboards, and rolled up his shirt sleeves. He made sure his radio and handcuffs were securely fastened to his belt. His leather holster was snug around him, the pistol a familiar and comforting weight. He quickly washed and dried his hands, and then opened the kit. When he glanced up, Rafael jerked his head away, his gaze returning to his twisting fingers.

"It doesn't make you nervous, does it?" Shane asked.

"No," he quickly insisted.

"I'd think you'd be used to guns by now."

Rafael's brow furrowed. "Guns? Oh yeah, I don't even think about them anymore. My parents took us to the gun range before we moved to DC so we could learn how they worked and understand them. You know, since we're surrounded by armed people all the time. They weren't encouraging us to, like, get our own guns and shoot things. They just wanted us to be educated."

"Makes sense. Up," Shane said quietly, and Rafael lifted his foot. Holding Rafael's ankle with his left hand, Shane eased out the glass with his right, pressing a bandage to it quickly to stem any further bleeding. "Didn't go too deep, I don't think." He held the bandage firmly in place. "We'll just wait a minute to stop the worst of it."

"Uh-huh." Rafael nodded. "So anyway, it's fine. I realize you guys totally know what you're doing. With guns, I mean."

"We do. In DC we have to re-qualify every month with our handguns. Quarterly on shotguns and automatic weapons."

"You must be a great shot. You guys do so much training. Seems like it never stops."

"Yeah, it's ongoing. We have to stay sharp. Run drills for all the possible scenarios." He shifted his grip on Rafael's foot and pressed harder against the wound.

Rafael laughed weakly. "Yeah, all the ways some wackos might kidnap us. I guess there are plenty."

In the silence of the kitchen, Shane could hear the anxious little hitches in Rafael's breathing. He cleared his throat. "I hope you weren't too shaken up after that false alarm the first day. I know it wasn't the most auspicious beginning. It seems like I make you nervous. If you're having trouble trusting me—"

"What? No. I'm not. I'm just…I'm sorry I snapped at you when you came up here. It was totally out of line."

"It's not a problem." Impatient or pissed-off protectees were a hazard of the job. Shane lifted the bandage for a moment, and then pressed it back into place. There was dark hair scattered on Rafael's arms and lower legs, and it tickled Shane's palm where he held Rafael's ankle aloft. He had the absurd urge to run his hand up Rafael's leg, and he almost dropped the kid's ankle like it was a hot potato.

"It's that I'm not supposed to be in here. My mom's away for a week. I shouldn't be cooking, but I figured she'd never find out if I was careful." His laugh was sardonic. "As you can see, it's working out really well."

Shane chuckled, and Rafael gave him a tentative smile. "Don't worry about it," Shane said. "You can try it again tomorrow. And you know your secret's safe with me."

"It's stupid anyway."

"What is? Cooking?" Shane knew he should finish the first aid and get back downstairs, but what was the harm in putting the kid at ease? After that false alarm their very first day, he wanted his protectee to feel safe with him. "I don't think it's stupid."

Rafael met his gaze, his eyes dark and luminous. "You don't?"

"No. Especially not when you make things that smell this good." Shane lifted the bandage again and lowered his head to inspect the cut. He ran his fingertips over the sole of Rafael's foot, making sure there was no more glass. Rafael gasped softly, trembling under Shane's touch. When Shane met his gaze, Rafael smiled shakily.

"Ticklish," he muttered.

Shane unpeeled a Band-Aid. "Well, at least this injury wasn't my fault."

"That was nothing. And thanks for your help."

"Anytime." Shane smoothed on the bandage, aware of Rafael's gaze on him. Maybe it was the stillness of the late hour and their proximity, but the moment suddenly felt unnervingly intimate. He let go of Rafael's foot and stepped back, rolling down his sleeves. "Good as new."

"Thanks." Rafael didn't move from the counter, and he stared at the floor beneath his dangling feet.

"Let me just give it another sweep to be sure." Shane busied himself with the dustpan and broom.

After a few moments, Rafael said, "It was roasted grape tomatoes with basil and goat cheese. I was just about to add the cheese and put it back in the oven when I dropped it."

"Sounds delicious." Shane put away the dustpan and medical kit before shrugging on his suit jacket. He'd lingered long enough.

"If I make it again tomorrow night, will you try it?"

Shane paused in straightening his collar. "I really shouldn't."

"Please? It would help me out so much to get your opinion. Besides, that way you'll know exactly where I am, and that I'm not being kidnapped."

It was probably a bad idea, but Rafael's eyes were so imploring. The kid was clearly lonely. "Okay. I'll come up around midnight for a taste. Only for a few minutes."

"Awesome. Thanks."

Shane hurried downstairs, but all was quiet and still. When he checked in with the command office, everything was in order, and the night went on as if he'd never gone upstairs at all.

Chapter Five

R AFA HAD A serious problem.

No one else had seemed to notice that time had slowed to the approximate rate of a sloth crawling on its belly through a vat of molasses. The aides and staff all bustled about like it was any other day, when it clearly wasn't. He was going to cook tonight, and Shane was going to taste it. This was happening in real life and not just his head.

He couldn't believe he'd actually said the words out loud, asking Shane to come back. And although he knew Shane was only being nice, excitement still simmered through him. Since his parents were out of town, Magda only made a quick appearance in the kitchen, and she was nice enough to load him up with supplies and even give him a quick brush-up on the proper way to chiffonade herbs.

Then Marissa called to talk about an upcoming foundation event his mother wanted him to chair, and Rafa forced himself to jot down notes, knowing he wouldn't remember a freaking word later. It was a good distraction for fifteen minutes, at least.

It was late afternoon when his phone buzzed. Rafa was flopped on his bed naked after another jerk-off session starring Shane and his thick cock, which alternated being cut and uncut in Rafa's imagination. Of course he had no idea what Shane's cock really looked like and never would, but in his head it was spectacular.

He reached for his phone, expecting Ashleigh and hoping it wasn't Marissa again. Instead, a text from his brother stared back at him.

How's it going?

That was Matthew—a man of few words. Affection and longing surged through Rafa. He realized he hadn't seen Matty since Christmas. His thumbs flew.

Okay. Mom's making me work with her foundation, but it's good experience, I guess. How's life in the pool?

Wet.

Rafa smiled fleetingly. Matthew had always loved swimming, but by his senior year of high school it had become an obsession. Even now, Rafa couldn't help but resent it just a little. With only two years between them, they'd been inseparable as kids. Now they saw each other on holidays when Matty couldn't come up with a good enough excuse to stay away.

Rafa asked: *Are you working on your backstroke?*

Mostly butterfly. Dude, why didn't you go to Paris with your girl? That way Mom at least has to cross the Atlantic to meddle.

Nausea waved through him. Not only did he barely see or talk to Matty—his brother didn't even *know* him anymore. But by the time Rafa had been ready to actually say it out loud in senior year, Matthew had been long gone to California. Adriana too, and Chris had really never lived at the White House. It hadn't been until Rafa had met Ashleigh that he'd been able to say the words.

Rafa typed out: *It hasn't been too bad.*

Matthew replied: *Mom's dropping by here on her way back to DC next week. Even more suits around. Just what I need.*

Of all of them, Matthew had rebelled most against the constant protection. Rafa could remember staring at his plate and spearing peas with the tines of his fork as Matty and their parents had argued about having agents at prom. Of course their parents had won. They always did. He typed again.

At least it'll be over in January. Not much longer.

The reply was: *LOL, always the optimist. You'll probably miss it all, you freak.*

Even though he knew Matty was kidding, it still hurt. He wanted to write back: *Just because I didn't scream and stomp my feet doesn't mean I like it.* Instead he typed: *Yeah. Probably.*

Later. My session's starting. Don't drink too much Kool-Aid.

Rafa wanted to reply, but he tossed his phone on the mattress. What was the point? He choked down his resentment. Matty had never understood why Rafa played by the rules and didn't make waves.

Besides, he was breaking the rules now, wasn't he? Asking Shane up to the third floor was...well, he supposed it wasn't against the *rules*, per se. And could Shane really say no? He was probably afraid Rafa would call his dad and get him in trouble if he didn't do as he asked.

Ugh. Was he, like, sexually harassing Shane?

No. It wasn't as if Rafa was hitting on him, or expecting anything other than a few opinions about his food. That was okay. It wouldn't even take long. It wasn't as if Shane was—

His phone buzzed, and he snatched it up. Maybe Matty had written more. But as he stared at the picture of his father, laughing on a hike they'd taken the last time they'd all been at Camp David, Rafa's stomach swooped. He hit the screen. "Dad?"

"Hi, Rafa. How are you?"

The line was so clear his father could have been right there in the room. Irrational guilt whooshed through Rafa since he'd been masturbating and thinking of a man—his Secret Service agent, no less. He tugged the duvet over him as if his dad could see he was naked and sticky. "Um, great. How are you?"

"Oh, fine. These Karelians are being stubborn. Russians too, but what else is new?"

Rafa forced out a laugh. "I'm sure you'll wear them down. You always do."

"Well, I try. But I want to talk about you, Raf."

Great. Since when? "Uh-huh? Everything's fine." It wasn't that his father didn't love him—he did, very much. But Ramon Castillo was a damn busy man.

"Enjoying your summer break?"

"Mmm-hmm. I'm working more with Mom's foundation."

"Good, good. When I get home, I'd like us to sit down and talk about your future."

I can't wait. "Sure. Well, you know I still have one term left of college, so…" Thank God for that.

"Of course." He paused. "Raf, are you sure everything's all right?"

His heart skipped. "Yeah. Why wouldn't it be?" He'd been telling his father everything was terrific for years and he'd never been questioned.

"You must miss Ashleigh."

Relief coursed through him. "Well, yeah. But she's getting such great experience. She wanted to thank you again for helping with the internship."

"Of course."

Rafa could imagine his father's self-deprecating smile and dismissive *who, me?* wave of his hand. As a conservative man of the people, he'd perfected his humble routine years ago. Not that Rafa thought he hadn't genuinely wanted to help Ash. It was just hard sometimes to know what his father was really thinking. "We appreciate it, Dad."

"Perhaps you should fly over and surprise her. We could easily arrange a plane."

"Oh! Um…that would be awesome, but like I said, I'm doing a lot of stuff with the foundation. I'm actually chairing an event in August." He was suddenly incredibly grateful Marissa had called. Not that he didn't miss Ashleigh and want to see Paris, but it made him uneasy for some reason.

"I just want to make sure you're happy. We worry about you."

You do? "I'm good, Dad. Honestly."

"All right." His voice went distant for a moment as he said something to someone else. "Raf? I'll see you next week. Love you."

"Love you too. Have fun with the Karelians."

After he hung up, Rafa laid there on his bed, staring at the artfully swirled paint on the cream ceiling. Jesus, how was he going to tell them the truth? He should have done it in high school, but his father's reelection campaign had been brutal. He'd barely squeaked out a second term, and Rafa hadn't wanted to distract him.

Then the bill had happened. His stomach churned just thinking about it.

S.J.Res. 19: A joint resolution proposing an amendment to the Constitution of the United States relative to marriage.

The battle over same-sex marriage had waged on for years, even after the Supreme Court's verdict declaring it legal in all fifty states. Then a junior senator from Oklahoma had introduced the bill to amend the constitution and overrule the Supreme Court. They wanted to call it "constitutional" marriage, and of course no same-sex couples need apply.

Even now, almost four years later, it made him sick to remember that night the week of Thanksgiving.

The TV lights were blinding as they stood on stage waving to hundreds of people gathered in some meeting hall or banquet room. Sweat trickled down his temple, and he hoped his neatly slicked hair would stay put. His mother's opal bracelet shone delicately as she waved. It was so noisy he could barely hear himself think...

When Rafa's father had addressed the crowd at the National Family Coalition, Rafa had listened with an automatic smile. His dad talked about marriage and family and God, and this new bill. About doing what he knew was right in his heart. All the while, Rafa had stood there frozen in the glare of the lights, still smiling while a chunk of his soul died.

Adriana had screamed at their father in the limo afterward, and Chris and Matthew had argued with him too. Their parents had insisted it was only politics—a party decision. Rafa had sat very still in the corner, not even hearing them after a while as a buzzing filled his head. His throat had been dry, palms clammy. He'd kept his head down and wished he could simply disappear. Even now, the remembered terror went bone deep. He'd always been afraid to tell his parents the truth, and after that night it had felt absolutely impossible.

Sighing, Rafa ran a hand over his face. He *would* come out. He wasn't going to live his whole life in the closet, not even if it meant losing his parents' love. He thought they'd come around after a while. That at least they wouldn't turn their backs on him completely. They were Catholic, but had never been regular churchgoers aside from during campaigns. His parents had always been much more vocally religious to appeal to voters than they actually were.

Gay marriage had been on the backburner during his father's election campaigns, and while Rafa had known his parents weren't exactly riding a rainbow float in a Pride parade, he'd never expected...*that*.

He knew it hadn't been personal—how could it be when his parents didn't know he was gay? But it had hurt him more than he'd ever thought possible. Then there'd been the guilt that if he'd come out before college, he might have influenced his father's thoughts on the matter. Although surely not the Republican Party's, and they were the ones making many of his father's decisions when it came down to it. It was the way of politics. Thank God the Democrats had managed to kill the bill.

Now it was almost over, and Rafa would be graduating and they'd all leave the White House. Maybe they could be a normal family again. Then he'd sit them down and tell them. Until then, he had to stick to the plan. The plan had worked all these years.

Blowing out a long breath, he checked the time on his phone. It was still early, but he had basil to chiffonade.

GLANCING IN THE reflection of the microwave, Rafa smoothed a hand over his hair. He'd tamed it with pomade after his shower that morning as usual, but now he squinted critically. Was it too much? *Maybe I should wet it a bit, or—*

"Oh my God," he muttered. "This isn't a freaking date. Chill."

The timer beeped, and he stirred the tomatoes and basil. He added the goat cheese before carefully putting it back in the oven. Lucky for him there'd been another casserole dish he could use. Then he checked the simmering ravioli, which he'd stuffed with caramelized onion and roasted Portobello mushrooms.

It had occurred to him Shane might be a vegetarian, so he'd played it safe. The gorgonzola cream sauce was thickening nicely, and he stirred it, splashing a little onto the cuff of his dark green button-down. He swiped it off with his finger and popped it in his mouth.

"Taste good?"

"Jesus!" Rafa whirled around to find Shane filling the doorway. His heart thumped stupidly, and he smiled. "I guess you'll be the judge of that." He nervously patted his hands on his chinos. "It's almost ready."

Shane checked his watch. "Great."

Rafa's smile faded. "Sorry, do you have to get back downstairs? I'm a little late. The timing is tricky—I'm still working on it. If you want to come back in a bit? Or we could just forget it. You're busy." Why had he even asked? The whole thing was dumb. His food probably sucked anyway.

But Shane shook his head. "It's fine. Besides, now that I smell it, there's no way I can leave without having a taste."

"Cool. Alan won't miss you?"

Shane's expression tightened. "He's not here. Probably won't be the rest of the week. His son's in the hospital."

Rafa paused in stirring the sauce. "Oh. I'm sorry to hear that. Is he going to be okay?"

"Hopefully. He has a rare disease. Something to do with the immune system." Shane was silent for a moment, as if weighing whether to say more. "It's brutal. Alan's daughter Jessica died of it last year."

"God. That's awful." Poor Alan. He seemed like a really nice guy. Dying kids was just the worst. Rafa shifted uncomfortably. "Tell him I hope his son will be all right."

"I will. Thanks."

The timer beeped again, and he slipped on his oven mitts and removed the casserole dish, depositing it onto a cooling board. "This needs to sit for a bit. Do you want to radio his replacement?"

"It's okay." Shane still stood in the doorway. "We're short-staffed, so I'm on detail by myself. We figured you weren't likely to be running around in the middle of the night."

"Oh. Yeah, not really my thing. But why didn't Brent tell me? I can make sure to stay in if that's easier for you guys." He'd seen Brent and Raul downstairs earlier, but they hadn't said a word.

"It's not your responsibility to make things easier for us, Rafael."

Rafa shrugged. "Why not? You're responsible for my life. It's pretty much the least I can do. Oh, and call me Rafa. Everyone does."

Shane regarded him for a moment before nodding.

"So it's just you and me all night?" The words were barely out when Rafa wished desperately he could reel them back. *This is why you shouldn't talk.* The tips of his ears burned, and he concentrated on the sauce, stirring it vigorously.

"Well, you and me and all the other security staff. Guess you're never really alone."

Okay, it seemed fine. Shane was being normal, and hadn't read anything sexual into what he'd said. Rafa exhaled. "Yeah. Not really. At school, my detail's always in the hallway. I get the closest to alone here, actually. The third floor's mine, for the most part. And when my parents are away and the second floor's empty, I can almost imagine there's no one around for miles." *Now you're babbling. Stop.* He drained the ravioli in a colander, and curiosity got the better of him. "Isn't it boring?"

As usual, Shane's expression was even. "What?"

"Protecting people. Spending hours and hours with me or whoever. Standing outside doorways, or in the corner of rooms. Watching crowds for danger. Do you even get to eat while you're working?"

"Sometimes."

"Sometimes you get to eat, or sometimes it's boring?"

"Both."

"Well, I hope you're hungry now."

"I can always eat."

"A man after my own heart." Rafa smiled, and—holy shit—Shane actually smiled back. It was just for a moment, a flash of teeth and the corners of his mouth lifting, but it was a smile. Butterflies fluttered to life in Rafa's stomach, and he wanted to make Shane smile again. He wondered what sort of things Shane liked. Did he have hobbies?

Stop thinking about him like that. This is NOT A DATE, you loser.

Keeping his eyes on his work, Rafa gently placed three ravioli in the center of a shallow bowl. Then he spooned the sauce over and sprinkled a few toasted pecans on top. "Um, here. You can try this while I cut the bread."

He picked up his bread knife and went to work on the warm baguette. The chopping board had been in the kitchen when they'd moved in, and Rafa loved all the old cut marks on the worn wood. For some reason it made him feel…safe, maybe. He glanced up. Shane was still barely inside the kitchen. "You can come in, you know. I won't bite." *Shit. Did that sound like a come-on?*

"Should I use my hands?"

"What?" Rafa dropped the knife, and it slid off the board and clattered to the floor, narrowly avoiding his leather-clad foot. He squawked out a laugh. "Whoops. And oh, uh, I'll get you a fork. Sorry." He laughed nervously again.

Shane only raised an eyebrow. "Should I get the first aid kit out just in case? Tonight you're wearing shoes, at least."

"Definitely learned my lesson." After rescuing the bread knife from the floor, Rafa opened and closed drawers, suddenly unable to remember where the cutlery lived. When he found it, he yanked out a knife and fork and thrust them at Shane, who leaned back. *Great. Stab the guy. That'll make things so much better.* "Sorry. Um, here you go."

Shane took the cutlery. With his bowl on the counter, he sliced into a ravioli and took a bite. After a moment, he mumbled, "Mmm."

Rafa exhaled and went back to the bread. *He likes it. Does he like it? It seems like he likes it. Play it cool.* "Do you like it?" he blurted. *Yep. Real cool.*

"I do." Shane took another bite and chewed thoughtfully. "Nice sweetness with the onion. The mushroom…it's good."

"No, the mushroom what? Don't just tell me what I want to hear. I have enough sycophants in my life."

The corner of Shane's mouth twitched. "Fair enough. The mushrooms might be a little salty."

"Okay. I'll check that. Thank you." Rafa speared a piece of

ravioli and tasted it without the sauce or pecans. "You're right—bit too salty." He hurried over to his notebook and scribbled. One day he'd perfect a signature dish that had all the flavor notes just right. He went back to the bread and served up the roasted tomatoes, basil, and goat cheese. "It's kind of like bruschetta, I guess. But hotter. More filling, especially with the olive oil. It's supposed to soak the bread a bit."

As Shane took a bite, Rafa anxiously shoved a piece of bread into his own mouth. The tomatoes and cheese tasted good, and the basil chiffonade looked almost professional.

"Mmm. This is excellent. Delicious."

"You think?" Rafa beamed.

"Absolutely." After a few moments of eating, Shane nodded at Rafa's shirt. "Why so dressed up?"

"This?" Rafa glanced down at himself. "This is my usual." He'd tried on four nearly identical button-down shirts before finally going with the one he wore.

Shane didn't comment, instead taking another bite of bread and tomatoes. He made a little satisfied noise low in his throat that threatened to transform Rafa's tingling arousal to a full-fledged hard-on.

Rafa cast about for something to say. "Did you always want to be in the Secret Service?"

"No." Shane sliced another ravioli in half.

"So what did you want to be?"

Eyes on his plate, Shane smirked. "An astronaut. But who doesn't?"

"Me. I think I'd throw up in zero gravity. I love food too much to risk it."

This time, Shane chuckled—a rumble that nearly had Rafa gripping the side of the counter. Shane checked his watch.

No, don't leave yet. "I'm going to Australia next year," Rafa blurted. "After the inauguration."

Shane seemed to ponder it for a few moments, leaning his hip against the counter as he scooped up more tomato mixture with a piece of bread, the goat cheese oozing. "Why Australia?"

"It's stupid. You're going to laugh." Rafa fiddled with a pot lid. Why had he said anything? He almost felt like he was outside his body, watching this surreal conversation unfold.

"I won't." Shane said it with his usual gravelly voice, but there was something else there too. An underlying tone of compassion, perhaps?

"Okay, well...there's a Cordon Bleu in Sydney, and other cooking schools. And in Australia hardly anyone will recognize me. Or at least it won't be as bad as here. I could go to Europe, but Australia's always seemed...I don't know. Magical somehow. Like another planet, as far away from DC as I can get. I can finally learn to cook from real chefs, and..."

Shane waited.

Rafa swallowed hard. "I've always dreamed of something else too." He forced out a breath, the words tumbling with it. "I want to surf. It's stupid, I know."

"Surfing's not stupid."

Rafa chanced a glance at Shane, who was smiling. In fact, his eyes were twinkling, and he was smiling so widely there were matching creases in his cheeks. "You don't think so?" Rafa asked?

"I grew up surfing. It's the thing I miss most about California."

"Really? You can surf?" Electricity zinged through Rafa.

"I could. Been a long time now."

"Where did you live in California?"

"Orange County. The regular burbs, not the gated communities. Laguna Beach was a couple of bus rides away. I practically lived there in the summer."

Rafa loved listening to Shane talk. There was something pleasing about his rumble-y voice, and he wanted to hear more. "That's so cool. I've always wanted to learn. I was obsessed with surfing websites as a kid. Did you have brothers and sisters? Did they surf too? My family always thought it was a weird interest considering I grew up in central Jersey."

"I was an only child." His expression tightened, and then he cleared his throat and didn't say anything else. He checked his watch. "I should get back down there."

Rafa was dying to ask more questions, but he also didn't want Shane to leave because he was being too nosy. "I tried it once in Atlantic City and wiped out big time." The humiliation washed over him, dulled by time but always there. "Someone recorded it on their phone and it went viral. I haven't tried again."

Shane frowned. "You shouldn't let what people think stop you."

With an incredulous laugh, Rafa filled the sink to scrub the pots. He liked cleaning up when he cooked; it was good practice for getting a job in a restaurant when he moved to Sydney. "I try not to, but…"

"Easier said than done. I get it."

"I just wish I could try it without people watching. I miss being outdoors so much. When I was a kid, sometimes I'd go camping with the neighbors. My parents never understood why I'd want to. I mean, Camila Castillo de Saucedo does not *camp*."

Shane laughed. "No, I don't imagine she does."

"But I always loved it—being under the stars and having a campfire. Even just going hiking for an afternoon. It would be so amazing to go for a walk by myself in the woods, or the mountains, or along a beach—anywhere, really. And actually be alone. Like, *completely* alone. No one else for miles, or at least no one in eye-shot. To have the freedom to just walk wherever I wanted without agents trailing me, or people taking pictures." He quickly added, "But I know you guys are just doing your jobs. I don't mean to sound ungrateful or whiny."

"You don't. I can't imagine what it's like having a detail twenty-four-seven. It would drive me nuts. You're everyone's favorite because you're so good about it."

Rafa looked down at his bowl, his ears getting hot. "Really? That's nice to hear. And you guys have always been cool. But man, I can't wait until I can go out by myself. I have a huge list of stuff to do in Australia. Hiking and swimming, and finally learning how to surf." He realized he was grinning like a fool just thinking about the freedom. "Anyway. Sorry, I'm talking your ear off."

"I don't mind. Makes the night shift a lot more interesting." Shane checked his watch again. "I really should get back, though. Thanks for this. Nice to have a home-cooked meal for a change. You really are very good at it."

"Your wife doesn't cook?" He went for a casual air and failed miserably.

Shane brought his bowl and cutlery to the sink. "No wife. I'm gay. No husband either. With the job, I tend to work long hours and travel at a moment's notice. Not conducive to serious relationships." As if he'd said too much, he quickly backed away. "Thanks again."

Oh. My. God.

Rafa's brain sputtered. *Did he just say he's gay? And single? Am I dead? Am I in heaven?* "Um…yeah. Good. Great. I mean, you're welcome." His mind buzzed. *Get it together! Say something!* "Oh, what about tomorrow? I have so many things to try. Please? You'd be doing me a big favor."

Fiddling with his sleeves, Shane didn't look at him. "I'll try. You did really good work tonight. Thank you."

With that, he disappeared into the little corridor, and Rafa listened to his quiet steps until there was only silence once more.

"Holy shit."

His mind replayed the last minute in his mind, and yep, Shane had said it. He'd said he was gay. And he'd said it like it was *nothing*. Even though lots of people supported LGBT rights nowadays…it still wasn't nothing. At least not to Rafa.

There were a lot of people who still thought it was wrong, and even though *he* knew it wasn't…the idea of saying it so easily was boggling. He wondered if it would ever be so simple for him.

Wow. Shane was gay. His wet dream fantasy man was *actually gay too*. Shane had undoubtedly had sex with men. Like, for real. It had happened. A lot. Images flashed through Rafa's mind, and blood rushed south.

Grinning, he hurried with finishing the dishes so he could go back to his room. There was nothing wrong with fantasies, right? Didn't hurt anyone. Rafa reminded himself that Shane was only being nice, but he may have even whistled as he worked.

Chapter Six

"HEY, KENDRICK." HARRIS nodded as Shane reached the top of the stairs on the main floor. His detail partner, Raul Guzman, nodded as well.

"Anything to report?" Shane asked.

"Nope," Guzman replied. He ran a hand over his short black hair and whistled softly. "This kid is boring as hell. You're in for another long night."

Harris smirked. "You'd rather be flying to Vegas with no toothbrush and just the clothes on your back?"

Guzman held up his hands. "You're right. After his sister's detail, I shouldn't complain. You know the story, Kendrick?"

"I've heard bits and pieces."

Guzman shook his head. "Ten o'clock at night, almost time for a shift change. Virtue up and jumps in her car and heads to the airport. No notice, no nothing. We're scrambling to make sure we can keep her secure at the terminal. And of course we have to go with her to Vegas. It was my wife's birthday the next day. I didn't get home until three days later."

"The glamorous life of the Secret Service," Harris said. "Travel at a moment's notice, unpaid overtime, and not enough money to deal with the bullshit. Especially now that they've slashed our benefits. Land of the free, and home of the overworked and underpaid."

Shane wondered when Harris had started getting bitter. Would that be him in ten years?

"All right, we'll leave you to it, Kendrick. Haven't heard a peep from the mouse. Have a good one." Guzman gave Shane's arm a slap, and he and Harris disappeared downstairs.

Shane sat in the wooden chair in the corner and wondered what Rafa had made for him to taste. The kid really did seem to have a flair for food, although Shane had admittedly never had a picky palate. Still, he found himself looking forward to it. Which he really shouldn't have been, since it wasn't in his job description to be Rafa's guinea pig in the first place. But what harm did it do if Rafa was safe?

Besides, it wasn't a bad way to spend some of the long hours of the night shift. There was no rule that said an agent couldn't enjoy him or herself sometimes. He'd spent plenty of pleasant hours on the ranch in Montana protecting former president Hamilton. Fortunately, the biggest threat there had been a gopher hole the former first lady had stepped in, leading to a badly twisted ankle.

He wondered if Rafa had been able to find the old surfing book he'd recommended. Shane wished he still had his copy to lend, but it had gone in the fire. The twist of pain and guilt knotted him up for a few moments, dull and familiar.

As it receded, he considered whether he should check the Amazon marketplace for it. But no, it wouldn't be appropriate to buy a book for his protectee. Still, it was nice to talk surfing again. Rafa had no practical experience, but he was far more up to date on the current state of the sport than Shane was.

When Rafa appeared ten minutes later, he smiled anxiously as he wound one of the strings on his navy hoodie around his finger and scuffed the toe of his sneaker on the carpeted runner on the stairs. "Hey. I've got a seafood lasagna in the oven. Béchamel sauce. I thought in the meantime, I'd go bowling. And you'd have to come with me, obviously. I mean, if that's cool."

"Of course. You know you're free to do whatever you want." Shane realized that must be why Rafa was in casual clothes and not his usual buttoned-up, neatly ironed outfits. His hair was still slicked, though. *Too bad he won't let his curls down.* Shane blinked at the strange thought. Why should it matter to him how Rafa wore his hair? Although he couldn't help feeling it would do the kid some good to let go a bit.

Rafa led the way downstairs to the basement bowling alley as Shane radioed their new location to the office. As they walked by the open door, one of the agents on the night shift inside gave him a nod.

There was a two-lane alley in the basement of the office build-ing near the West Wing that Shane had heard hosted tournaments between White House staffers and the Secret Service, but here in the residence there was a narrow room with a single lane.

Rafa opened the door and flicked on the overhead fluorescent lights. "It's kind of lame, huh?"

Shane blinked. He'd been to almost every room in the White House, but not this one. "It's very...patriotic."

Nose wrinkling as he smiled, Rafa sat in one of the molded plastic chairs and untied his shoelaces. "When we moved in it was painted this gross coral color, with big cheesy bowling pins on the walls. So my dad asked Henry to get it repainted, and I guess his instructions were something like, 'imagine what would happen if an American flag puked all over the room.'"

Shane couldn't hold in his burst of laughter, and Rafa's smile grew wider. Shane surveyed the stars and stripes painted over the walls—red, white, and blue everything. There was even an eagle taking flight at the end of the lane. "Sounds about right."

"What size are you?" In his socks, Rafa crouched in front of a wooden cubby holding about twenty pairs of bowling shoes in various sizes.

"Oh, I can't bowl. You go ahead."

Rafa didn't look up from the cubby. "You can't as in, bowling is beyond your capabilities, or you can't because you're not supposed to?"

"The latter. If there's an emergency, I can't run out of here in bowling shoes. You go ahead. I'll keep score."

"The computer keeps score." He stuffed his feet into shoes. "Come on, you can just do it without the right shoes. I won't tell. Hardly anyone uses this bowling alley anyway. It's no fun to play against myself."

"Don't you have any friends who could come over?"

Blinking, Rafa dropped his head. "I guess. Not really. Sorry, I know I'm bugging you." He jammed his palm against a button on the wall, and the bowling alley came to life, the mechanism at the end resetting the ten pins and the computer screen on the wall flickering on. At a console on a little table, Rafa typed in his name and hit enter.

Shit. Shane hated seeing Rafa's shoulders hunch like that. "That's not what I meant. You're not bugging me at all." What the hell. "All right." He walked to the console and added his name. "Let's see what you've got."

Rafa smiled tentatively. "Yeah? Okay. Cool." He picked up a green globe and moved to the edge of the alley. Holding the ball up in front of him, he breathed silently for a few moments. Then he took three steps and gracefully unleashed the ball, his legs bending and his arm arcing up, his shirt pulling over lean muscles. The ball slammed into the pins, sending all ten scattering. He pumped his fist and spun around. "Beat that, old man." His smile faltered.

Shane realized he'd been staring, and he could see the worry on Rafa's face as the kid likely wondered if he'd gone too far. But Shane picked up his own ball and strode by him. "Watch and learn, Grasshopper."

"Grasshopper?" Rafa's nose wrinkled. "Is that from something?"

"An old kung-fu show. I had to Google it when one of my instructors called us that during training." He swung his arm back and took a few steps.

Shane hadn't been bowling in years, and he knew as soon as the ball left his hand it was no good. As it careened off the wooden lane and headed for the gutter, Shane gritted his teeth.

"Um, what am I supposed to be learning, exactly?"

Ignoring him, Shane picked up another ball. He lined up the sights and pulled his arm back. This one rolled into the other gutter.

"If you want, I can put down the bumpers?"

He shot Rafa a glare that only made the kid smile wider.

"Good effort. Keep it up." Rafa picked up his next ball. "That's what my little league coach used to say when I whiffed my at-bats."

Shane laughed. "All right, let's see what you can do. Prove that wasn't a fluke."

Rafa did just that, scoring a spare with his two balls in the second frame. Shane lined up his next shot. This time it hit one pitiful pin on the left side.

"You're twisting your arm too much," Rafa noted.

"All right, Grasshopper. How do I fix it?"

"Okay, pick up the ball."

Shane did, and suddenly Rafa was standing behind him. Very close. He put one palm on Shane's back and ran his other down Shane's right arm. When he spoke, his breath tickled the back of Shane's neck and ear.

"So when your arm goes back, keep it straight, like this." He guided Shane's arm into position. "You see?"

"Mmm." Shane's heart was beating too fast.

"Then when you throw it—" Rafa moved even closer, his hip

meeting Shane's ass. "Take the last step and keep your arm straight as you go."

Shane's mouth was alarmingly dry, and he jerked forward, his fingers gripping the holes in the ball. "Got it. Thanks." He tried to focus on the pins and the arrows on the lane, but his mind was full of white noise as his body thrummed. What the fuck was wrong with him? Clearly he needed to get laid if he was getting turned on by physical contact that was purely innocent.

His next shot took out three pins, so that was a vast improvement.

Rafa clapped. "There you go! See, I'll give you bowling tips, and you can tell me about surfing."

Shane managed one more pin in his frame, and shook his head as Rafa knocked down almost all of them with his next ball. "I think at this point your advice is a lot more useful than mine. Haven't been on my board in forever." With a pang, he thought of his trusty Infinity, long gone now. His parents had kept it for him in the garage. He could still hear his mother's teasing now.

"We're keeping this board hostage so you'll visit. Come back soon!"

But he hadn't. He'd gotten caught up in work. Caught up in everything except what really mattered.

"Why not?"

"Huh?" Shane blinked back to attention.

Rafa took his next shot, taking out the final two pins for another spare. "Why haven't you surfed more over the years?"

"After training, my first assignment was the field office in Omaha. No waves in Nebraska. Then it was Greensboro, and then Albany. Montana. Me and surfing just weren't meant to be, I guess."

Rafa leaned against the wall as he watched Shane take a ball. "Don't you ever go back to California to visit? Do your parents still live there?"

"No." He rolled the ball, sending it into the gutter near the end of the lane. It was stupid that the pain still tugged at him, clammy and insistent even now.

"I'm sorry. Did I say something wrong?"

Shane forced himself to meet Rafa's gaze. "No. It's... My parents were killed. Six years ago now. A house fire caused by faulty wiring."

"God. Shane, I'm so sorry." Rafa took a step, reaching out with his hand and then letting it drop to his side. "That must have been terrible."

He kept his voice even as he lined up a shot. "House was completely gutted. It all burned. My dad had kept a family picture on his desk at the school where he taught. It's the only thing I have left of them." *Why am I telling him this?* He threw the ball and managed to keep it on the lane. "Anyway, like I said, hasn't been any opportunity for surfing since I finished college." Stepping back, he waited for Rafa to take a ball, but Rafa only watched him with sad eyes. Shane cleared his throat. "It's your turn."

"Oh! Um, yeah." Rafa bowled, his ball spinning into the gutter.

Shane forced a triumphant smile and a light tone. "Ah, the master shows weakness. Things might be turning around here for the old man."

Rafa put on his own shaky grin. "You wish. I was just faking you out." He took his next ball, and sure enough it was a strike. "*Bam.*"

"Impressive comeback, I'll grant you that. But let's see what the rest of the frames have in store."

What they had in store was resounding defeat, and when the game was over, Shane shook his head. "All right, you win this round."

Rafa pulled his phone from his pocket and glanced at the screen. "Just in time for lasagna. Hope you're hungry."

"Always."

As he changed his shoes, Rafa glanced up at Shane. "Hey, where did you go to college?"

"UCLA."

"What did you major in?"

"English. I always liked reading, and I needed a degree to join the Service."

"Cool. What's your favorite book?"

"*The Hunt for Red October.*"

Rafa's face lit up. "Really? Most people would say something totally old and pretentious."

Chuckling, Shane shrugged. "I've certainly enjoyed my fair share of literature, but for sheer pleasure, it's Clancy's earlier work. What's yours?"

"Well, usually I'd say *The Grapes of Wrath*. I mean, I have to say something American, and I do think it's a good book. But for pure reading enjoyment? Harry Potter." He laughed and ducked his head as if he was expecting Shane to mock him.

"Which one in particular? I'm partial to number four."

Springing to his feet, Rafa grinned. "Me too! The Triwizard Tournament is the best. The whole maze sequence was so amazing. Uh, excuse the pun."

Shane found himself laughing, which felt...damn it, it felt *good*. "And the graveyard scene was a gut punch. I really need to reread the whole series."

"Yeah, me too. We should read them together." He waved his hand, his smile fading. "I mean...not actually *together*. We should just both reread them. Although I guess we shouldn't be talking about books anyway." He turned off the lane. "But now I need to know: least favorite book."

"Anything by James Joyce aside from *The Dead*. I know they say *Ulysses* is genius, but I'm a fan of punctuation."

"Oh my God, *right*? I only had to read a few chapters for my

English historical survey class, and it was torture. I just do not see the genius."

"I don't think anyone does, but they're too afraid to admit it."

"Exactly!" Rafa exclaimed. As Shane opened the door, Rafa flicked the lights and paused in the shadows. "Hey, do you think you'll ever try surfing again?"

The thought simultaneously filled him with a swell of joy and the heavy drag of grief. He hadn't been in California since the funeral. Not that he couldn't surf in other places, but for some reason surfing was all tied up in the fire, lost in the ashes. "I don't think so."

"But you never know, right?"

"I'm not much of an optimist."

Rafa smiled then, sad and sweet. "That's okay. I'll be one for you."

Shane followed as Rafa headed to the stairs, trying to banish the wave of happiness that filled his chest.

Chapter Seven

AFTER DIPPING HIS finger in the jar of pomade, Rafa went after the rogue curl over his ear, cursing at it under his breath. "Stay put, damn you."

Of course it wouldn't, and it really didn't matter anyway since it would be dark. And it's not as if Shane would care what his hair looked like. Maybe he should just have another shower and let it curl naturally. Frowning at himself in the bathroom mirror, Rafa imagined it.

Ch-ch-ch-Chia.

He snapped off the bathroom light and grabbed his burgundy hoodie. It had been a little cooler that day, and he might need it down by the water. He zipped it over his tee and hesitated. Maybe he should wear nicer clothes like usual. He hoped they wouldn't encounter anyone, but what if they did?

So what *if you do? No one will care, you freak. And Shane's seen you in your boxers. What does it matter?*

The thought of being in his underwear in front of Shane predictably made his dick swell, even if there'd been nothing sexual about it. Checking his watch, Rafa considered jerking off before going downstairs—it wouldn't take much—but it was almost midnight.

He laced his sneakers and then picked up his knapsack before taking the back staircase down. As he reached the main floor, his heart skipped. Shane stood in the hallway glancing at his watch.

He frowned.

"Everything all right? I was just going to come up."

"Yeah. I actually wanted to do something different tonight. Go for a walk."

Shane's frown deepened. "Okay. On the grounds?"

"By the river, actually. The Potomac," he added. He winced internally. *No shit.*

"By the Memorials?"

"No. Farther upstream. It's not too far, though. Shouldn't be anyone there this time of night. Or morning, I guess."

Shane was still frowning. "Why do you want to go to the river in the middle of the night?"

"The moon's almost full, and there's this cool little waterfall. It's peaceful. I don't know. I just want to go." Rafa suddenly felt foolish with the picnic he'd carefully packed in his knapsack. He'd been planning for it all day as if he and Shane were going out on a date, and it was ridiculous. Irritation flashed through him. "I'm allowed to go where I want. I'm not a prisoner."

Shane's frown morphed into the placating half smile that the Secret Service must drill into its agents during training. "Of course you can go. Let me give them the heads up downstairs and put in a call to the Joint Ops Center at headquarters. They monitor all the protectees' locations. We might want to enlist one of the uniforms to come with us."

Rafa's heart sank. "I don't think we'll need to. Seriously, there'll be no one around. And no one's even interested in me."

"I'll be back in a minute."

Grumbling to himself, Rafa waited. If someone else came, it would... *What? Ruin your date that's not a date?* Rafa should just abort. This was a terrible idea. They could go back up to the kitchen and eat the food there. It wasn't even that fancy. He should have made something better than roast beef sandwiches, even if he'd made the garlic horseradish mayo himself and even borrowed a bread maker from Magda for the sour dough buns. They were still just sandwiches. Why had he ever—

As Shane reappeared, Rafa attempted a smile.

"Okay. I'll drive you in the Suburban. Since it's a pop-up at this hour, we should be fine without another agent. Just this once."

Rafa knew that was what they called it when a protectee went on an unplanned excursion. "Great." He stuffed his hands in his pockets so he wouldn't fidget. "Cool. Thanks."

The ride to the river was quiet and didn't take long. Rafa directed Shane, who kept his eyes on the road and the mirrors, and his hands at ten and two on the steering wheel. Since he was the only agent, he didn't wear the radio earpiece, but when they arrived at the falls, he called in immediately and had a terse conversation that lasted no more than ten seconds.

Then there was silence as they sat in the front seat of the Suburban. Rafa had been right—there didn't seem to be a soul around for miles, and the little waterfall gleamed in the moonlight, the river flowing over the rock formations. Maybe they could go for a hike, but he supposed it would be too dark in the woods.

Shane cleared his throat. "So here it is. Do you want to get out?"

"Oh. Yeah." Rafa's palms were slick, and he tried to breathe steadily as he climbed out of the vehicle. This had been a dumb idea. What had he thought would happen? He'd take Shane to the river under the moon and...*what*? And *nothing*.

Part of Rafa wanted to just tell Shane to take him back, but that would make him look even more foolish, so he grabbed his pack and left it on a rock before picking his way to the water's edge.

"Careful."

Rafa bit back a sigh of irritation. "I know. I'm not going to fall in or anything." When he glanced behind, Shane was standing with his hands clasped in front of him, his head turning as he steadily surveyed their surroundings. Rafa sighed again. "There's no one here. I'm sure it's fine."

Shane pressed his lips together into a thin line. "I still have to do my job."

"No one wants to kidnap me. Trust me."

Shane's nostrils flared. "Why do you do that?" He turned to survey the trees beyond the Suburban.

"Do what?"

After a long moment, Shane answered, "Put yourself down."

"I don't." Rafa bent and picked up a stone to toss into the river, which rushed by with a low hum.

His back still turned, Shane made a noise that might have been a snort.

Rafa wanted to ask Shane what was so great about him, but it was far too needy to say those words out loud. He tossed another rock. "Of the first kids, I'm just not the one people pay attention to. My sister's always been a little wild. Christian is the hot one and Matthew's the athletic one." He shrugged. "I'm the other one."

Shane was quiet for a few moments as he continued surveying the trees. "Maybe that's the way you've wanted it. To stay hidden. But that doesn't mean you're not just as important."

Rafa couldn't help but smile and feel...well, *good*. "You'll get along great with Ashleigh when she comes back. She says I don't value myself enough."

Shane's back was still turned to Rafa and the river. "Sounds like an intelligent young woman."

Rafa smiled. So Shane thought he should value himself more too? "Yeah. Ash is awesome. I'm really lucky."

"You must miss her."

"Of course, but she's having an amazing time in Paris. She's interning at *Vogue*. My dad pulled some strings. At first she didn't want me to ask him, but I convinced her that people use their connections all the time."

Shane faced Rafa again, and his brows drew together. "You don't worry?"

"Huh? About what?" Rafa picked up another stone.

"About being apart for months. Pretty girl like that in Paris with all those French guys?"

Tossing the stone, Rafa laughed. "Nope. Frenchmen are wasted on Ashleigh. Now French—" He bit off the *women* just in time. Keeping his gaze on the river, Rafa laughed again, a reedy sound this time. "Um, French pastries are more her indulgence. She'd never cheat. No worries."

"Hmm. Glad to hear it." Shane's voice was even, but did he sound a little…skeptical? Suspicious?

He's gay too. He'd understand. Maybe I should just tell him the truth. Maybe he'd even…

Shaking his head, Rafa grabbed another stone from near his feet and launched it. Maybe Shane would what? Like him back? It was crazy to even fantasize about it. But he couldn't deny that it would be wonderful to be out to a man he could trust. Not that Ashleigh wasn't understanding, but sometimes he really wanted to talk to another guy.

He went to the pack and pulled out the thermos of cold water. He gulped some down and offered it to Shane, who eyed the bottle. Rafa flushed. "Oh, sorry. I forgot cups. Shit."

"It's fine." Shane's fingers brushed Rafa's as he took the thermos. "Thanks."

Rafa watched Shane's throat work as he swallowed, and heat shot through him. Ducking his head, he busied himself with the food. "I made sandwiches and stuff. Nothing fancy. You probably don't even want one."

"You brought food?" Shane smiled. "Of course I want some."

"You do? Cool. Um, here." He thrust up one of the foil-wrapped sandwiches.

After he took it, Shane glanced around again. "Thanks."

Rafa sat on a flat rock by the water's edge. "Why don't you sit?"

Shane shook his head before taking a bite. He moaned softly, and Rafa dug his nails into his palm. "Damn. This is amazing. Did you make the bread?"

He couldn't help but beam a bit. "Yeah, earlier this evening. It was still a little warm when I wrapped up the sandwiches."

"Mayo too?" Shane glanced left and right.

"Yep. I didn't make the beef, though. Or the provolone."

Shane smiled, his cheeks creasing. "Would be a challenge to make a cow." He peered into the trees again.

"It's seriously fine. There's no one out there."

Shane peered down at him. "Those are what we call famous last words, Rafa."

Hearing Shane say his name gave him a highly inappropriate thrill. "Good point." He got to his feet so Shane wasn't looming over him. "There are some cookies too. Peanut butter snickerdoodles. Oh, I should have asked if you have allergies."

"I don't. Love peanut butter." Shane took another bite of his sandwich. When he swallowed, he asked, "So why are we here in the middle of the night?"

Because I wanted to go somewhere it was just the two of us for miles. Rafa shrugged. "I like this spot. I thought it would be pretty with the moon. Guess I'm getting a little stir crazy at home. Probably because it's not really a *home*. Even with the third floor to myself, staff still come up there. You're never really alone in the White House."

Shane watched him with an intense gaze. "You're not alone here either."

"I know, but it's different with you."

"Different how?" Shane still watched him.

Rafa grabbed the thermos off the ground and took a drink. "I dunno. You're cool or whatever." He put down the thermos and the rest of his sandwich before stepping up on a rock right by the water's edge. "It's peaceful here. I love water."

"Don't get too close."

Rafa rolled his eyes. "I'm not going to fall in."

"Let's not make those famous last words either."

"I know you wouldn't let me fall." As the quiet words left his mouth, Rafa's smile faded, and the air suddenly felt electric. The river hummed, and Shane watched him, his half-eaten sandwich still in his hand.

To break the strange tension, Rafa forced a laugh and went right to the very edge and stood on one foot. "Not even if I did this. Or—"

Rafa swung his arms to keep his balance as the traitorous rock shifted beneath him, but in a blink he was in the water, the cold stealing the air from his lungs as his ass hit the rocky bottom and the current tugged hard at him. Then Shane was there hauling him up, his hands gripping Rafa's upper arms.

Blinking, Rafa looked at Shane, then down at where the water rushed around their knees. Lifting his head, he met Shane's gaze, and after a frozen moment, they burst out laughing.

"I think I'm okay." Rafa snickered. "I can just...you know. Stand up."

His shoulders shaking, Shane still gripped Rafa's arms. "I told you not to get too close."

"You did. You totally, explicitly told me so." He tried to stop laughing, but standing there with the water flowing around their knees, it was all just so silly.

But then Shane tugged him forward and wrapped his arms around Rafa's back, and a giggle died in Rafa's throat as he held his breath. His arms were pinned at his sides, and Shane...Shane was *hugging* him.

"I've got you," Shane murmured.

He was warm and big, and Rafa's face was at the collar of Shane's shirt. If he turned his head he'd be pressing against Shane's skin, and—

Jerking back, Shane stumbled on the rocks, managing to catch his balance as he reached solid ground. His gaze darted around, and he ran a hand over his shorn hair. "I… We'd better get back. You'll catch a cold."

Rafa's pulse rushed in his ears over the sound of the water. *What just happened? Did he…why did he do that? Does he…? No. It's impossible. Shut up.* Rafa carefully climbed back up on the rock. He unzipped his sodden hoodie and wrung it out. "I'm sorry. I didn't mean to… Sorry."

Shane's voice was strained. "It was an accident. Come on."

Rafa quickly packed up the thermos and their abandoned half sandwiches and hurried to the vehicle. Inside, Shane turned on the engine and adjusted the heat.

Rafa pulled his panic button from his pocket. "Um, do these still work if they get wet?"

Shane glanced over. "Yes. Don't worry."

"I'm not worried. You're here, so…"

Silently, Shane shimmied out of his jacket and rolled up his white shirt sleeves. Leaning over, he brushed against Rafa as he turned on the vents. It was lukewarm air as the engine warmed.

Rafa's throat was dry as he shivered. "Did you…are you very wet? I'm so sorry. Are you going to have to stay in a damp suit all night?"

"It's fine. I got splashed, but it's mostly just my legs."

Rafa reached out and ran his hand over Shane's damp forearm, as if he could dry him off. "I'm sorry." He stopped moving his hand, and it rested on Shane's arm. *What are you doing? Stop touching him!* But Rafa didn't budge. He could feel damp hair under his palm, and barely resisted the urge to roll the hair between his fingertips.

Shane stared at Rafa's hand on his arm, and his Adam's apple bobbed in his throat. When he lifted his gaze, it was so dark and intense that a breathless shiver spun through Rafa.

Then Shane moved, putting the Suburban in drive, and Rafa yanked his hand back to his lap. He cleared his throat, praying he could speak without squeaking.

"And your shoes. Ugh, wet socks and shoes are the worst. And they're leather too. I'll replace them."

"They'll dry. It's fine, Rafa." Shane kept his eyes on the deserted road as they wound through the trees, but his face softened into an almost-smile. "As long as you're okay, everything's good."

He knew it was Shane's job. He knew Shane didn't mean anything more than that. But it still made Rafa warm from the inside out.

Chapter Eight

A T THE FOOT of the stairs, Shane checked his watch. Eleven fifty-nine.

He held his walkie to his mouth for his report. "Checking in. Valor secure. Over and out."

The radio crackled. "Ten-four."

Aside from the one night by the river—which Shane tried very hard not to think about—it had been four nights now that he'd slipped up to the third floor at midnight to eat Rafa's creations and linger far too long listening to the kid talk.

Rafa.

He should think of him as Valor or Rafael, but the nickname always came to mind first now. Which was fine—most everyone called Valor that. But it wasn't his role to be spending this much time with his protectee up in that kitchen.

And it definitely wasn't his role to be *hugging* him. Even if he'd been ridiculously relieved that Rafa was okay after he'd toppled off the rock. *Of course I was relieved. Keeping him in one piece is my damn job. That's all it was.* Yet it had felt alarmingly natural as they'd laughed to wrap Rafa in his arms.

He sighed. Good thing he had the next day off before rotating to the day shift. Alan would be back too, and things would return to normal.

But Shane couldn't stop the pang that echoed through him at

the idea of not spending time with Rafa alone anymore. He'd really enjoyed their late-night talks and tasting sessions. *Maybe a little too much.*

Not that anything had *happened*, but girlfriend or not, there was no question in Shane's mind now that Rafael Castillo was gay, or at least bi. The desire practically came off the kid in waves. Shane should never have mentioned his own sexuality, but he hadn't thought about it at the time as being an issue. Not that it was an *issue* now. But the kid clearly had a crush on him.

On one hand, it was sweet and harmless. Rafael Castillo was likely closeted and lonely, and Shane didn't want to hurt his feelings. But he was treading on dangerous ground. A situation like this could blow up in his face. Aside from a few unfortunate incidents involving alcohol and prostitutes on foreign details, there hadn't been any scandals in the Service the past decade. He sure as hell wasn't going to cause one now by encouraging this crush and having it go south.

Especially since that dangerous ground was becoming more and more treacherous by the day. It was harmless enough for Rafa to have a crush on him. It sure as hell wasn't for Shane to have a crush of his own. And of course he didn't. The idea was absolutely absurd.

Yet that night at the river, when Rafa had touched him—only an innocent touch of his hand on Shane's arm—Shane had felt it right down to his balls. And on the drive back to Castle, he'd been compelled to share an embarrassing story about falling in a pool at a barbecue in college while trying to balance a case of beer on his head. It had made Rafa laugh and wrinkle up his nose, and Shane wanted to tell him more personal stories.

He shook his head. He couldn't remember the last time he'd met someone and wanted to spend so much time with them. Of course the irony was that he'd be spending hours a day with Rafa, and it was time to get his shit together and stop blurring the lines.

But he couldn't just not show tonight—not when Rafa was making avocado soup because it was Shane's favorite. He could imagine how Rafa's face would fall if he didn't show. As he started up the stairs, his pulse fluttered uneasily. *Christ. What do I have to be nervous about? Go eat the soup and call it a day.*

The smell of roasting tomatoes—and mmm, bacon—filled the third floor. Shane stopped in the doorway as he reached the kitchen and watched Rafa ladle soup into a bowl with great concentration. Rafa wore jeans and a worn green T-shirt, with flip-flops on his feet. His hair was unfortunately still slicked down, and Shane wondered, with a strange pang of regret, if he'd ever see it curly again. The denim hugged Rafa's slim hips and the curve of his ass, and Shane mused about what kind of underwear Rafa had on…

As heat rushed through him, Shane jerked his gaze up and cleared his throat.

Rafa's face lit up as he glanced over. "Oh! Hey, Shane. The soup's almost ready. I've just got to…" He reached for a small bowl. "I cooked and diced a few strips of bacon as garnish. Thought it was worth a try."

"Bacon's always worth a try."

Rafa laughed. "That's what I figured. And I made the roasted tomatoes and basil again, but this time with Boursin instead of goat cheese. So you can tell me which one's better. But here, soup first." He thrust out a spoon and handed Shane the bowl.

"Aren't you going to have any?" Shane hesitated. Rafa had a habit of just watching him intently, and it could be unnerving at times. Largely because he looked at Shane like Fred Flintstone eyeing a rack of brontosaurus ribs.

"Oh, yeah." Rafa went back to ladling.

Shane took a mouthful of the soup. "Mmm. Damn, that's good." The creaminess of the cold avocado and the salty hint of warm bacon was perfect.

"Really?"

Nodding, Shane had another spoonful. And another. As he ate, Rafa talked. Everyone thought of him as so quiet, but once he got going, he wasn't so shy, and he had a lot of interesting things to say.

"And we're talking about the actual King of England here. I seriously almost tripped him in the entrance hall. But he was just like, 'Steady on, old chap. Pip, pip,' or something ridiculously British. And this other time, you won't believe what I saw in the Blue Room."

Shane chuckled as Rafa continued. Rafa talked with his hands, his voice never getting very loud, but his eyes sparkling. His teeth were even and white, and gleamed as he smiled.

"Oh, I watched that movie—*Endless Summer?* You're right, it was really cool even though it was old."

"Glad to hear it. It's dated, but it's a classic." Why should he care if Rafa liked the movie or not? It made no sense whatsoever, but Shane was pleased. "There was a sequel too. From the nineties, I think. Kelly Slater's early era."

Rafa's face lit up. "Kelly Slater? He's a legend. I still have a poster of him in my room." He laughed nervously. "Wow. That sounds super lame. It's from when we first moved in. I just haven't bothered taking it down. I'm not...I don't put up posters anymore."

"It's okay. My old room at my folks' house was like a time machine." As the words left his mouth, he tensed. He never talked about his parents, but with Rafa the words somehow just came out. Somehow it felt...safe. Shane kept his gaze on his shoes.

But Rafa didn't push the subject, instead simply saying, "Thanks for understanding. Okay, that's totally next on my list. Have you seen *Riding Giants?* Laird Hamilton was a beast. I wonder if he still surfs. He's gotta be pretty old now."

Shane breathed easily again. "Probably. He'll still be out there when he needs a walker."

"Hey, did you ever surf Rincon in Santa Barbara? I saw a thing on TV about the point break there. Looks so cool."

"No, but I did the Trestles when I could catch a ride. About half an hour south of Laguna, and it was a trek to get to the beach. Some gnarly breaks, though. It was worth it."

Rafa burst out laughing and raised his hand. "I'm sorry."

Shane found himself smiling. "What's so funny?"

"Hearing the word 'gnarly' come out of your mouth."

"Fair enough," Shane laughed. "But hodads don't get to make fun."

"Wait, what's a hodad?" Rafa popped a piece of tomato in his mouth.

Shane watched as he swallowed. "Uh, it's…a hodad is a non-surfer, but one who hangs at the beach. A poser."

"Hey, I'm not a poser!" Rafa puffed up with mock anger. "Trust me, I'll be surfing my ass off in the new year. I'll be a, what do they call it? A grommet?"

"You're a little old for a grommet, but just don't be a kook."

"What's a kook? I definitely don't want to be that." Rafa was serious again, looking like he was ready to take mental notes.

"A newbie who causes trouble. Gets in the way and doesn't follow the rules. Wherever you end up surfing, make sure you find out how the locals operate. Don't get in anyone's way."

Rafa nodded. "I won't." He ate a bite of tomato and bread. "I think I prefer the goat cheese."

"Me too. Boursin is nice, but I think the goat cheese was more… It didn't compete with the basil."

"More neutral, but in a good way." Nodding, Rafa flipped open his notebook and jotted down a line. He toyed with his soup spoon, swirling it through his bowl. "Did you have a favorite spot at Laguna?"

The old ache was still there, but Shane smiled. "Brooks Street.

Swells were usually just right. Not ankle busters, but not too big. Plus, Maddie's is there. Not much more than a shack, but she's got the best slushees. I'd have a watermelon-pistachio every day." His smile faded. "Long time ago now."

"It sounds awesome. So, you didn't do the big waves? No riding giants for you?"

"Nah. I wasn't good enough. I didn't want to end up with a sand facial." He grimaced. "I went over the falls once at the Trestles—wiped out over the front of my board as the wave broke. Got dragged along the bottom."

"Ouch. Were you hurt?"

"A little. Got a cool scar I showed off to all my friends. It wasn't so bad." He remembered how Jimmy Clarkson had blown him afterward behind the Carl's Jr. The day had ended pretty well, all things considered.

Rafa's eyes lit up. "Can I see it?" His cheeks flushed. "Um, I mean if you can show me. Like, if it's on your hand or something. Forget it. That was stupid to ask."

"It's okay." Tugging at his tie, Shane undid the top button on his shirt and pulled down his collar to show the pale, jagged scar at the juncture of his neck and right shoulder. "Coral did a number on me."

"Whoa." Rafa stepped close, leaning in. The puff of his exhalation was warm on Shane's skin. "That must have hurt."

They were standing only a whisper apart, and Shane's breath caught in his throat as Rafa traced the three-inch mark with his fingertip, running it up and then down. A shiver raced down Shane's spine, and he stepped back, quickly buttoning up and straightening his tie. *What the fuck am I doing?*

"Hey, I was thinking…if I went to visit my sister in LA or my brother up at Berkeley, maybe I could try surfing. You'd have to go with me out on the waves, right? Just in case a shark tried to kidnap me." He smiled tentatively.

Before his brain could kick in, happy anticipation swelled through Shane, warm and tingly, and for once, the guilty grief only flared for a moment before fading away. He imagined Rafa beside him, all eager smiles, his freckles standing out across his cheeks and his hair curling over his forehead. He could almost smell the salty air and feel the warmth of the sun as they paddled out past the break…

No.

This was not how he was supposed to feel about his job. He wasn't supposed to look forward to spending time with his protectee. It was one thing not to hate it, or to find it pleasant. But it was another thing all together to daydream about it like he was a kid with a crush. There was a reason they didn't want agents getting attached. It clouded judgment. Put the protectee at risk. Put other agents at risk.

I should never have come up here. This is it. I'm done.

He kept his tone even and non-committal. "We'll see." *Finish your plate and get back downstairs.* A bit of oil spilled as Shane popped the last tomato into his mouth, and he swiped at his lower lip with his finger. He looked up to find Rafa watching him with wide eyes, and the air was suddenly charged and heavy, like a storm was close by.

Shane wiped his hands on a paper towel, his heart kicking up despite himself, skin prickling all over. "I'd better get back. Have a good night."

Rafa only stared, and then the few feet between them were gone, and their lips touched. His fingers dug into Shane's arms, and he crushed their mouths together desperately. He was warm and sweet, and smelled like bacon and lemons, and Shane wanted to bend him over the counter and dive into him like the ocean at high tide.

But even more than that he wanted to push his tongue between Rafa's lips and really taste him. *Fuck*, he wanted to make

Rafa feel good. Show him how amazing it could be. He wanted to lose himself.

Shane opened his mouth to suck in a breath and break away, but Rafa's lips parted against his so tantalizingly. He swept his tongue into Rafa's mouth while his mind screamed for him to stop.

Rafa moaned into the kiss, his tongue tentatively meeting Shane's, and all the blood in Shane's body rushed to his cock. Rafa pressed closer against him, and Shane swept his hands down Rafa's back, heading for his ass—

Jerking away, Shane broke the kiss and yanked his hands back to his sides. Rafa followed, his eyes dark, lips red and parted as he sucked in a little gasping breath that sent even more blood rushing straight to Shane's dick.

But Shane pushed firmly against Rafa's chest with his palms and gritted the words out. "No. This can't happen." He shook his head.

But God, he couldn't remember the last time he'd felt like this. If he ever *had* felt like this. He'd been with dozens of men over the years, but he'd never wanted them in the way he wanted Rafa. He'd never *cared*. What the hell was wrong with him?

The flush in Rafa's face deepened, and he backed away, his hands and head dropping. "I'm so sorry," he croaked. "I don't know what... I didn't mean to... I'm sorry."

Shane concentrated on keeping his voice and expression calm. He let the mask slide into place. "It's all right. I'm going now."

"Shane..." Breathing hard, Rafa raised his head, pain and longing shining in his big eyes.

"This was my fault. It won't happen again."

He turned on his heel, because the urge to take Rafa into his arms and tell him everything would be okay was over-fucking-whelming and *unacceptable*. Shane managed to walk calmly out of the kitchen, although his heart was thumping painfully. He should have known this was coming. If it cost him his job, he damn well deserved it.

"THREE MORE BURGERS. Got it!" Darnell called as he closed the screen door behind him. He peered up at the clouds as he joined Shane by the barbecue. "Think it'll hold off long enough?"

Shane shrugged and dropped on three more patties. "Probably not. Guess we'll find out."

"Well, I guess we will, Mr. Philosophical." He nudged Shane's shoulder. "What's up with you today? Why so dour?"

Keeping his gaze on the meat, Shane shrugged again. "No more so than usual."

"Mmm-hmm. If you say so. I've been inviting you over all summer and you've never showed. I was shocked you actually read my text, let alone answered it and graced us with your presence."

"Ha, ha."

Darnell scoffed. "You think I'm kidding. Sometimes it's weeks." He held up his finger and thumb a fraction apart. "I'll be *thisclose* to breaking into your apartment for a welfare check to make sure you aren't being eaten by starving cats."

"When have I ever had cats?"

"Right, because *that* was the point of my diatribe. Why don't you go in and watch the game? I'm supposed to be doing the cooking. It's my barbecue, after all."

"I don't mind. You're the Orioles fan, D."

"Uh-huh. And...?" Darnell's eyebrows disappeared beneath his baseball cap.

Shane sighed. "Guess I'm not feeling particularly social. Should have stayed in bed." But he hadn't been able to, because God damn if he hadn't woken up hard as a rock, thinking of Rafael Castillo and that kiss. God damn if he hadn't thought about the kid all day, wondering what he was doing and if he was okay.

God damn if he wasn't *missing* him.

"Well, I could have canceled and joined you." Darnell winked.

That was exactly what Shane should have needed, but the thought left him shrugging again.

"I'll try not to take your lack of enthusiasm personally. Okay, cough it up. Did something happen at work?"

Rubbing his face, Shane nodded. After a few moments of hesitation, he confessed, "He kissed me."

Darnell's brows drew together. "Who? Your partner on the detail? With the sick kid?"

"No. I wish. Well, I don't. Fuck." Shane took a chug from his beer bottle, gripping the foam cooler. "Rafael Castillo."

Eyes wide, Darnell whistled softly. "The other one kissed you?"

An insane surge of protectiveness filled him and he snarled, "Rafa's not that gangly little kid anymore."

"Whoa." Darnell held up his hands. "It's Rafa now?"

"Everyone calls him that." Shane waved dismissively.

"But everyone doesn't kiss him."

"*He* kissed me."

Darnell regarded him silently for a few moments. "You didn't kiss him back? Not even a little?"

"Well..." Shane sighed, remembering the hot slide of Rafa's tentative tongue, the feel of his body, and his little gasp. "Just for a few seconds. It was like my brain temporarily shut down and my dick took over. But I put a stop to it fast."

"Okay. Good save. But the question is, did you want to keep kissing him? And then some?"

Shane was silent for too long.

Darnell sighed heavily. "This is dangerous territory, my friend."

"I know. Fuck, I know. I just met him a few weeks ago, but there's something… I can't explain it. I mean, he's not even my type. I don't know what's gotten into me. This is beyond inappropriate. I'm practically twice his age." Sure, Rafa was twenty-one and an adult, but he was still a kid. A smart and thoughtful one that Shane liked to talk to, but that was irrelevant. Entirely fucking irrelevant.

"But this is not a typical situation. Be careful, Shane. You may be older, but that kid's the one with the real power. He could tell his father anything, and who would they believe? Your career would be over."

"I know. Fuck, man. I have no idea what's wrong with me. I've protected way hotter guys. Hell, I once drove Bradley Cooper around DC with the California senator. I barely even looked at him. I've never let it distract me. But Rafa makes me…"

"Horny?"

Shane glared. "No. Well, yes." He groaned. "This is not how I do things. Jesus, he's probably a virgin. At least as far as men go, or his other details would have known. I'm almost forty. I have no business messing around with a virgin. But…" He realized he smelled smoke, and quickly flipped the charred burgers. "But he's been so isolated. So held back. He's a really good cook, but his parents don't want him anywhere near a kitchen. He wants to move to Australia and learn to surf. And for some bizarre reason…I want to teach him."

Darnell whistled softly. "As I live and breathe. Mr. Independent is taking the fall."

"Shut up." Shane rolled his eyes. "I'm not in love, for fuck's sake."

"Not yet. But you could be down the road, couldn't you? You always said you'd never found someone you wanted to wake up to every day. That's how you'd know he was the one. Are you wondering how Rafael Castillo looks with bed head?"

"Don't be ridiculous. I barely know him." *His curls would be all over the place, falling over his forehead...*

"Well, you're certainly in lust, and you'd better reel that in quick."

He sighed. "I know."

"Could you ask for a transfer?"

Gripping the spatula, Shane shrugged. "I could. They usually say no. They'd rather transfer us at their whims, not ours. Moved me to three different field offices in seven years, and then the PD in Montana."

"Right. Protective detail on our illustrious ex-president. I still want details of just how batshit that guy really is."

Shane tried to smile. "Maybe one day if you get me drunk enough. Anyway, I finally worked my way to DC last year for the first time since training. Gotta be honest—I really don't want to go to another field office. DC's the big time. I could get on PPD in the next couple years. Guarding the president."

"The big show. I hear you. Well, then you'd better get yourself back into your usual control. This is a phase. You can outlast it. Just lock that shit down, and keep your eyes on the prize. And off Rafael Castillo's tight little ass."

Shane huffed out a laugh. "I thought you said his brothers were the hot ones?"

"Well, he's still got a nice caboose. There aren't many tight asses I can't admire. So he's gay, huh? Or bi? It's about time we had a queer in the White House. Woo boy, I bet his parents will not be happy about this. His momma might choke on her pearls."

One of the guys called from inside Darnell's bungalow. "Hey, runners are on first and third with no outs!"

"Coming!" Darnell yelled. He scooped the patties onto a plate. "Now just make sure you don't come anywhere near Rafael Castillo."

"Thanks for the sage advice as always." Shane followed inside, hoping beer, burgers, and baseball would help clear his mind.

He and Rafa might both be gay, but nothing was ever going to happen. Could never and would never, so there was zero point in even thinking about it. Zero point in thinking about the fact that there was something about Rafa tugging at Shane in a way he couldn't explain. Zero point in thinking about how Rafa's nose wrinkled when he smiled for real, instead of for the public or his mother or whoever.

Zero point in thinking about how much Shane wanted to kiss him again. Zero point in thinking about how he wanted to make Rafa smile. And how Rafa made *him* smile, and feel lighter than he had in a long, long time.

No point at all.

Chapter Nine

★★ 🏛 ★★

A S THE UNDERWATER bing-bonging that signified a Skype call filled the air, Rafa muted the TV and picked up his tablet. It was Ashleigh, of course. His finger wavered over the answer button, but guilt kicked in, and he tapped it. He hadn't spoken to her in more than a week aside from the odd text. He picked up the tablet and propped it on his knees, his feet braced on the coffee table.

"Bonjour, ma *cheri*! Or *cher*, perhaps? I don't know, my French is still *très* basic." Ashleigh smiled as she twisted her blonde hair up into a knot on her head. "I'm getting ready for bed, but we haven't talked in forever. Things have been crazy here, sorry." She tilted her head. "Where are you? I thought you'd be in the kitchen." Behind her, he could see pillows and the bottom of a painting of high-heeled shoes on the wall.

"Solarium. Just watching TV." Along with the traditional couches and potted plants in the windowed room, they had a big-screen TV with surround sound. The White House had its own little movie theater, which had been fun when he was younger, but now Rafa would rather flop on the couch. Especially on a day like this.

"Okay, what's wrong? You look like warm spit."

He huffed out a laugh and ran his hand through his tangle of waves. He hadn't bothered slicking them back since he had no plans to venture off the third floor, and he most definitely didn't have to fix his hair for Shane. Even if Shane had been on duty, no way would he have come upstairs after what Rafa did. "You're great for my ego, Ash."

Her brow furrowed. "But seriously, what's up? Are you sick?" He could tell from her expression that if they'd been in the same room, she'd have pressed the back of her hand to his forehead.

The lie was on his tongue, but instead he shook his head. "It's not that. I'm fine. Just mopey or whatever. Tell me fun things about Paris. Any good art showings?"

But she ignored him. "Tell me what's wrong."

He sighed. "I screwed up. Like, big time."

"Like, you-said-something-that-mortified-you-and-no-one-else-gave-a-second-thought-to kind of screwed up? Or more like sophomore year, accidentally deleted your term paper and had to engage the White House tech squad to dig it up?"

"So much worse." His stomach churned, and he thought it was very possible he might cry before this Skype conversation was through.

"I bet it's not as bad as you think. Let's work through it. Jump in the way-back machine and start at the beginning."

"I can't, Ash. It's...we can't talk about it like this. Only in person."

Her eyes widened for a second. "Oh. Okay. Well, let me tell you about my wonderful week in the City of Lights."

She talked for a few minutes, making him smile and even laugh a few times. Then, as he knew she would, she brought the conversation back around. "You would have loved this motorcycle I saw. Little Japanese number, all slick and chrome plated. Seen any good rides in DC lately?"

His mouth was dry, and Rafa swigged from a bottle of soda. "Yeah, actually. A really great one. The best I've ever seen in real life."

"Wow. Tell me more. Contemporary or classic?"

"Classic. Harley. A little rough around the edges. Tough, but…really cool. Intriguing."

"Hmm. Did you want to take it for a test drive real bad?"

"I…I actually tried to." His face flamed, and he wished she couldn't see him.

Ashleigh's eyebrows shot up. "Whoa. Seriously? That's a first."

"And last," he muttered. "It was such a mistake. I'm so stupid."

"Why? It wasn't…a good fit?"

"No, it was. It *so* was. But it was highly inappropriate. Not the right bike for me." He scrounged for ways to keep the motorcycle code going. He'd never even kissed a guy before. "I knew it, but I couldn't resist."

"Okay." Ashleigh seemed to be processing it. "Where'd you see this ride?"

He shifted. "Um, here."

She blinked owlishly. "Wow. That was unexpected."

"I know. Believe me."

"Well, that explains why you look like someone just ran over your dog and mounted it over the fireplace. This classic Harley…how classic are we talking? How much older than you?"

Rafa bit his lip. "Um, a couple decades, I think."

"Well, that is a classic indeed, Rafael Castillo. Go big or go home, huh? Are you going to see this bike again?"

"Definitely. Like, every day. Especially when I go out."

Her jaw actually dropped open, and then her eyes narrowed. "Wait. Does this Harley come with its own radio?"

Closing his eyes, he nodded.

"*Raf!*" Ashleigh looked like she didn't know whether to laugh or not. "That's definitely a risky ride to take. And here I was thinking I was naughty for seeing one particular painting at the Louvre three times this week." She grimaced, her teeth pressing together. "I may have even touched it, which was totally against the rules. Alarm bells were ringing."

Ashleigh had always insisted her vibrator would do her fine until they were out of college and out to their parents, especially after one girl she'd slept with in high school had tried to blackmail them. She was sure her Tea Party-leaning mom and dad would take it worse than Rafa's, and they had bet a bottle of Dom Pérignon on it. They'd always talked about crushes, but now it was suddenly becoming real.

"Maybe you should just go for it, Ash."

"I don't know." She stuck out her lower lip and blew strands of her hair up off her forehead. "Part of me thinks we should wait. But shit. It still feels so far away, you know? We've always had our four-year plan, though."

"Yeah. Well, I'll be too freaking humiliated to even look at another Harley for about five years at least."

She winced. "That bad?"

"Worse. Whatever you're imagining, times it by a hundred." He'd replayed the kiss over and over, and each time the mortification grew, cold and clammy in the pit of his stomach. Even though it seemed like…just for a few seconds…had Shane kissed him back? *He had, hadn't he?* At the thought, Rafa shivered hot and cold all over. Their mouths had been open, and he could still imagine the heat of Shane's touch on his back, moving down his body…

But the memory of Shane's hands firmly pushing him away overshadowed everything else. Not that he blamed Shane at all. Even if they were two regular people who met at a bar, what would Shane ever want with *him*? A gawky virgin likely wasn't high on Shane's to-do list. "It was like…I have no idea what came over me. Temporary insanity."

"Shit, babe. I'm sorry."

"I mean, as if some scrawny geek like me has any place trying to ki...ride a Harley." And God, being with him was Shane's job, And Rafa had put him in this terrible position. "Harleys are so out of my league."

"Hey." Ash drew her brows together and gave him her *I mean business* expression. "That's bullshit. You may still think of yourself how you did when you were fourteen, but you're all grown up. You're hot. You can't see it for some bizarre reason—you probably need a therapist to unpack why—but trust me. You are Harley-worthy."

"But..." He wanted to believe it was true. He knew he'd grown a lot, but he still had those freckles, and his hair, and—

"Stop cataloguing all your perceived faults."

Rafa had to chuckle. "Okay, okay." He sighed. "I'm dreading tomorrow. Mom's coming home from California, and the Harley will be back around. Wasn't here today. I can't hide up here forever." He groaned. "And I bet my mom has more public speaking for me to do. I just wish I could hit fast-forward, you know?"

"I know. Stay strong. We can do this. Keep me posted, okay?"

"Yeah. Get to bed, Intern. Those lattes won't get themselves tomorrow."

"Sadly true. But hey, Raf? It'll be okay. I bet it's not as bad as you think. It never is. So stop torturing yourself. That's an order."

He gave a mock salute. "Ma'am, yes ma'am. Love you."

Ashleigh blew him a kiss, and the connection terminated. He tossed the tablet beside him and groaned softly. No matter what she said, it really was as bad as he thought. There was no way it couldn't be.

IT WAS DEFINITELY, one hundred percent as bad as he feared.

In fact, it was worse, because when Rafa forced himself down-

stairs to the main level, Shane and Alan were there by the Red
Room talking to a few of his mother's agents. As Rafa entered the
hall, they all glanced over, the chatter ceasing.

*Do they know? Did he tell them? Oh my God they probably all
had a good laugh, and right now they're thinking about what a loser I
am.*

Their collective gaze felt like lasers on him, even though he
knew Shane would be crazy to tell anyone his professionalism had
been compromised. Panic clawing at his throat, Rafa dropped his
eyes and kept walking toward the main staircase, hurrying down it
and nodding to aides that passed by.

He knew Alan and Shane would follow, and he stopped outside the China Room when he reached the basement. The China
Room was one of those places in the White House that probably
seemed like a good idea at the time, but now was just weird. Who
needed ornate display cases of china settings?

"Good morning, Rafa. Are you off somewhere?" It was Alan's
voice. He couldn't bear to look up.

"There you are, darling." Heels clacking, his mother swept
down the stairs in a navy pantsuit, her aides and agents trailing
behind. "Did you have breakfast?"

"Uh-huh," he lied. He'd attempted a piece of toast and given
up after one choking bite.

"I'm going to greet some visitors in my office and give them a
tour. Would you like to join us? I'm sure they'd be thrilled."

Sure they would. "Sorry, I can't. I'm going to meet with Marissa," he lied. "About the project."

"Excellent." She beamed—truly beamed—and guilt sliced
through Rafa. "Have a productive day." She strode away toward
the East Wing.

As staff passed by, Rafa nodded and tried to smile. During the
day there were so many more people around, and he wished he
could run back up to the third floor and hide in his kitchen. But

then he couldn't talk to Shane, so he'd have to suck it up.

"Did you want us to drive you?" Alan asked.

"No, I'll take my car. It's been a while." Rafa could see Shane in his peripheral vision, but kept his focus on Alan, who had dark circles under his eyes. "How's your son doing?"

"Better." Alan smiled genuinely. "Thank you."

"I'm glad to hear it. Um, so…" He glanced around. "I actually want to see a movie. Not meet Marissa. Not right now, anyway. I'm seeing her this afternoon."

"Okay." Alan glanced toward the East Wing, which housed the movie theater. "After you."

"Oh, no. I want to go out. To a real theater. The AMC? It's not far."

Alan and Shane glanced at each other and seemed to have a silent conversation. Then Alan said, "Pop-up shouldn't be an issue."

"Cool. Thanks." He started walking toward the West Wing, leaving through the Palm Room and going along the covered outdoor walkway, past a row of white columns. The West Wing bustled with activity, and Rafa smiled and nodded as he made his way past the Press Secretary's office and the Cabinet Room, leaving through the other side and hurrying to the parking lot beyond. Shane and Alan followed, and Rafa resisted the urge to look back.

His Toyota chirped as he pressed the key fob, and despite the knot of tension threatening to cut off his airway, he smiled as he slid behind the wheel. He couldn't freaking wait until the day when he could drive whenever and wherever he wanted, without anyone following or needing to know where he was going. He grabbed his Yankees cap from the passenger seat and tugged it over his slicked hair.

The Suburban pulled up, waiting. He couldn't really see them through the tinted windows, but he wondered what Shane was

thinking. He continued wondering as he drove to the theater.
Is he:

A) *Furious*
B) *Embarrassed*
C) *Disgusted*
D) *All of the above*

Rafa knew that if anyone found out he'd kissed Shane, it would be Shane that suffered. He'd probably lose his job, or end up on some terrible field duty in Podunk, USA. It had been unbearably selfish. It really had. Shane had been so nice to him, and this was how Rafa thanked him. The urge to apologize and clear the air burned in his empty stomach.

At the AMC parking lot, he waited to get out of his car until Shane and Alan approached, just like he was supposed to. Alan walked ahead to the theater, scanning and talking into his wrist, and Shane's presence behind Rafa felt like…he didn't know what. It was somehow awkward and electric at the same time.

After getting the nod from Alan, Rafa went inside. In the quiet lobby, he bought his ticket at a machine while Alan bought theirs. Rafa would have just picked them all up, but his agents had always insisted on protocol. Alan would expense the tickets and get his money back eventually. Still wearing his cap, Rafa approached the ticket taker, bypassing the snack bar, because vomiting popcorn and M&Ms wouldn't help his case.

A kid who looked about fifteen took his ticket. "Enjoy the show." Then he did a double take, and stared with wide eyes at Alan and Shane, who handed him their tickets. "Uh…enjoy the show too," the kid sputtered.

As they walked to the theater, a young woman in business casual clothing approached, smiling widely. Shane stepped toward her so she didn't get too close. Rafa smiled at her. "Hi."

"Hello! Welcome to AMC. How wonderful to have you. If

there's anything I can do to make your visit better, please let me know."

Alan spoke up. "If you could keep any looky-loos out of the theater, that would be very helpful. And ensure that your staff don't start tweeting that the president's son is here."

"Absolutely. Consider it done." She smiled at Rafa again. "Did you want any snacks? On the house, of course."

"Thank you so much, but I had a big breakfast."

Outside theater thirteen, which Rafa hoped wasn't a bad omen, he waited with Shane while Alan did a sweep. The previews were already playing from the sounds of it, but Rafa didn't mind missing them this time. All he could think about was Shane. He could have reached out and touched him, but instead kept his hands shoved in his chino pockets. Shane surveyed the lobby silently.

Alan appeared. "All clear."

They walked inside up the slanted dark hallway to the stadium-style theater. As Rafa had guessed, there was hardly anyone at this morning weekday screening of the latest Superman movie that had come out more than a month ago. He and Ash had seen it in Charlottesville before she left for Paris. It had kind of sucked, but it didn't matter.

An older man sat near the front, and a younger couple were huddled in the middle, giggling and kissing. They didn't even glance up. Rafa went all the way to the top, and Alan murmured to Shane.

"I'll take the front." He went back down, taking a seat a few rows up from the entrance.

At the very back row, Rafa started toward the middle, stopping when Shane didn't follow. He felt like he'd swallowed glass. "Are you coming?"

"I'll stay on the aisle."

Rafa stood there until Shane finally met his gaze. "Please? I really want to talk to you. And it's not as if I can text you like a normal person."

After a heartbeat that felt like an eternity, Shane nodded. He still left one seat between them as they sat. With the wall behind them, at least Rafa knew no one could eavesdrop. Shane murmured into his wrist, and then pressed against it. Turning off the mic, Rafa realized. He eyed the coiled clear plastic disappearing from Shane's earpiece beneath his collar.

He decided to start with some small talk. "Why don't you use wireless? I've always wondered."

Shane kept his gaze forward. "Not reliable enough. Too much could go wrong. If my earpiece falls out, it'll dangle and I won't lose it. A bluetooth could be gone in an instant in a crowd. They've tested it all. The old radios are still the best. We can turn the mics off and on now. That helps cut down on chatter over the wire."

The glass in Rafa's throat was accompanied by gritty sand. Maybe he should have gotten a gallon-sized soda after all. "Oh. Cool. I've never thought about it. I don't know why, since I'm surrounded by Secret Service agents." He laughed weakly. A preview for the next *Wonder Woman* movie played, and he gathered his courage. "Um. I just wanted to… I'm so sorry for what I did. For kissing you."

"You don't have to be sorry. There's really no need to discuss this. But…I'm sorry too."

Does that mean he did *want to kiss me back?* "Okay. You didn't tell anyone, right? I mean, I'm sure you didn't. I just want to double check."

Shane kept his gaze forward, looking left and right every so often. "Of course not. Besides, there was nothing to tell. It's already forgotten."

It shouldn't have hurt, but damn it, it did. Rafa's eyes burned. *Do not even think about crying right now.* Before he could stop himself, he blurted, "I can't forget my first kiss."

Oh yes, this is helping. Tell him you're a lame virgin. Way to go, genius.

He stumbled on. "I mean…not that it was a *real* kiss. I know you didn't want it to happen, and I basically jumped you, which was really not cool. It was so wrong." The movie was starting, and after the blare of the previews, it was suddenly very quiet. Even though there was no one in earshot, he whispered, "I just wanted… It's hard. When Ashleigh's not around, there's no one I can talk to. Which is so not your problem. Anyway, I'm sorry. It won't happen again. Any of it."

Shane was silent as Superman hung around the Fortress of Solitude and looked mopey. "I know you must be lonely. Confused. It's okay. You'll be okay."

"It's not even that I'm confused. Just…so fucking sick of the closet. And…I like you. I've never felt like this about anyone. But that's no excuse."

Shane's nostrils flared. "I…" His gaze darted around the theater. "You know this is not a thing that can ever happen."

Rafa's pulse fluttered. Did that mean that if things were different, Shane would actually *want* something to happen? Before he could summon the courage to ask, Shane went on.

"Stop beating yourself up," he murmured in his low growl. "We're good. Okay? I let the situation get out of hand. It won't happen again, and I'm not upset."

"You're not?" Rafa watched the side of Shane's face, light from the movie flickering over his skin. "Thanks. I really like talking to you. You're cool." He winced internally. He sounded like a dumb kid. But it seemed like Shane definitely *had* kissed him back, and not just out of instinct.

Not that it matters, because it's never going to happen again. "I'm sorry I put you in that position. But to be honest, I'm not sorry it happened. Because I can't think of anyone I'd rather have my first kiss with."

Shane looked at him then, his stoic expression unreadable. Was he mad? Touched? Ambivalent?

Rafa rambled on. "Um, I just want you to know that I wouldn't do anything to get you in trouble. Well, I told Ash, but it's all in code. And she would never talk."

Shane nodded, and they both turned to the screen. Rafa took off the hat and ran his hand over his stupid hair, hoping it wasn't sticking up now. Maybe he should put it back on. Maybe—

"She knows the real you?"

As Superman flew off to battle the latest version of Lex Luthor, Rafa nodded. He glanced at Shane, who didn't look at him. "We've never been a real couple. Just best friends. Neither of us could come out." Oh shit, he wasn't supposed to be outing Ash. "Shit, you can't tell anyone that," he quickly added. "Not that you would, but…"

Their eyes met in the darkness. "I wouldn't."

There was something about Shane's steady gaze and voice that just made Rafa feel so safe. He nodded. "I know."

"It must be hard. Hiding who you are."

"You never had to? From your parents?"

Something—perhaps affection and a stab of pain—flickered over Shane's face, and his Adam's apple bobbed as he swallowed and looked away. "They were very accepting. It was never an issue."

"That's good." Rafa wanted to ask a million more questions about them, but it wasn't his place. "So, we have a plan. Me and Ash. It's all worked out, how we're going to break up, and finally come out to our folks. We've only got one semester left, and my dad will be out of office in January, and then…"

Shane glanced over and waited.

"And then anything, I guess. Everything." The thrill of anticipation put a smile on his face. "My life will finally begin. In

Australia I can surf and cook. It's going to be perfect."

Shane smiled at him, and Rafa's stomach swooped like he was on a rollercoaster. "Sounds like a good plan, Rafa." Shane turned his head back to the movie, although Rafa knew he wasn't paying attention to it. His eyes darted around, always watching; protecting Rafa from any possible threat. Rafa wondered what he was like off duty, totally relaxed and himself. No suit, or ear piece, or eagle eye. Just Shane.

Of course thoughts of no suit immediately morphed into thoughts of Shane naked, and that was *not* a good mental path to travel unless Rafa was alone in his bedroom with his hand down his shorts. He forced himself to focus on the movie and the lackluster action scene involving a monorail and screaming passengers heading to certain doom. Naturally, Superman saved the day.

The man in front got up and left the theater. He came back in a few minutes, and Shane lifted his wrist to say something to Alan that Rafa missed in an explosion of glass onscreen. Shane glanced over and gave him a reassuring smile—a quick tug of his lips.

Rafa put his feet up and finally breathed deeply for the first time in days.

Chapter Ten

ALTHOUGH THE WHITE House was generally always bustling with people and activity during the day, when the president returned, it went into high gear. Shane stood on the South Lawn with Alan and other agents as Marine One and its two flanking escorts approached, the rotors of the helicopters thrumming. The countersnipers in strategic positions on the roof reported in, and Shane pressed against his ear piece to better hear the command center's response as the noise from the choppers grew.

Rafa, his mother, sister, brother, and a few aunts and uncles waited on the lawn with wide smiles and neatly pressed clothing. The eldest brother, codename Vacation, was enroute with his wife from New York City. The last report was that they'd be wheels down in thirty after a canceled flight the night before thanks to torrential rain on the eastern seaboard.

There had been some concern that the president himself might not make it back from Europe in time for his own birthday party that night, but here he was. Would probably be jetlagged as all hell, Shane mused.

As the summer wore on, the heat had settled into DC, and sweat prickled the back of Shane's neck. The sun was bright overhead, and even with his polarized sunglasses, he had to squint as he peered around the grounds. Sometimes people asked about Secret Service agents and if there was some covert reason they wore sunglasses, but the truth was they were to block the god-damn sun.

Press Corps photographers were huddled on the lawn with zoom lenses at the ready, and the armed emergency response team was concealed in the bushes around the perimeter. Beyond the fountain was the fence and the street, and in the distance across a long stretch of grass looking toward the Washington Monument, Shane could see tourists gathered, undoubtedly with iPhones at the ready as the helicopters passed them overhead.

When he'd finished a visual sweep, Shane brought his attention back to Rafa. It looked as if he'd gotten a haircut, although it was hard to tell for sure with it slicked down. In his usual preppy uniform, Rafa laughed at something his sister said to him. Shane was glad to see him smiling, even if he knew he shouldn't give a damn one way or the other. Even if he knew Rafa probably wasn't truly happy, and wouldn't be until he could come out.

In the past two weeks, things had mostly gone back to normal. Mostly. It had all been very polite and proper. He and Alan trailed Rafa to foundation meetings, and otherwise Rafa had stayed upstairs in the residence. Shane filed his reports and checked in with Harris and Nguyen, and the brass at HQ. It was all by the book. No more going upstairs to sample Rafa's latest creations. No more bowling matches. Everything was the way it was supposed to be.

So why was he so goddamned miserable?

Marine One hovered over the South Lawn, the wind kicking up and blowing skirts and hair. The noise was deafening. The other two helicopters circled the area, and the snipers reported in ready as Marine One landed safely. The rotors slowed as the stairs were lowered and President Castillo appeared, smiling and waving as the photographers leaped into action.

Ramon Castillo—codename Vagabond—greeted his family with kisses and hugs, and as he embraced Rafa, Shane found himself wondering what the man would say when he found out his son was gay. He'd supported that bullshit anti-gay bill dressed up as a marriage issue, and had always been conservative even for a Republican.

As an agent, Shane tried not to think too much about it. His job was to protect, no matter who it was and what they stood for. The Secret Service didn't play political favorites, probably making it the only agency in DC that didn't.

As the first family reentered the White House, Shane, Alan, and the other agents followed, now joined by part of Vagabond's detail. The family had brunch waiting for them in the dining room, and Shane and the others stopped in the corridor, taking up their positions. It wasn't effective to clump together, so they spread out, trying to blend into the background unobtrusively. Alan nodded to Shane from across the wide hallway.

Chang, one of the guys on PPD, told Shane about the trip back from Europe, which had been delayed by the eastern storm. "I haven't slept in forty-eight hours. So ready for my bed."

"I can imagine. Did you do the advance over there?"

Chang grimaced. "Yep. The Russians sure as hell didn't make it easy. They know our protocols, and I swear they go out of their way to fuck with them." He rubbed a hand over his lined face. He was about fifty, with an enviably thick head of black hair. "And of course Vagabond decided on a last-minute excursion to shake hands and kiss babies. Hopped out in the middle of a crowd in Austria for an OTR after the peace signing with the Karelians."

Shane shook his head. Off the record stops were incredibly dangerous—not to mention stressful as hell for the protective detail—but the president didn't seem to care. "Sometimes it's like they want to get nailed."

"Yep. Too bad Venus wasn't there. She would have had his ass back in the limo pronto. But no, he was taking selfies as the crowd got bigger and bigger. There was a man in a trench coat getting near, and there was no room to even frisk him."

"Did you lock him down?" Shane had done it in crowds him-self—thrown his arms around a suspect, pinning their arms to their sides to keep them immobile.

"Yep. Smelled like beer and fish. Turns out he didn't have a weapon; guess he was just expecting rain later. How's it going for you and Pearce with Valor?"

"Good. No complaints." That was true, at least. Shane thought of the lie detector test he'd had to take during the application process to become an agent. He wondered how hard he'd fail it now if they asked him questions about Rafa.

"You lucked out with that one. The mouse, right? He's easy."

Shane stretched his neck. "Uh-huh." It felt strangely disloyal to talk about Rafa.

"He'll probably end up arrested with blow and hookers one day. Wound too tight, that one."

Shane bit back the flare of annoyance. "I dunno. Think he'll turn out just fine."

"Yeah, I guess the hookers and blow is our department." Chang smirked. "At least that's what people love to think. One of my wife's friends asked me at our last dinner party how often we have wild parties expensed to the government."

"Wouldn't it be nice?" Shane shook his head. "Did you ex-plain that it's only happened a handful of times in decades and it's been more than ten years now?"

"Would have been a waste of breath. I spun her a tale about jello shots with White House interns in the emergency tunnels. It was quite a rager, as my son would say."

"I bet it was."

The catering and decorating staff were in and out of the East Room at the end of the corridor preparing for Vagabond's birthday party that evening. Shane and Alan were working a double with so many visitors expected. When Chang and the rest of the PPD left for the West Wing, Rafa and his siblings were shepherded into the oval Blue Room for an interview with a reporter from *People*.

Shane slipped in to stand just inside the door while Alan remained in the hall. The reporter had of course been cleared by security, but each of the protectees had one agent in the room.

The White House PR flacks sat off to the side on an ornate blue and gold couch, while Rafa and his brother and sister perched on matching chairs positioned in a semi-circle facing the reporter. The wooden floor was polished to a high shine, and when Shane glanced down at his feet, he could make out his faint reflection.

From where he stood off to the side, he could see Rafa's profile. Virtue sat between her brothers, with Velocity on the far side. The reporter opened with some light banter about their brother Christian being stuck at the airport and how Mother Nature didn't cut the first family any breaks.

They all laughed on cue, and Rafa fiddled with one of his finger nails, toying with the cuticle. He glanced to his right at Shane, his lips twitching into a quick smile before he refocused on the reporter. Shane kept his expression impassive. But damn it, he wanted to smile back.

As back to normal as things were, if Shane was being honest with himself—something he hadn't attempted much lately—this still wasn't a normal detail. He was keeping his distance and following protocol to the letter, but Rafa was an itch under his skin that he couldn't scratch away. It was ludicrous. Even if they were two strangers who'd met by chance, Rafa was too young for him. What the hell did they even have in common?

Yet he found himself looking at recipes online and wondering whether Rafa would like to make them. He thought about surfing every day, the memories of his youth now mixing inextricably with Rafa. As he'd tried to sleep the night before, his mind had spun as he'd imagined Rafa in a wetsuit, damp curls on his forehead as he laughed under the sun. Shane ached to see that.

Christ. He was acting like a teenager.

But he couldn't forget the sensation of Rafa's lips against him, and the sound of his breathy little gasp. The youthful daring of the kiss had only made it sweeter, and the knowledge that Shane was the first man Rafa had ever kissed stirred up a possessive instinct he wasn't proud of. The thought of anyone else touching Rafa sent his blood pressure through the roof.

The Castillo siblings took turns answering the usual types of fluffy questions about life as the first family. Adriana waved her hand as the reporter asked about growing up in the White House.

"You'll have to ask Raf about that. Chris and I escaped to college, and Matthew was only a couple of years behind. But Rafa did a great job holding down the fort."

Rafa laughed, but Shane could tell it was half-hearted. "Yeah, they all abandoned me as soon as they could."

The reporter didn't seem to pick up on the tension in Rafa's smile. "Must have been terrible to have your own movie theater and bowling alley, huh? And a chef to cook you dinner every night. What will you miss most when your father's term is up?"

After a silence that threatened to grow awkward, Rafa managed to smile again. "The bowling alley. Definitely."

When the reporter moved on to the subject of romance, Matthew jerked his thumb at Rafa. "Since Chris isn't here yet, you'd better ask my little brother. He's practically married, and Ade and I aren't even close."

Shane wished they'd just leave Rafa alone. He glanced at the PR staff, but they didn't seem concerned. Rafa smiled tightly again. Could these people not see that he didn't want to talk? Were his brother and sister just clueless, or cruel?

"Um, there's not really much to say. I've got a great girl-friend," Rafa replied. "Ashleigh's my best friend. I'm very lucky."

"And such a beauty!" the reporter gushed. "You must miss her this summer. How is she enjoying Paris?"

"She loves it. She's always had a passion for the fashion world, and she's also getting a chance to explore art and everything Paris has to offer." He glanced at his sister. "But you should really ask Adriana about that reality TV star she's been dating." He leaned forward and stage whispered, "He's a bit of a bad boy, they say."

As the reporter's eyes practically gleamed, the PR flacks sprang into action, redirecting the interview to a few final questions about the president's last birthday celebration in the White House.

When they were finished, Adriana glared at Rafa, who quickly took the chance to hurry out of the Blue Room. The west side of the entrance hall was clogged with staff, so instead of crossing to the back stairs, he took the main staircase. Alan and Shane followed to make sure he got up safely, and as he reached the second floor, Rafa turned back.

Shane could see the turmoil on his face, but he could only stand there as Rafa opened and closed his mouth, and then disappeared up to the family's private floor, his shoulders hunched.

SHANE'S EARPIECE SQUAWKED as the command center spoke. "Negative. Request denied. All guests will be magged. No exceptions."

Beside him, Brent Harris rolled his eyes. He kept his wrist at his side and didn't speak into his mic, but murmured to Shane, "And tell the freaking White House staff that we're in charge of security for a reason." He shook his head. "They always want to cut corners. And what happens if we don't put everyone through a metal detector and someone has a gun? Well, it would be our fault. They're always in such a goddamn rush."

Shane nodded. The use of magnetometers was time consuming, and often a bone of contention between Secret Service and the White House staffers, who seemed to care more about appearances and PR than safety. "They think it's enough we run a security check on the invite list. As if someone's social security number and a clean record will tell us the whole story. Like a movie star can't go nuts and try something." As far as they were concerned, no one was above suspicion.

"I'm just about done with this whole damn place. All of it." Harris's cheeks puffed as he exhaled.

Shane frowned. "With the Service?"

"Yep." Harris shook his head. "Ah, hell. Don't listen to me. I'm in a mood."

"It's all right." Shane watched as Rafa stood with his mother in the entrance hall, nodding every so often as the guests they spoke to said something. Wearing a tuxedo that hugged his body, Rafa looked like he could have been a movie star himself. *Stop thinking about him like that. Stop.* Shane had never understood it when people talked about not being able to get someone off their minds. People came and went, and he usually didn't think about them much at all. So why was Rafael Castillo different?

Shane tugged at his collar, adjusting the coiled cord that hooked his earpiece to the transmitter clipped to his belt at the small of his back. The Service provided agents with formal wear, and it had been a while since Shane had worn his tux. He preferred his usual suit since the collar of the tux was just a little too tight.

He cleared his throat. "What's bugging you?" *Because I sure can't talk about what's bugging me.*

"What isn't?" Harris replied. "I've always loved this job, Kendrick. Serving my country. Keeping people safe from harm. And hell, obviously we're all adrenaline junkies at least a little bit. When I joined, all the travel and long shifts seemed exciting. But I've missed my kids growing up. And now they're hell and gone in

California and the fuckers in charge won't transfer me. I offered to pay my own moving costs. No dice."

Shane had heard of other agents who'd faced the same stubborn bureaucracy. "What are they doing in California?"

"Sharon's company transferred her to Santa Barbara. So I figured, okay. I've been in DC now more than a decade. Time to get some sun. LA field office is still big and active, and it's a hell of a lot closer to Santa Barbara than DC. So I put in for a transfer. Denied, of course. They can't spare me, and there are no openings in LA. Okay, fair enough." He pressed his lips together. "So I asked them to put me on a waiting list."

Shane kept his eyes on Rafa, as well as surveying the people around him. Alan was on the other side of the entrance hall doing the same. "That's a bitch."

Harris barked out a laugh. "Yeah, especially when the bastards put up an internal notice not a month later asking for agents to move to the LA office. Paid moving costs and the whole nine. Well, I just about broke my damn arm waving it to volunteer. Nope. They said they can't replace me. Look, I know I'm a superstar, but come on. This detail isn't rocket science. But they give me this spiel about 'the needs of the Service' and how duty has to come first."

"That's a crap sandwich, all right."

"Want to hear the cherry on top? They ended up forcing one of my buddies in Philly to transfer. He didn't even want to go, but you know—the needs of the Service. It makes no damn sense."

Shaking his head, Shane whistled softly. "Guess I'm lucky I don't have a wife and kids. I can go anywhere." But the thought of moving again and leaving Rafa filled him with unmistakable dread.

"Sometimes I think they try to drum us out so we can't get our pensions. Use us up and spit us out. After everything I've sacrificed for this job, I deserve more."

Shane blinked. It was normal for agents to bitch to each other, but Harris's bitterness gave him pause. As the detail leader, it was unprofessional for him to complain to an underling. Not wanting to encourage it, Shane said, "I hear you. But we should probably cut the chatter. I'm heading to the east vantage."

Harris raised his hands. "You're right. Geez, don't listen to me, Kendrick. Like I said, I'm in a mood today."

"No problem. We all have those days, right?"

"Yeah." Harris was quiet for a few moments, his gaze focused across the hall. "You and Pearce are doing a great job with Valor. But how's Pearce doing? Insists he's fine, but he's looking rough around the edges. Understandable, what with his family situation."

Shane looked over to Alan's position. It was true that the circles under Alan's eyes were only getting darker. He'd been increasingly distracted and distant at times, but Shane kept that to himself. "He's good. He won't let us down."

"Okay. If anything changes on that front, let me know."

"Will do."

As he walked the perimeter of the entrance hall, he nodded to Alan, who maintained his position. Shane stood near a pinky-white marble column, surveying the crowd. *Like I'm one to criticize Harris for unprofessionalism, or Alan for being distracted.* Watching Rafa fiddle with his cufflinks and look like he wanted to be anywhere else, Shane wished he could take him far away.

Chapter Eleven

"WHY DO YOU always get the hot ones?" Adriana mock pouted as she peered at Shane and Alan standing in the corner of the grand East Room. Around the perimeter between golden drapes, wall sconces, and oil portraits, agents in tuxes stood every few feet. More in black tie and gowns were dispersed through the crowd.

Rafa tried not to stare at Shane, who looked amazing in regular suits, and in a tux was out of this world sexy. He gave himself a mental shake as he started imagining Shane *out* of the tux. "Because the Secret Service knows you too well," he answered, adjusting the cuffs on his jacket to make sure his wrists were covered. His arms had always been a little too long, and even though the tux had been tailored, he double checked self-consciously.

Adriana only smiled, flipping back a lock of her dark hair, which had been gently curled just so. "Touché."

Champagne flute in hand, Christian appeared and knocked Rafa's shoulder lightly. "Are we having fun yet?" They were just about the same height, and Rafa bumped him back.

"We're about to witness Celine Dion's first live appearance in five years," Adriana said. "What could *be* more enjoyable?"

"What indeed." When Chris smiled, his cheeks dimpled perfectly. His short dark hair was thick and neat, with nary a curl in sight. "I'd say watching the Knicks game in my underwear with a cold beer and a bowl of pretzels."

Rafa looked around for Chris's wife, Hadley, spotting her blonde up-do near the stage. Beneath the huge chandeliers, her hair glittered with several embedded jewels that managed to be glitzy, yet tasteful. "Don't tell me Hadley would rather be on the couch."

Chris laughed. "No, no. This is her idea of heaven. Where's our brother?"

Adriana huffed. "That little prick's nowhere to be found. He appeared for about five fucking minutes before vanishing. Mom will have his balls for breakfast if he's not back here for the cake. Of course it's not like the agents don't know where he is, so I'm sure he'll be hunted down shortly." She sipped her champagne. "I wonder if Mom and Dad will take permanent protection once it's all over."

Rafa frowned. "Of course they will. You think Mom would let Dad say no? Too dangerous."

She shrugged. "If someone really wants to trade their life to kill the president—or an ex-president—there's only so much the agents can do. I can't wait to finally be free."

"You already are," Rafa scoffed. "LA's a million miles from DC."

"I still have agents watching me take a dump."

"Adriana, stop it," Chris hissed, glancing around. "You know the press is here."

"Yeah, yeah. They're occupied with your wife, don't worry. Sometimes I just wish we could sing happy birthday to Dad without hundreds of strangers and Celine freaking Dion on hand."

"We're almost there. Not many months left now." Chris squinted across the room. "Is Uncle Juan already tipsy?"

"Yup," Rafa answered. "Mom will love it." They'd had a big

breakfast with his aunts and uncles, and it was nice to see them again, but they were little more than strangers.

Chris took another drink. "But really, who among us doesn't need some liquid courage to get through this party?" He sighed. "We'd better stop that kind of talk. We don't want to sound ungrateful."

"You're right," Rafa agreed. "But sometimes it's just so…"

"Motherfucking exhausting to live in a fishbowl?" Adriana drained her glass. "I'd better hit the can." Her beaded green dress swaying, she strode off, her tuxedoed agents following discreetly. Adriana barely topped five feet, but with her stilettos and swagger she was bigger than life.

Rafa and Chris could only laugh. Rafa knew part of the reason Adriana had started swearing like a sailor was to bother their mother, and he wondered if she'd ever outgrow it. She had an amazing capacity to smile sweetly for the public while hiding her true feelings. He supposed they were more alike than he'd thought.

He and Chris plucked fresh champagne flutes from the tray of a passing waiter, and Chris shook his head. "I keep forgetting you're old enough to drink now. Do you like it? Have you ever even tried a beer at college?"

Rafa sipped the fizz. "I like it okay. Ash got me drunk on my birthday. It was fun. The hangover not so much, but what can you do?"

"Well, I'm glad to hear it, baby brother. You're way overdue for fun. Matty would guzzle every drink I'd slip him, but never you."

Rafa chuckled. "Remember after the second inauguration when he yacked in a ficus pot? Yeah, I wasn't too eager to follow his lead."

"How could I forget? Our details totally covered for him and cleaned up the mess. They do not pay those people enough to deal with all our shit. Not that they get any trouble from you." He looked to the side of the room. "Adriana's right—they are hot."

The champagne almost squirted out Rafa's nose as he coughed and choked. He smiled tightly as a few people looked his way, waiting until their attention was elsewhere to ask, "What?" in as casual a tone as he could muster. *My ears must be clogged. Or broken.*

"Your new agents. Especially the one with the muscles and steely gaze?"

Cheeks flaming, Rafa tried to keep his voice steady. He gripped his glass to keep his hand from shaking. "Why would you say that?"

Chris tilted his head, sighing. He glanced around before speaking softly. "Come on, Raf."

Rafa was suddenly putting one foot in front of the other, ordering himself not to run as buzzing filled his head. He made it out of the East Room, but of course the hall was clogged with guests. The stairs were too hard to reach, so he veered left into the Blue Room.

Chris called his name as he shoved up the window at the south end of the oval and yanked the short double doors inward. Not many people knew about this secret door to the portico, but he hadn't spent seven and a half years in the White House for nothing.

As he raced down the stairs to the South Lawn, Chris caught his arm.

"Raf, wait. I'm sorry. Are you okay?"

Rafa jerked his arm free. At the top of the stairs, Shane, Alan, and Chris's agents appeared. "I just need some fresh air," Rafa announced loudly. "I'm fine."

Of course Chris followed him to the lawn. Despite the heatwave, the grass was lush beneath his dress shoes, and Rafa wondered when the sprinklers would come on. He hoped it was any minute now, because an untimely soaking would be an excellent excuse to escape to his room.

"Rafa, would you stop and talk to me?"

Exhaling sharply, Rafa spun around. "Fine. But there's nothing to talk about."

Chris raised his eyebrows. "Are you sure about that?" He kept his voice quiet, even though their agents were well out of earshot at the top of the portico stairs by one of the thick white columns.

"Of course I am. Why would you even say that stuff in the first place?" His heart thumped, and he was sure Chris could hear it.

Gazing at him with unmistakable sadness, Chris shook his head. "I didn't want to upset you. I shouldn't have said anything—at least not in there. Not tonight. It just came out, I guess. Excuse the pun."

Rafa's mouth was bone dry, and he couldn't seem to find any words. *How does he know? He can't know. No one does. Right?*

"I've wanted to say something for a long time. I just want you to know that you don't have to be afraid. That I love you and accept you the way you are."

"I have a girlfriend," Rafa blurted hoarsely.

"I know. And I'm not saying you don't love her or care about her."

"Then what are you saying? Why are you saying any of this?" His palms were clammy, and his skin prickled all over.

Chris rubbed his face. "I'm doing this all wrong." He inhaled deeply and blew it out. "Okay." He met Rafa's gaze steadily. "What I'm saying is that I think you're gay. I've thought that for a long time."

The words were shards of glass in Rafa's throat. "Why?"

"I don't know. There was always just something about you. When you were a kid, you had a soft voice, and there was something…gentle about you. And I know gay people aren't all the same and I shouldn't put any stock in stereotypes, but you had this way of…sparkling. But over the years that's disappeared bit by bit. Maybe you're in denial, or maybe I'm completely wrong and you're not gay at all. But I can see that you're miserable. You've always put on a smile and stayed quiet, and…we let you. But you're not happy, are you? And I hate it, because I want you to be. Maybe it's not my place to say any of this, but you're my baby brother. I love you."

Rafa's throat was so thick he could barely swallow. "I love you too." He blinked rapidly, glancing at the stairs. He couldn't let Shane see him cry like a baby.

"I'm sorry to confront you like this. I know this was the wrong time and the wrong way. Hadley always says my timing's for shit. But you never seemed interested in girls, or even had a girlfriend until Ashleigh. And I know you care about her. But if you're repressing who you really are for her sake, or Mom and Dad—"

"I'm not." He cleared his throat. "I'm not in denial."

Chris nodded. "Okay."

"I know I'm gay."

The words hung there in the lank June air, no hint of a breeze coming to float them away in the night.

Blinking, Chris smiled tentatively. "Really? Raf, that's great!" He reached out to squeeze Rafa's arms briefly. "You have no idea how happy I am to hear you say that."

"You are?" Rafa had never let himself think much about how his family would react when he did come out. It had been too terrifying to contemplate. His heart swelled, and he returned his brother's smile.

"Of course!" Chris's white teeth gleamed in the darkness. "I was worried you'd keep it bottled up for years still. Are you and Ashleigh…?"

"She's a lesbian. It's been fake all along. I mean, I do love her; she's my best friend."

"Yeah, of course. I have to say, you guys are good. If I hadn't grown up with you, I probably would never have guessed."

Rafa's head spun. *Chris knows. I just told him. Out loud. I said it.* "But you can't say anything. Not about me or Ash. We have it all planned out."

"I won't breathe a word, I promise." Chris yanked him into a hug. "Just let me know what you need from me and when, and I'll be there."

Rafa let himself relax in his brother's arms, hugging him back. "I never thought... I'm surprised you even noticed."

When Chris drew back, his face was pinched. "I know I wasn't here enough. After Dad took office, I couldn't wait to escape to Yale. Ade and Matty were here with you, but not for long. Matty got that early scholarship, and you were alone until you finally got to leave for college. Mom's...well, she's Mom, and Dad's been a little busy being the leader of the free world and all that. I was so wrapped up in myself. You never got into any trouble, so I think...we all just let you do your thing."

"That's the way I wanted it. It was easier than being in *People* and *US Weekly* all the time, or partying like Ade, or trying for the Olympics like Matty. You didn't do anything wrong."

"Debatable, but I'm going to make up for it now, okay? Man, we have so much to talk about." Chris grinned, his eyes gleaming. "Do you have a secret boyfriend?"

"Are you crazy?" Rafa barked out a laugh. "No way. There are no secrets here. You know that. Ash and I talk in code. Once this is over and we go back to normal, or normalish, then I can date. But not yet. Can you imagine what Dad would say?"

Chris grimaced. "Yeah, I think Dad's afraid you'll bring home some muscle queen in hot pants, as if gay people dress like they're on a Pride float every day." He rolled his eyes.

Rafa laughed, but then he tumbled Chris's words over again in his mind. "Wait...Dad? But he doesn't know." His pulse kicked up again, sweat beading on his forehead. As Chris's gaze flickered away and he took a deep breath, bile rose in Rafa's throat.

Chris sighed. "Raf, look… I know this is hard."

"He doesn't know. Of course he doesn't." Rafa shook his head back and forth. "He *can't* know."

"Not for certain. But we talked about it once." Looking at him intently, Chris squeezed Rafa's shoulder. "I know this must be a shock to you, but—"

Rafa jerked away. "What about Mom? Ade and Matty? Do they know?"

"Raf, just listen for a minute."

"Holy shit, they do." The sheer humiliation was acid on his tongue. "Do you all sit around talking about me? Laughing about how stupid I am to think it was a secret? About how hard I tried to pretend? It must be hilarious."

"No!" Chris shook his head earnestly. "I swear to God we've never talked about it. It was only one time with me and Dad. It was late, and he'd had a few drinks."

"When?" Rafa crossed his arms, his fingers digging into his sleeves.

"You were still in high school," Chris admitted.

Nausea swelled, and Rafa thought he might vomit all over the pristine lawn. "He knew all this time? Mom did too, didn't she?"

"I don't think much gets by her. But we've never talked about it. I haven't with Ade or Matty either. But I think they probably have their suspicions."

"God, I'm such an idiot." He wished the South Lawn would open up and swallow him whole. "What…what did Dad say?"

"I don't know. It was a long time ago. It doesn't matter now."

"Of course it matters!" Then it hit him, and he actually staggered back. "The bill. That bullshit traditional marriage bill that he supported."

Chris winced. "I know. That was awful."

"He suspected then that I was gay. He knew, and he didn't care. He still did it. He still made me get up there in front of the world and smile while he shit all over gay people's rights." A sob choked him, cracking his voice. "He *knew*."

"Not for sure. Raf, it doesn't mean anything. You know he loves you."

"It means everything," Rafa whispered. "That was *me* he was fighting against. My rights."

Chris took Rafa's shoulders. "We all love you. Please believe me," he implored. "I—"

A female staffer called from the portico, "Boys! It's time for cake. We need you inside, please."

"Time to smile for the cameras." Rafa shook off his brother and turned back before Chris could say more. At the bottom of the stairs, he paused. Chris stopped too, but he waved him on. "I need a second."

Nodding, Chris mounted the curving staircase. Rafa watched him go, concentrating on breathing in and out. As Chris disappeared inside with his detail, Rafa forced his feet to move. At the top of the stairs, he met Shane's intense gaze.

"Okay?" Shane asked quietly.

Rafa's heart skipped. God, how he wanted to throw himself into Shane's arms and block out the rest of the world. Wanted to tell Shane everything, and hear what he thought about it and get his advice. From the corner of his eye, he saw Alan stop and glance back from the door. Rafa jerked his head in a nod, his eyes stinging, and hurried inside.

As Celine led them all in a rousing rendition of "Happy Birthday" and his parents beamed, Rafa stood beside his family and smiled while his soul burned.

Chapter Twelve

"WHAT WAS THAT?" Alan asked as they made their way around the West Wing to where their G-ride was parked.

"What?" Shane said, as if he didn't damn well know. Rafa's face filled his mind—his eyes luminous with *hurt* that Shane wanted to take away. Maybe it was fucked up to want to take care of him, but he did. He wanted to hold Rafa in his arms. He wanted to find out what was wrong so he could make whoever was responsible suffer. He wanted to make Rafa smile again.

Alan cocked an eyebrow. "Asking Valor a personal question. You know we're not supposed to get involved."

"I didn't get *involved*. Obviously he was upset. It was nothing."

"Look, he's a nice kid, but you know it's not the job to get caught up in his drama. You can't get too close."

Shane rounded on Alan, who jerked to a stop. "Are you accusing me of something?"

Alan opened and closed his mouth. "Of course not. Jesus. Don't get bent out of shape."

As Shane pressed the button to unlock the vehicle with a *beep-beep*, he bit the inside of his cheek. "I asked one question. It won't happen again."

Alan sighed. "I'm not trying to bust your balls, man. But you know they'll yank you off the detail in a heartbeat if they think you're getting too friendly with the protectee. Since I came back, it feels like there's a weird tension between you two."

He was completely right, and all Shane could do was nod. "It won't be an issue."

Alan stalked around to the other side and climbed into the Suburban. "Great."

As they left the White House, Shane gripped the wheel. He blew out a long breath as he pulled up to a red light. "Sorry. I know you're not trying to be a dick. And you're right. So thanks for saying it."

Laughing, Alan shook his head. "Nope, definitely not trying to be a dick, but I guess I succeed despite myself sometimes."

Shane laughed too, the tension dissipating. "No, I'm the dick here. It won't happen again. Like I said—not an issue."

"Clearly the kid was upset about something. I thought he might burst into tears when they were cutting the cake."

"Yeah." Shane shrugged, as if he wasn't dying to know what had happened with Christian to upset Rafa so much. He told himself he just wanted to know if Rafa was okay. It was just normal human kindness and concern. Nothing more. *Because it can never be more. I shouldn't care. I can't care.*

"I just think… Sometimes the way he looks at you? I know he's got a girlfriend, but I dunno. He wouldn't be the first protectee with a crush on an agent. Might only be a hero worship thing. I'm just saying you need to be careful. Don't encourage it."

Too fucking late for that. "You're right. Won't happen again."

They drove on silently, Shane eager to get this night over with.

"So, um…" Alan laughed humorlessly, rubbing his face. "Don't feel that you have to, but I know Jules would really love it if you came tomorrow morning. I figure we can catch a nap before we start work, since we're on second shift. And if you can't make it, don't worry."

Shit. He'd totally forgotten. *Here I am with my head up my ass when Al's kid is dying.* "Of course I'll be there. Wouldn't miss it."

"Thanks. I don't know why they're even doing this breakfast. It's the neighborhood group. Not that I don't appreciate them trying to raise money for Dylan. I do." He sighed heavily. "It's just so much if we have any prayer of trying this treatment. Even if it was in the States and not Sweden—the treatment itself is going to be so much money. Too much to ever raise."

"I'll be there bright and early. I'd love to see Dylan and Jules. It's been too long."

"Okay. You're a good pal." Alan tipped his head back and closed his eyes. "Thought that party would never end. Celine just doesn't know when to stop, does she?"

Shane chuckled. "Her heart will go on."

"And on, and on, and fucking *on.*"

They laughed, and he gave Alan's shoulder a quick squeeze. Shane had to remember that there were people with problems much bigger than his inappropriate little attachment to Rafael Castillo. It was time to get over it and put it out of his head for good.

THE SUN PEEKED out from behind a bank of white clouds, gleaming off the colorful streamers and balloons festooning the large backyard. Shane scanned the clumps of people and headed over to where Alan and Julianna stood talking with guests.

"You remember this troublemaker from Albany," Alan said to his wife, nodding to Shane.

"Hey, Al. Jules, it's great to see you." Shane hugged her briefly and kissed her cheek. She was a tiny thing, barely reaching Alan's shoulder. Dark circles that makeup couldn't cover shadowed her eyes.

"Shane. It's wonderful to see you. I was so glad to hear you and Al were partners again. You're keeping him out of trouble?" She winked at her husband, tucking a strand of dark hair behind her ear.

"More like the other way around."

The couple Alan and Jules had been talking to introduced themselves as the hosts of the party, and pointed out the breakfast buffet and silent auction items lined up on a table under the shade of an old oak. The woman gave Jules a squeeze before she and her husband circulated with the other guests. Children shrieked and chased each other near the vegetable garden.

Shane tried to pick out Dylan. "Is that Dylan playing the water balloon darts?"

"It is. He's a lot bigger than the last time you saw him, huh?" Jules smiled, but it didn't quite reach her eyes.

The boy was indeed much taller, although he was noticeably gaunt, and his sandy hair was thinning. "He's looking good. How is he feeling?"

"Much better than last month," Alan answered. "He's okay for now. We're thankful for that. Not sure for how much longer, but I guess there are never guarantees, are there?" As he watched his son, the ache in his gaze made Shane want to comfort him. What could he say?

Jules seemed to read his mind. "It's okay. We've heard all the sympathy and platitudes. It is what it is. We'll fight it with everything we've got. It's all we can do."

Shane reached into his pocket. "I brought him an Amazon gift card. I don't have a clue what kids are into, so I figured he could pick what he wants."

"Oh, you didn't have to do that." Jules waved him off.

"I'm happy to. And of course I'll donate."

Jules opened her mouth and then shut it. She took the card and put it in her pocket. "Thank you. Everyone's been so generous. Cathy and Bob organized this party, and hit up their friends for silent auction items. It's so kind." She blinked rapidly, and Alan rubbed the back of her neck. "Ugh, I'm a mess today. Enough about us. Shane, tell me all about you."

"Hasn't Al told you everything already?" Shane smiled.

"Not the important stuff. For example, are you dating? And if you aren't, why not?" She poked his polo shirt with her index finger.

"Nah. Not really the romance type, it seems." But heat crept up his neck.

Jules didn't miss it, of course, narrowing her gaze. "Ohhh, the gentleman doth protest too much. There *is* someone, isn't there? Come on, I only ever dated this one, so I have to live vicariously. Spill it."

"Hey, why do you say that like it's a bad thing?" Alan nudged her playfully with his hip. "We got it right straight out of the gate in high school. We were dating savants."

"We were indeed. When you joined up instead of going to college, I never thought we'd last." She smiled up at her husband. "But I guess it was fate. Or stubbornness. Everyone told me I'd make a terrible army wife. Although sometimes I think being a Secret Service wife is worse. Thank goodness you landed a good boy who doesn't take off for days at a time. Al says he's a real nice kid. You like him, Shane?" She raised her hands. "Not that you have to like him to protect him. I know, I know. Just curious."

"I do like him." *Too damn much.*

"Oh, and don't think you're off the hook. I still want to know who this mystery man is." Jules leaned in and murmured, "Is he in the Service? Is he here right now?" She gazed around at the guests, some of whom were agents Shane recognized. "Come on, throw me a bone."

Shane had to chuckle. "He's not here."

"A-ha!" Her face lit up. "So he does exist. All right, husband of mine. I expect you to get it out of him on your next shift. Use any methods necessary. The people demand the truth."

As new guests arrived, Jules left to greet them. Alan shook his head with a smile. "Sorry about that. But gossip is a good distraction. It helps to talk about normal stuff." He looked over at Dylan, who ate chocolate-dipped strawberries with a friend. "Even though there'll never really be a normal again. Not the way it was." He watched Jules go to Dylan, kissing his forehead and wiping chocolate from his cheek. "I don't know how she can stand to even look at me. She says she doesn't blame me. But how can she not? How can she not hate me?"

Shane frowned. "Al, it's not your fault. There's nothing you could have done. Genetics aren't something we choose."

Alan's distant gaze was still on his family, his voice strained and thready. "I'd do anything, you know? To save him. To make this easier for her."

"Of course you would. They know that. We all know that." Shane put his hand on Alan's arm and squeezed.

Blinking, Alan snapped back to attention. "Shit. Sorry. Just letting my brain get away from me." He smiled and waved to someone. "It's so fucking weird, you know? We're worried all the time, but we want him to be happy. We want him to enjoy everything he can. We try to still joke around, and keep things light. But when I laugh, or feel good, I remember Jess, and I think: How could I have laughed just then? How could I feel even a moment's happiness when my baby's gone? When my boy's going next."

Shane wished to God he knew what to say. More and more people arrived, and they'd surely want to talk to Alan. "Hey, let's go for a walk around the block. Get away from the party for a few minutes. Regroup."

Rubbing his face quickly, Alan took a deep breath. "No, it's okay. I'm okay. I'd better go talk to people." He slapped Shane's back. "Thanks for listening. I'm fine. Really."

"Anytime." Shane caught Alan's arm. "I mean it, okay? Anytime."

He nodded. "Yeah." He tried to smile. "Hey, is Jules right? You seeing someone?"

"It's nothing." Shane waved his hand.

"Hmm. Anyone I know?"

Shane glanced around the backyard, looking anywhere but at Alan. "Nah."

"If you say so." Then to someone else, he called, "Good morning," and squeezed Shane's arm as he left.

Blowing out a long exhale, Shane went over to chat with other agents and make the highest auction bids he could. He rarely used any of the hefty insurance settlement he'd received after the fire, and he couldn't think of a better way to spend it.

Chapter Thirteen

I T WAS LATE afternoon by the time Rafa emerged from his room. He'd claimed a migraine when his mother had knocked on his door that morning, and fortunately his family had left him alone. Chris had asked to come in, but he'd gone away when Rafa told him to.

Now Rafa was showered and dressed, his shirt crisp and his oxfords polished. As he reached the stairs, Chris's wife joined him, wearing a green floral dress that brought out her amber eyes and golden hair perfectly.

"Hi, Rafa. Are you feeling better?" Her pretty face pinched in concern. He didn't really know Hadley well, but she'd always seemed nice. "Chris was worried."

Does she know I'm gay too? Probably. "Uh-huh. Thanks."

"Oh, good. You look great. All ready for the photo shoot? Your favorite thing, right?"

"Yeah. More in your wheelhouse. Oh, congrats on that new movie."

Hadley's teeth gleamed as she smiled. "Thanks, Raf. I'm pretty excited. It's a more dramatic role than I've had. I'll actually get to act and not just stick out my boobs and wait for the hero to rescue me. And hey, just think—before long you won't have to deal with *People Magazine* unless you want to."

On the second floor of the residence, they joined the rest of the family aside from his father. Adriana and Matthew tapped their phones. Matty's hair was a too-long mess, and he was ignoring their mother as she nagged.

"Shouldn't you cut that mop for aerodynamics?" Camila asked.

Matty shrugged. "It's under a cap in the pool." At least he'd changed his usual flip-flops and shorts for slacks and a buttoned shirt.

Chris watched Rafa with a furrow between his brows, and their mother turned to peer at Rafa closely.

"How are you feeling, dear? You didn't look well last night." She licked her finger and patted down a stray lock of his slicked hair.

"I'm good." He forced a smile. "You look beautiful." And she did, wearing a subtly patterned purple dress that flowed around her knees.

"Thank you, my darling. They've requested an Oval Office shot. Let's walk over."

They trooped down the stairs, picking up a tail of agents when they reached the first floor and headed to the West Wing. Rafa only let himself glance back at Shane once, keeping his gaze on his feet the rest of the time. Shane hadn't been looking at him, which shouldn't have hurt, but it did.

I'm such a freaking mess.

He'd wanted to call Ashleigh after the birthday party torture had finally finished, but it had been the middle of the night in Paris. By morning he'd curled up in bed with the curtains drawn, and even talking to Ash had seemed like too much of a mountain to climb.

Ramon sat behind his desk in the Oval Office, talking to a few of his aides. The middle-aged PR staffer sitting on one of the couches stood as they filed in, and their security details waited in the hall. There were three agents already stationed inside the office, standing silently around the room.

The PR woman smiled brightly. "Good afternoon! The *People* reporter and photographer are just coming through security. Are we all ready? Do you have any questions about the talking points?"

"Do you know I'm gay too?" Rafa asked.

He hadn't planned on saying anything at all, let alone *that*, but somehow the words were suddenly out, and the PR woman's eyes bugged as the air was sucked from the room in a giant *whoosh*.

In the silence, Rafa could feel the heat of everyone's gazes on his skin. He didn't breathe, and it didn't seem like anyone else did either. He managed to get out, "Is that why you get the reporters to ask so many questions about my girlfriend? To try and convince anyone who suspects that we're the perfect little hetero couple? Because apparently I haven't been fooling people as much as I thought."

As he stood, Rafa's father barked to his aides, "Out." As they scurried away, he ordered, "Cancel the interview" to the PR staffer. The woman rushed out, and the three agents glanced at each other. Ramon flushed red. "You too. *Out.*" They obeyed silently, the detail leader closing the door behind him.

"Rafael, what is the meaning of this?" His mother stared at him, and it was the first time he could remember her appearing truly flummoxed. The rest of the family watched with wide eyes.

"Don't pretend you're surprised." Rafa's voice was amazingly steady considering his heart was close to pounding right out of his chest. "If Dad suspected, there's no way you didn't."

His parents shared a glance, and Camila sighed. "This isn't the time for this discussion, and it certainly isn't the place."

Ramon shook his head. "Certainly not, Rafael. Son, I don't know what's gotten into you, but—"

"You knew all these years, didn't you? *Years.* Do you know how hard it's been, trying to hide who I really am? How hard I've worked at it? I was so scared to tell you. So scared to mess things up for you. Terrified you wouldn't accept it. Wouldn't accept me. But you already knew, and you never said a word. You never...dropped any hints that would let me know you'd be okay with it. Because you're not."

His parents had another silent conversation. Then Camila motioned to the couches. "Why don't we all sit down and talk about this reasonably."

"No! Why didn't you say anything? Why did you let me pretend? Even if I wasn't out to the world, I could have stopped hiding with you guys."

His mother shook her head. "Darling, I thought... It didn't seem necessary."

"Wait...what?" Matthew's mouth gaped. "You're seriously gay? I thought you, like, grew out of it or whatever."

"Oh my God." Adriana glared at their brother. "Is your head really that far up your ass?"

"Everyone lower your voices," their father commanded. "Now. And watch your language, young lady."

Adriana replied, "For fuck's sake, Dad." She turned to Rafa. "Why didn't you tell me? You know I'd accept you. Don't you know that? I have a million gay friends. It's not an issue even a little bit." She blinked rapidly, tears forming in her eyes. "Didn't you know you could trust me?"

"You're never here," Rafa whispered. "We hardly ever talk. You all left a long time ago."

Adriana said, "I thought you'd tell us when you were ready. I wanted to ask, but my friend Billy told me not to push. I always push and fuck things up. I didn't want to do that with you." She swiped a tear from her cheek. "But I guess I fucked it up anyway."

Rafa wanted to tell her that it was okay and not to cry. "I should have told you. You're right."

Chris cleared his throat. "I think we all made mistakes. Why don't we just—"

"But what about Ashleigh?" Matty asked, frowning. "Jesus, I really am clueless. I'm so sorry. Raf, I thought you guys were tight."

"Of course they are," Camila said. "Rafa..." She paused, the silence stretching out. "Your father and I suspected you had certain...inclinations. But you and Ashleigh have a wonderful relationship. A very successful relationship. Since you never spoke to us of being unhappy, we assumed we were all on the same page."

"The same page," Rafa echoed dully. It was surreal to actually be having the conversation, and it was almost like he was hovering outside his body watching.

His father walked around the wide desk. "Rafa, there are many people who maintain a respectable marriage while keeping the other part of their life...private."

Respectable. He ached all over, his chest hollow.

"This isn't the twentieth century, Dad." Chris shook his head. "Gay marriages are just as respectable. They're just *marriages* now, no matter how many right-wingers try to change it back. Maybe equality isn't popular in your Republican circles, but Rafa shouldn't have to hide who he is." Beside him, Hadley nodded strenuously.

"I'm not marrying Ashleigh, Dad." Rafa's own voice sounded far away. "I was never going to marry her. We were going to come out in January when you left office."

Camila took a step toward him. "Dear, let's not do anything rash."

"It isn't rash." Rafa gritted the words out. "We've planned it for years. Did you really think I was going to stay in the closet my whole life?" As his parents stared at him, he realized they did.

Oh my God, they really, actually did.

"Rafa, you have to think about your future," Ramon said

quietly. "Your career."

Adriana rolled her eyes. "Gay people have careers, Dad."

"I'm not going into business anyway," Rafa said. "I'm not going to work in some corporate office."

Camila's tone was sharp. "Well, what on earth do you plan on doing? Do you expect us to support you while you do what, exactly?"

"I'm going to Australia."

Another silence filled the room. Camila folded her hands in front of her, her rings visibly digging into her white fingers. "And what do you plan to do in *Australia*?" She said the word as if she'd found it stuck to the bottom of one of her Louboutin heels.

"I'm going to apply to the Cordon Bleu. I'll work in a restaurant to pay the bills."

"Oh for God's sake!" she shouted, her eyes flashing. "Why are you so obsessed with this ridiculous idea of cooking?"

"Why are you so afraid of it?" he yelled back. "It's what I love to do, Mom. It's what I'm going to do. Why does it bother you? Because you think it's *gay*? Even though there are a million straight guys who are chefs? All these years I've played my part and done what you wanted. I tried so hard to be good. To be the son you wanted. But I never will be."

"Rafa, you know we love you," his father said solemnly. "No matter what, we love you. We always have, and we always will."

Tears burned behind his eyes. "Then how could you do it?"

"Do what?" Ramon shook his head.

"That bill!"

His parents shared a puzzled glance. "Darling, what bill?" Camila asked.

They don't even remember.

Rafa spat, "S.J.Res. 19: A joint resolution proposing an amendment to the Constitution of the United States relative to marriage."

Ramon frowned deeply. "That had nothing to do with you."

"How can you say that?" Chris demanded, as Rafa's head felt like it would explode.

"It was politics, dear." Camila looked at Rafa with such genuine confusion. "It wasn't anything to do with you."

Rafa clenched his hands into fists. "How—how can you seriously say that to me? It was a bill to take away gay people's rights. It felt like I'd been hit by a truck that night, but I told myself that you didn't know." He looked to his father. "That you'd have never supported it if you knew it was my rights you were trying to destroy. It was bad enough you supported it at all, but I told myself you would never do that to your own son."

"It was a party decision, Rafa." Ramon steepled his fingers and brought them to his chin. "It was about those people who insist on—"

"*I'm* those people, Dad! But no, you thought I'd live in the closet and marry a woman. That was never going to be my life. It never will be. One day I do want to get married, and I'll be marrying a man. At least it's still legal, no thanks to you. But you made me stand up there in front of all those people, smiling while you talked about traditional marriage, and God, and the Bible, and all that hate disguised as religion."

"The party has a platform, Rafa. These decisions aren't always mine," Ramon insisted.

"If you didn't even believe it that makes it worse!"

His mother stepped toward him, beseeching. "Rafa, we've always tried to guide you on the right path. You and Ashleigh are happy together! We thought it was the best for your future if we—"

"I can't do this. I can't." His breath coming short and fast, Rafa's head spun. He tore open the west door, hurrying along the little corridor past his father's private study, and into the small dining room where his father and staffers often ate. At the open door to the main corridor, he stopped in his tracks. Shane and

Alan undoubtedly thought he was still in the Oval Office, and were stationed with the other crowd of agents in the main hallway by the northwest door.

He was alone.

"Rafa?" his father called.

He patted his chino pockets, heart soaring as he grasped the hard metal of his car key. He'd toyed with the idea of taking a drive to clear his head after the interview, but now it was a burning need. Fuck his parents. Fuck the White House. Fuck the Secret Service. Fuck them all.

There was no time to waste. Heart thumping, he edged out of the little dining room and into the main hallway, walking as fast as he could past the senior advisor's office and the chief of staff's. He kept his head down as he went, ignoring anyone he passed, resisting the urge to run.

Of course when he rushed by the security on the outside door, they called his name, and now he did run, racing to his car and hopping in as Shane and Alan burst out of the West Wing. In the rearview, he could see them hightailing it to their Suburban, and Rafa stepped on the gas. At the gate, he nodded and smiled to the guard, who raised the barrier just before he undoubtedly received a radio message, his expression changing as he called, "Wait!"

But Rafa wasn't waiting. He roared away, and of course the Suburban followed. For a crazy moment he considered trying to ditch them, but it wouldn't do any good, and would likely get them in trouble.

"Fuck!" His voice was hoarse. "I just want to be alone!" He sped along the streets of DC, making turns to avoid stopping when he could. He had to keep moving. Had to. Seven years hiding in that place, and he was done.

In his pocket, his phone buzzed. He ignored it. When he was forced to stop at a red light, the Suburban was two cars behind him. His phone buzzed again, and he pulled it out. The caller ID only said *United States Secret Service.*

Of course they had his cell number, but only called when they really had to. Was it Shane? The thought of hearing his voice was too much to resist, and he hit the speaker phone as the light went green.

"Rafa?" It was indeed Shane, and Rafa's eyes burned as his chest swelled. He wanted to pull over and tell Shane everything— pour out all the words that clogged his throat and threatened to choke him.

But he couldn't, because the echo on the line indicated he was on the speaker in the Suburban, and because Shane was his Secret Service agent. He wasn't his boyfriend. He wasn't even his *friend.* Rafa was a job to him. He was nothing. *Nothing.* "Leave me alone," he gritted out.

"I know you're upset. Just tell me where you're going. You can go wherever you want. Okay?"

The pain and fear and resentment tore through him with jagged teeth. "I know I can. I'm not a prisoner! Just let me go and leave me alone. *Please.*"

"You know we can't do that." There was a pause, and Rafa could hear the murmur of Alan's voice, probably talking to command. Probably calling more agents to come and box him in. "We just want to help."

"No you don't." He took the freeway entrance, stepping on the gas and heading toward Virginia. "Everyone just wants me to shut up and smile and be a good boy."

"Rafa, I know it feels—"

"No!" Rage sliced through him, icy hot. "You don't know anything about how I feel." He hung up and gripped the wheel.

The miles ticked by, and the Suburban stayed behind him. No other Secret Service vehicles appeared, at least. The gray clouds darkened, and rain splattered the windshield. Rafa had no idea where he was going, but he kept driving on to West Virginia as the afternoon waned. He knew he should turn around and get back to the White House—go "home," what a joke—but he couldn't bear having to talk to his family again. At least in his car he was alone. As alone as he could get until January.

His phone buzzed every so often, Chris, Adriana, Matty, and their parents all trying him. Finally he turned it off. Even if it wasn't fair, and even if it was selfish and childish, he ached with betrayal.

They'd known.

Maybe not for *certain*, but still. They'd let him pretend. They'd let him hide away who he really was, keeping it locked up, not letting anyone but Ashleigh see. No one but Shane. He felt unbearably foolish and hurt.

"*It was politics, dear.*"

He took the next exit, not knowing where he was. The rain poured now, but he kept going through the forest and eventually along a side road that started to wind up into the hills. A car passed the other way, its lights glittering in the rain, but the road was deserted as he approached a lookout and rest stop. The urge to pee had become too much to ignore. He pulled over, screeching to a stop, tires sliding in the wet ground.

The rain was a curtain over the hills, the world gray and murky as the sun set in the west. As he stepped out, Rafa tipped his head back, letting the water flow over him, not caring as he got soaked. Then the Suburban pulled in behind him, and he hurried to the squat brick bathroom.

Inside, fluorescent lights flickered over the dank concrete. Opposite a row of urinals there were two stalls, and Rafa locked himself in one just as Shane appeared. Leaning back against the door, Rafa squeezed his eyes shut. "Go away."

"I just want to make sure you're all right." Shane's voice was low and steady as always.

It sent traitorous warmth through Rafa, and he shoved it away.

"Can't I piss in private anymore?" He yanked open his chinos and pulled out his dick, punctuating his question with a stream of urine into the toilet. Shane didn't answer, and when Rafa was finished he stood there, his chest rising and falling.

"Are you done?" Shane asked quietly.

"No." Rafa knew he was being petulant and stubborn, but it was almost as if he was outside himself, and the mess of his emotions had taken over. "Jesus, I want to be alone. Can't you understand that? Maybe I want to, to…to jerk off! Just go."

"We both know you're not going to do that." Shane was still infuriatingly calm.

"Oh yeah?" Rafa shoved his open pants and boxers down to his hips and gripped his cock.

Shane sighed. "Come on. You wouldn't."

"You don't think so?" Screw him. Screw them all. They didn't know him. He was done holding everything inside.

Leaning back against the stall door, Rafa spread his legs and stroked roughly, the slapping sound of his flesh echoing off the concrete and metal. "Maybe I'm sick of being the good boy who does everything he's supposed to. Who jumps through their hoops and always smiles when he feels like screaming. Fuck it. What has that gotten me, huh?"

He spit into his palm once, twice, and slicked the way as he lengthened and swelled. His breath caught on a gasp as he teased the ridge under his shaft, and then words were pouring out and he was powerless to stop them, a distant part of him watching in horror as the rest of him went all in.

"I wish it was you, you know. I wish you were touching me. Fucking me. I know I shouldn't. I know it's wrong, but I want it so bad. I want to get on my hands and knees and take you inside me. Want you to pound my ass so I'll feel it tomorrow." He moaned softly as his cock throbbed in his grasp.

Shane didn't make a sound, but Rafa knew he was still there.

He could feel it like fireflies dancing in the air, buzzing around him. "I've dreamed about what you look like naked. Are you hairy? I bet you are. Bet it would feel so good against my skin. Rough. You'd be on top of me, and I'd do anything you wanted. Anything you asked." He was getting close, his balls tingling as he jerked himself in a shaky rhythm. "I want you to show me what it's like. I want you to show me everything."

It was so wrong, and the thrill of it just made him harder. He'd kept all of this locked up so tightly, and now his dirtiest fantasies surged out of him.

"I want to eat your spunk. I want you to fill me up until it's dripping out." Rafa was hot all over, his cheeks burning, but the words kept tripping off his tongue. "I know I'm not supposed to. But that's what I *want*. I want your cum, Shane."

There was a sharp, unmistakable intake of breath on the other side of the stall door, and Rafa came, spraying the floor and toilet, his knees trembling as the pleasure burned. Gasping, he bit his lip, riding out the waves as he emptied.

Then it was over, and he was standing in a gross roadside toilet with his messy dick in his hand, Shane still out of reach.

Oh my God, what did I just do?

Humiliation spiraling through him, Rafa tore off a wad of rough toilet paper and cleaned up. *Please let me wake up now. Please let this not be real.*

But he knew no amount of wishing or praying would help. Shane was waiting.

Chapter Fourteen

*J*ESUS. CHRIST. ALMIGHTY.

Shane's pulse thundered in his ears, cock straining against his briefs. He curled his hands into fists, willing his body to calm. The last thing he needed was Alan coming in to find him with a raging hard-on. *Get a fucking grip. NOW.* He should have left the building as soon as Rafa started touching himself, but his feet had been stuck in virtual cement.

In the stall, Rafa was breathing hard, his little pants filling the air and echoing off the walls and ceiling. Shane still couldn't believe Rafa had actually done it, but done it he had.

And God, the things he'd said.

His voice had been raw with need, and hearing his fantasies made Shane harder and hotter than he'd been in…maybe ever. Had Shane really once thought Rafa was nothing to write home about? An unremarkable kid? Lust burned his veins, and in a perfect world he'd yank open the stall door and fuck him so hard and good that Rafa would come again.

But this was reality, and the reality was that tomorrow he was going to request an immediate transfer. There was no doubt he wanted his protectee in his bed, and it wasn't just about sex. Yes, Rafa turned him on something fierce, but beneath it Shane ached to find out what was wrong. To make it better. He wanted to hold him close and keep him safe. Not just physically, but in every way that mattered.

Enough. Take control of the situation. He breathed deeply, and his erection began to subside. *Mind over matter.*

Alan's voice filled his ear. "Okay in there?"

Hoping the brick building had muffled enough of Rafa's cries, Shane pressed the little button on his cuff to reactivate his mic, which he'd fortunately turned off before coming into the rest stop, thinking Rafa might want to talk in private. "Fine. Valor needs a few minutes. Perimeter?"

"Secure."

"Copy that."

Clearing his throat, Shane muted his mic again and walked a few steps from the stall to face the streaked mirrors. "Can you come out now?"

Rafa's laugh was thready and bitter. "That's the question, isn't it?" After a few moments, the stall door opened and he shuffled out, flushed, with his wet hair dipping over his forehead rebelliously. He'd straightened himself, although his chinos and blue button-down looked ready for the laundry hamper. He didn't meet Shane's gaze as he hurried to the sink and scrubbed his hands. His head low, he mumbled, "I'm sorry."

Shane watched him in the mirror. "Don't be."

Head still down, Rafa laughed—a harsh, staccato burst. "Come on. That was fucked up. I should never... You're just trying to do your job. You don't need this. Some pathetic little loser jerking off in front of you."

The urge to tell Rafa that he wanted him, to reassure him that he wasn't pathetic in the slightest, burned in Shane's throat. He clasped his hands behind his back tightly. "You're not a loser. And I shouldn't have dared you."

Rafa scrubbed his hands again, the soap frothing. "What am I, twelve? I can't let a dare go? I'm supposed to be a grown-up. I just feel so..."

After a moment, Shane quietly asked, "What?"

"Forget it. They don't pay you to be my therapist. I just had a bad day."

"Is it about what happened at the party last night?" The question popped out before he could stop it.

Rafa blew out a breath and glanced up tentatively, meeting Shane's gaze in the mirror. He was still flushed, and his dark eyes shone. "Yeah. Bad night too."

Shane desperately wanted to ask more, but he'd fucked up enough for one day. "Come on. Let's head back. Have you eaten? We'll stop along the way. You'll feel better."

Rafa nodded. "Will you ride with me? I promise I won't..." He flushed. "I won't do anything inappropriate."

"Of course. Rafa..." Shane sighed. "I know it's hard to see right now, but everything will be okay."

"Will it?" he whispered. He wrapped his arms around himself, trembling.

Reaching out before he could stop himself, Shane cupped Rafa's cheek, stroking gently with his thumb. Rafa leaned into the touch as Shane nodded. "Whatever's happened, or whatever does happen, you'll get through it. You're tougher than you think."

Stepping away, Shane dropped his hand. Time to haul ass back to Castle before he did something else he'd regret. His leather shoes scraped on the rough concrete as he pushed open the door.

Light flashed in the darkness and agony seared into Shane's skull, a *crack* exploding in his ears as he suddenly dropped to the ground, no more air in his lungs.

Rafa!

He tasted mud, and a ringing filled him, echoing in his head too loudly. He blinked, but his vision was clouded with white, and his arms and legs wouldn't follow his commands to move, move, *move! Where is he? Where is he?* Shane beat the swell of panic back, forcing in a deep inhale and exhaling it sharply. The ground vibrated, and as he blinked, he saw a flash of red.

No, no, no!

This time, Shane let the panic sweep through him, adrenaline clearing his vision as he got his knees under him and pushed to his hands. Something warm and sticky flowed over his left ear, and the side of his head burned. He had to get up. He raised his hand to the side of his head, his fingers finding the gouge where the bullet had scraped his skull. Didn't matter. Had to find Rafa.

Move!

Where was Alan? As his eyes focused, he scanned the area, seeing only their Suburban and Rafa's abandoned Toyota through the rain.

Then he looked down.

Shane staggered to his feet and closed the distance between them, hitting the emergency contact shortcut on his phone, which would connect him immediately to headquarters. "Agent down." He could barely hear his own voice, the ringing in his ears was so loud. "Repeat, agent down. Request immediate medical evac. Valor has been intercepted. Need immediate backup." His mind went alarmingly blank for a moment, and then he rattled off their coordinates.

No one answered. Could he not hear over the ringing? Shane slammed to his knees and pressed his hands over the growing red stain on Alan's shirt and jacket. So much blood. Too much.

His Adam's apple bobbing and eyes wide, Alan tried to speak. He croaked, "Jammed."

The confusion was clearing in Shane's head. He realized there was static in his ear. The radio signal connecting him and Alan had been scrambled. He tried his phone again. Nothing. He pressed down hard on Alan's wound and tried Alan's phone. No signal. No satellite connection at all. Nothing.

Alan gurgled. "Tell Jules…" He gasped. "Tell her…sorry to leave like this. Love her."

"You're not fucking going anywhere, you hear me?" Shane's throat was raw, and the words still distant to his ears. "It's okay. You called in this location to Harris and Joint Ops when I went inside. They'll come when they can't reach us. Hold on."

"I'll be waiting for Dylan." Gulping, Alan shuddered. "Me and Jess."

Shane desperately looked over each shoulder, but there was nothing but the rest stop and the empty road, dark in both directions in the rain and fog and night. He tore off his suit jacket and tied the arms as tight as he could around Alan's chest as a makeshift tourniquet, Alan screaming as he pressed the folded material against the wound.

Alan's breath came in little gasps and whimpers. "Van. West."

"Hold on. You're going to make it, Al." As Shane desperately uttered the lie, he could see the fear and acceptance in Alan's eyes. "Hang in there."

There was nothing else to say.

With a final squeeze of his friend's hand, Shane forced his legs to move. Forced himself to do his job and leave Alan behind on the wet, muddy ground, his blood seeping out of the hole in his chest with each last beat of his heart.

Hauling himself to the Suburban, Shane extracted the protection package and yanked out the night-vision goggles from beneath the driver's seat. Killing the lights, he put it in drive. As he peeled away, he watched the dark lump that was Alan lying so still in the rearview, hating that he couldn't stay with him until the end.

Then he was around the bend, and there was only the road. There was only finding Rafa. The fear and grief and adrenaline coalesced into fury. *If they hurt him...*

With his left hand, Shane yanked his shirt out of his pants and tore off a strip. Hot blood soaked his ear and neck, and he pressed the wadded material to the wound on his head.

Shane summoned the memory of the area map he'd glanced at as he'd driven from DC. From the passenger seat, Alan had pulled up the map on their dashboard screen and reported in their locations to Harris and HQ.

The trees and twisting road unfurled before him now in a clear, thermal image. Abandoning his wound for the moment, he gripped the wheel with his left hand and tried the Suburban's radio. The signal was still being jammed. But the vehicle had a transponder that was the newest technology and supposed to be impervious to interference. Harris would be calling out the troops any minute. They'd soon be out of touch for too long.

Shane's mind spun. They'd followed all their protocols for a pop-up. No one had followed. *How the fuck did they find us?*

As he sped around a slick corner, he shook his head. It didn't matter. All that mattered was getting Rafa back. He clutched the wheel, his nostrils flaring. It was every agent's worst nightmare to fail, but heavy underneath it was an agonizing fear that he'd never see Rafa again—a gut-clenching despair that was about so much more than the job.

But the thought of how terrified Rafa would be poured more iron into Shane's veins, chasing away any other emotions except his conviction to get him back.

"If they wanted to kill him, they would have already." Shane's own voice sounded distant. He spoke again, trying to ground himself. "He's alive. I'm getting him back."

The fuckers had headed farther into the West Virginia back-woods, and they were only minutes ahead. But they thought Shane was dead, and in the dark and rain, they wouldn't see him coming. He focused on his breathing, clearing his mind. Slowing just a bit, he opened the protection box and took out the M-16. He didn't know who had cut down Alan and stolen Rafa.

But it was going to be the last thing they ever did.

Chapter Fifteen

*C*AN'T SEE.

Blinking, Rafa struggled to open his eyes again. Why was it dark? Why couldn't he see? Where was he? His pulse raced, head aching as if he'd had too much to drink. The remnants of a harsh chemical singed his nose and lingered in his mouth as he swallowed over and over, terror mounting.

Through his grogginess, Rafa jerked his hands up to his face, slamming his elbows into hard metal as he did. His panic amplified in the confined space with a jolt of hot terror. He pressed against his eyes, confirming that they were indeed open.

But there was only blackness.

He was curled on his right side, and his shoulder and hip were jammed against the unforgiving metal. His heart pounded so hard his eardrums were practically vibrating, and the metal surrounding him might as well have encircled his chest, squeezing like a boa constrictor. A scream tore out of his dry throat as he flattened his palms on the smooth wall a few inches in front of him. His harsh pants filled the dank air.

He was in a box.

Kicking his curled legs, he cried out as his feet hit solid metal. The rubber soles of his oxfords squeaked as he dragged them across. The box wasn't even as big as a coffin. He couldn't stretch out. Holding his breath, he wriggled around onto his left side, feeling for the wall there. In the blackness, he searched the smooth surface and pushed at the lid above with trembling hands. It didn't move even a fraction.

Hyperventilating, he cried out again, thumping his fists against the lid.

Have to get out. I'm blind. Can't breathe! Fuck! Help me! Jesus, please!

Rafa's body seized, and he barely managed to avoid pissing himself. He was hot all over, a sickening flush that dampened his hair and trickled down his spine. He gasped through his mouth, kicking again and pushing against every surface he could reach, trying to swallow his screams.

Trapped. Dying. No no no no no!

He tasted salt as tears streamed down his face. The air felt thin, and his lungs burned. How much oxygen did he have left? Was he buried alive? Was he going to die like this? Where was he? Where was Shane?

Shane.

Sucking in a jagged breath, Rafa remembered. Gunshot. Shane jolting and dropping to the ground like a marionette with cut strings. An arc of blood from his head.

Is he dead? Please don't be dead. Please, no.

Rafa's sobs consumed him in the tiny space, filling his ears, tears and snot coating his face. Like a Vine video on a loop, he saw it happen over and over in his mind—how he'd stood there uselessly, frozen as Shane had fallen.

How he'd watched him die.

There was nothing in Rafa's memory after that. Until now, in this box where he'd suffocate before long. Now he saw a flash of Shane's surprisingly broad smile, and the way his cheeks creased and his stony face softened. He heard an echo of Shane's husky chuckle, and the bursts of real laughter that had rang out sometimes. The way he moaned softly when he tasted something he liked. How his lips had felt against Rafa's in the kitchen, and the slick heat of his tongue as the kiss had deepened. The way his face had lit up when he talked about surfing and the sensation of catching a wave—of soaring.

He never got to surf again.

Squeezing his eyes shut even though it was just as dark with them open, Rafa remembered how Shane's breath had puffed over his neck when he'd shoved him to the ground that day at the park, and how safe Rafa had felt beneath his weight. How Shane had held his palm tenderly against Rafa's cheek tonight, and how desperately Rafa had longed for one more kiss.

"You're tougher than you think."

But he wasn't. Oh God, he was trapped, and Shane was gone. There were so many more things Rafa wanted to say. Things he wanted to talk about. Questions he'd never been able to ask.

He wondered what Shane had thought about when he woke up that morning, not knowing it was his last day. That he was going to die trying to protect Rafa. It wasn't supposed to be like this. Shane must have had dreams and ideas and hopes for the things he'd do, and in an instant it had all been taken away. It was over.

He's dead because of me.

Rafa let the screams out and wished with every ounce of him that he could take Shane's place.

When he opened his eyes again to the blackness, he had no idea how much time had passed. Probably only minutes, but he felt as though he was in a dream world. His throat hurt, and he choked down another swell of panic, forcing out a long, slow exhale. Concentrating on what was beyond his tiny prison, he realized the box was shifting slightly, and there was a rumble beneath him. Not buried alive, then. At least that was something.

A fresh sob stuck in his throat. Shane was still dead. Rafa pressed his lips together and inhaled through his nose. Time to be strong. Time to be a man. To be tough, like Shane thought he was.

Rafa blew out a shaky breath, the warm air making the box even stickier. Sweat dripped down his skin. He had to stop freaking out, or he'd use up all the air. How much was left? Were they—whoever *they* were—going to let him out in time? His heartbeat spiked, and he tried to focus.

He was in some kind of vehicle; likely a car or truck as opposed to a boat. Now that he was able to think beyond his frenzied terror, he could feel the odd bumps and sways of a road. He strained his ears, but couldn't hear his captors.

He'd seen the shapes of men, but had only focused on the gun as the bullet had taken down Shane. He supposed it didn't really matter who these people were. What mattered was what they planned to do with him.

How had they found him? Why the hell would anyone kidnap *him*? Not that he wished this on his sister or brothers. *Oh God, are they okay? Please let it just be me. Please let them be okay.*

As he tried to stretch his cramping limbs, Rafa remembered. He knew his phone was gone from the absence of weight in his pocket, but twisting his arm, his heart tripping, he tried to dig his fingers into his other pocket. He bent his wrist back, his fingers groping for the hard little piece of plastic. But he only felt the cotton seam of his pants.

No panic button, and he obviously hadn't pressed it when he'd had the chance, in that awful moment as he'd watched Shane jerk and drop to the ground, the gunshot so loud Rafa was sure his ears still rang with it.

The darkness overwhelmed him, and he fought down another surge of panic. His heart pounded, and he ran his hands over the metal box again. He needed light. Needed air. Needed Shane.

That he'd never see Shane again was an ache and regret choking him as he curled his cramping legs tighter to his chest. Would he ever see his family again? Or Ash?

He'd gotten what he'd asked for. Rafa had never been so well and truly alone.

THE TWO *POPS* echoed dully in Rafa's metal prison, and then his heart swooped as the vehicle jerked. *What—*

But there was no time to even finish his thought as the box careened wildly, sliding and slamming into a barrier before tipping onto its side. Rafa scrambled to brace himself, the blood pounding in his ears as he tried to hold his head off the side of the box, which was now the bottom.

He was upside down, and new panic clawed him open as he slammed himself back and forth, trying to tip the box over. His pulse raced as more gunshots peppered the night. It seemed like the vehicle was stopped. *Please please please. Help me.*

The weight of his body was pressing his head painfully into the metal, and his fingers tingled. Spasms of pain tore into the cramped muscles of his neck, and he started hyperventilating, kicking uselessly with his feet and crying out. The gun battle continued in a barrage of shots and muffled shouts, and he could only pray the good guys were winning.

He gasped as a sound that had to be an explosion rocked the air. Pushing with all his might, he used the momentum to tip the box over. At least now he wasn't on his head, and he wriggled around until he was on his side, feeling the seams of the box with his fingers again. He couldn't even tell which side was the top, and an iron band squeezed his chest as he tried to breathe. He kicked uselessly with his bent, cramped legs.

My coffin. Going to die in here.

His throat and mouth felt like they were coated in sand and glass, and sweat dripped down his forehead. More shots, closer this time. *If they're going to kill me, just do it!*

Then the box was moving, and he was rolling with it, on his stomach now as it was heaved over. The rush of cool air hit his back, and strong hands grabbed around his waist.

"Rafa!"

The voice sounded just like Shane, and the man hauled Rafa to his feet, lifting him out of a van, which had crashed onto its side. Rafa jerked his head over his shoulder, sure he was hearing things. The surge of relief as he blinked at Shane's wet, bloodied face brought tears to his eyes.

"*Shane.*" His voice was barely a hoarse whisper, and he couldn't get his legs to work.

But Shane held him up, tossing aside a pair of shattered goggles as he spun Rafa and hauled him near, wrapping him in his arms. "I've got you. You're okay. Got you."

Rafa's knees wouldn't hold, his leg muscles cramped and numb. He sagged against Shane's chest, burying his face against the wet cotton of his shirt and clinging to him with every ounce of strength he had, gripping the leather of his holster. Rain poured down in torrential sheets now, and it felt so good after the confined heat of the box.

"I've got you." Shane held him so tightly. "Safe now."

Rafa's legs trembled as he tried to get his footing in the mud. He lifted his head, meeting the glimmer of Shane's gaze in the flickering orange light. "They shot you in the head. You were dead."

"Only nicked me. I was lucky." Shane turned his head, showing Rafa the wound. The rain washed the blood from where it had coated Shane's ear. Rafa gently wiped it clean with his sleeve.

As Rafa took in their surroundings, he realized the orange light was fire coming from a burning vehicle that was likely the Suburban. He blinked at Shane. "Now what?"

Shane brushed his hand over Rafa's head, his eyes searching. "Did they hurt you?"

"No. Just put me in the box. I couldn't move. It was so small."
He sucked in a shaky breath. "Are they all…?"

"Dead."

When Rafa looked around, he saw bodies strewn in the mud.
They were on a dirt road, hemmed in by trees and the shadows of
mountains. "Alan? Where did he go?" Rafa's heart sped up as
Shane's expression tightened.

"He was shot."

"Oh my God. Is he okay? Where is he?"

"The rest stop. They should find him soon. He might…"
Shane broke off, his voice thickening. "You never know. He's
tough."

Rafa's knees gave out, and he would have dropped into the
mud if not for Shane's powerful grasp. "It's my fault. I shouldn't
have come out here. Oh my God. You should have stayed with
him. Saved him. Let them take me." He sniffed as tears flooded
his eyes.

"You know I'd never let them take you." Shane brushed his
thumbs over Rafa's cheeks.

"I know it's your job, but…"

"It's more than my job," Shane whispered hoarsely, taking
Rafa's face in his hands.

The kiss was wet and hard, their mouths opening as they met
in a desperate rush, the wind howling and rain streaming down.
He was kissing Shane, and Shane was definitely, a hundred
percent kissing him. But it was over in a heartbeat as Shane pulled
away, still holding Rafa's face.

"We have to get back. Can't…" He exhaled sharply, rubbing
his thumb over Rafa's lips. "We can't."

Before Rafa could hope to argue, the roar of an engine and
slash of lights cut through the din of the downpour. Lunging for a
weapon that looked like a machine gun, Shane tugged Rafa into
the trees, shoving him roughly as they slip-slided their way down a

hillside.

"What if it's the police, or other agents?"

"Then we'll find out in a minute, and no harm done." Shane urged him on faster.

Rafa's hair was plastered to his forehead, and his oxfords squelched with mud. His legs shook, and he was about to argue when shouts in a foreign language exploded in the night, lights glaring into the murk. *Oh shit.* Rafa forced his legs to go faster, his pants harsh in his ears. Shane guided him, not seeming to even breathe hard at all, the big weapon in his hand and his expression calm.

Voices behind them. Getting closer. More lights. *Oh fuck, they're going to catch us. No no no!*

"Inside!" Shane hissed, jerking Rafa to the left and maneuvering him into a black chasm in the side of the hill. Rafa stumbled into the cave, brushing the top of his head against the stone ceiling. "Get back as far as you can," Shane ordered. "Carefully." He pulled a clip from his back pocket and loaded it into the machine gun. "Stay down. Get on your belly."

Rafa did as he was told, reaching his arms out into the blackness, stepping tentatively. He pressed himself against the side wall and dropped down to his knees and then his stomach. Shane was a dark shape silhouetted against the mouth of the cave and the slightly brighter forest beyond it. As Shane stretched out on his belly too, it was like looking at different shades of black, and Rafa rubbed his eyes.

Then light and sound exploded as Shane gunned down whoever was outside. In the stark silence that followed, Rafa's ears rung. Another voice called, and Shane turned to Rafa. "Okay?" he whispered.

Rafa murmured, "Uh-huh," inhaling heavily through his mouth.

So they waited. And waited. He dug his blunt nails into his

palms, concentrating on breathing in and out. *It's okay. Shane's here. He's alive. He won't let them hurt me. He won't.*

When the others came, the noise felt as though it shattered Rafa's eardrums, the thunder of the shots rattling his spine as he clamped his hands over his ears. Rocks tumbled down from the mouth of the cave, and in the sudden silence after Shane stopped firing, the patter of falling stones filled the air. Shane scrambled back, reaching for Rafa. "Move!"

But it was too late.

With a rumble, a barrage of rocks sealed the mouth of the cave, and the blackness was complete. Just like in the box—but this time Shane was there, his hands on Rafa, covering him with his body as they coughed on dust and dirt. Rafa thought of that first day on the sidewalk, and Shane on top of him. It was the same now—Shane's breath hot on his skin.

But it was so dark.

As the dust settled, Rafa lifted his fingers to his eyes to make sure they were open. "Shane?" Why wasn't he saying anything? Oh God—

"Are you hurt?" Shane whispered, shifting off Rafa, his hands roaming over him, poking and prodding.

Rafa whispered back, "I don't think so. You?"

"I'm good." Shane paused. "Relatively speaking."

"Did you get them all?"

"I think so. Hard to say a hundred percent." Shane pulled Rafa up to sitting.

They sat there, waiting and listening. Minutes ticked by. Shane still held Rafa's arms tightly, as if he was afraid to let go. His strong hands anchored Rafa in the darkness.

They waited. And waited.

Finally, Shane exhaled loudly, his breath brushing Rafa's face and sending a shiver through him.

Shane murmured, "If any are left, they must be heading for

the hills. The troops will be coming. They jammed our signals, but the G-ride blew big. They had some kind of grenade. Good for us, because we may be in the middle of nowhere, but that'll be a beacon for the choppers."

Light flared, and Rafa blinked in the sudden glare of Shane's phone. Shane shook his head, glancing around. "Still no signal."

"Don't you have a satellite phone or something?"

"Yep. They still managed to jam it. Must be some new tech. But the Service can still track my location." Tapping the screen, he turned on the flashlight app, shining it around the cave.

The space extended for about ten feet toward the back, where it narrowed steadily to a space they'd have to slither through on their bellies.

Rafa's heart kicked up. "How are we getting out?"

"Too many variables if we tried to go deeper. Unlikely there's a way out back there." Shane kneeled and examined the new pile of rubble in the mouth of the cave, flashing the light up to the roof. "The whole thing might collapse if we try to dig out."

"So where does that leave us?"

"We wait. They'll find us." He passed the phone to Rafa. "Shine it there." On his hands and knees, Shane moved stray rocks away from a spot against the wall. "Come sit here. Unless you need to lie down?"

"No. I'm okay." Rafa crawled over and settled himself. He and Shane were both soaked to the skin and dirty, Shane's jacket gone. Shane sat beside him and took the phone.

As they plunged back into darkness, Rafa sucked in a breath. "Can't we have the light?"

"Might need it later. Best to save the battery for now." Shane found Rafa's hand and threaded their fingers together. "I'm here with you. I won't let anything happen."

Rafa gripped his hand. "I know. Thank you."

"Well, anything *else* that is. I'm sorry. I don't know how it happened."

"Don't be sorry. It wasn't your fault. I thought…God. I swear, they shot you in the head. I thought you were dead." He swallowed down the growing lump in this throat.

"A few millimeters and I would have been. Think it's stopped bleeding now."

"Thank God. If you'd…there are so many things I never…" Rafa tingled all over. *He kissed me. It's not just me. He* kissed *me.* "Shane…"

"You should try and rest."

Shane gently tried to pull his hand away, but Rafa held tight. "No. We almost died. We still could tonight." Screwing up his courage, Rafa let go of Shane's hand and felt his way as he crawled over Shane's lap, straddling his thighs. Rafa wasn't that much smaller, and his knees scraped on the rocky floor, but he didn't care.

With a little groan and a puff of breath that brushed over Rafa's cheek, Shane's hands stroked up Rafa's thighs, settling on his hips. In the pitch-black, Rafa tentatively ran his hands over Shane's shoulders, and up his neck to his face. His fingers rasped over the five o'clock shadow on Shane's cheeks, and he explored gently, finding the groove where the bullet had grazed Shane's head.

Shane inhaled sharply. Leaning in, Rafa pressed a kiss to his temple.

"We can't do this." Shane gripped Rafa's hips. "Can't. Shouldn't."

Rafa pressed their foreheads together, running his hands down Shane's arms. "But you want to?" he whispered.

"Rafa…" His fingers dug in, and his breathing was loud in the darkness.

"You want me?"

"Yes." It was barely more than an exhale, and Shane brushed

their lips together. "I want you."

To hear him say it sent heat and joy spiraling through Rafa. Rolling his hips slowly against Shane's, he fumbled for the buttons on Shane's shirt, desperate to feel skin. "How do you want me?"

Shane groaned again. "I shouldn't…"

"I told you what I want." Rafa spread open Shane's shirt as far as he could with the holster. He flattened his palms over Shane's chest. "Mmm, you *are* hairy."

He caressed in circles, his fingers finding the nubs of Shane's nipples and teasing. As much as he wanted to see Shane, somehow it was easier to be bold when they were invisible. "Everything I said in the bathroom was true. I tried not to want it, but since we met, I can't stop myself."

He rubbed his cheek against Shane's in the blackness, their stubble scratching. His cock strained against his chinos, and he rolled his hips again, feeling Shane's growing hardness. Rafa trembled all over, and he was going to shoot in his pants if he wasn't careful. With his fingertips, he searched for the scar on Shane's neck. When he thought he'd found the line of raised skin, he licked over it, making Shane shudder and inhale sharply.

Squeezing Rafa's ass, Shane yanked his head up and kissed him, teasing his lips open, both of them laughing as they bumped noses in the dark. *Laughing*, and it felt so good and right.

They tilted their heads, and Shane deepened the kiss, sliding his tongue into Rafa's mouth, exploring. Their little gasping breaths were loud in the cave, the wet, smacking sounds of their kiss turning Rafa on even more. He moaned, sparks shooting from his cock and balls and licking out over his whole body.

They kissed and kissed, and Rafa thought he could just kiss Shane forever and that would be enough. It would be *everything*. But then Shane worked Rafa's shirt open, and his hands were rough and gentle on Rafa's skin at the same time, and okay, maybe kissing wasn't *quite* enough.

Rafa moaned as his dick strained. Shane stroked over his chest and back, teasing down his spine. Then he undid their belts and flies. Rafa lifted up as Shane pushed his chinos and briefs down his hips. Rafa cried out as a callused palm wrapped around his cock.

"Shh, shh. We have to be quiet."

"Right. Could be…more kidnappers." Didn't want more bad guys finding them. Or the Secret Service hearing them have sex— *oh my God, we're having* sex—or another rock slide starting.

What if they can't find us? What if we're trapped in here forever?

Rafa ruthlessly pushed those thoughts away. Damn it, he wanted to scream and shout, because another man was actually touching his cock. And not just any man—*Shane.* Biting his lip, he thrust blindly into Shane's hand.

Shane gritted out, "Are you sure? If you want me to stop…"

Rafa moaned softly, searching for Shane's mouth to kiss him again and muzzle any talk of stopping, because *hell no.* But Shane broke the kiss, one hand flat on Rafa's chest, the other still holding his cock.

"I can't see you. You have to tell me yes. I need to hear it."

"Yes, yes, yes. Don't stop. Please." Rafa gripped Shane's shoulders. "Unless you don't want…?" Was he doing it right? Shane had to be used to experienced guys, not over-eager virgins. "I know I'm not… I've never…"

Shane let go of his shaft, and Rafa's heart sank. Then he had Rafa's right hand, and he guided it to his own cock, which throbbed in Rafa's grasp.

"Feel how hard you make me?"

Gasping, Rafa nodded before remembering Shane couldn't see him. "Yes." Aside from playing a jerk-off game once in Bobby Simpson's basement in middle school, Rafa had never held another cock. And Shane was every inch a *man.* Rafa touched it from the cut tip to the thick base, wishing he could see what it looked like. He ran his fingers into Shane's thatch of hair before stroking him again.

Shane was hot in his hand, licking and sucking at the juncture of Rafa's neck and shoulder while he caressed Rafa's back and chest.

"That's for you," Shane muttered. "Want to fuck you every way there is. Want you in my bed. Want to make you come. Do you want to come for me?"

"Yes, yes." Rafa was whimpering, but he couldn't help himself. "Please."

With sure hands, Shane urged Rafa's hips closer. It took a couple of tries before they were lined up right, and Rafa cried out as Shane took both their cocks in his big hand, stroking them together.

Rafa was leaking, and Shane used it to slick the way, both of them moaning softly. Rafa rocked his hips, getting into the right rhythm as he slid his hands under Shane's shirt and onto his shoulders beneath the holster, holding on.

It was almost like they were floating in outer space—nothing else left in the universe except for the two of them. It was all touch and taste and sound, and he kissed Shane messily before he could only pant, their warm breath gusting.

Shane's other hand dipped down the back of Rafa's briefs and into his crease. "Have you ever been touched here?"

"No," he gasped. "Not by someone else. Want it to be you."

The low pull of Shane's gravelly voice pinged down Rafa's spine. "Bet you're so tight, aren't you?" He circled a finger around Rafa's hole. "Do you ever fuck yourself?"

"Uh-huh. My fingers."

"How many?" Shane inched the tip of his finger inside.

The rough push had Rafa gasping. "Two, usually. Want more." His dick was on fire, his balls ready to explode. He wanted it to last, but the need to come burned through every pore as Shane worked their cocks together.

"Bet you'd spread yourself for me, wouldn't you? So beautiful. And I'd lick you open until you begged for my cock."

Groaning, Rafa thrust desperately. "Yes. God, Shane. Want that. Want you." *He thinks* I'm *beautiful.*

"Still want to eat my cum?"

Crying out, Rafa spurted, the orgasm tearing through him so hard he swore he saw stars in the blackness of the cave. He shuddered as the pleasure split him open, and when Shane clapped his hand over Rafa's mouth, it sent another wave pulsing through him.

"That's it, Rafa."

Hot bliss burned him inside out, the explosion receding into aftershocks. "Oh God," he muttered. "*Shane.*"

Shane was still pumping their cocks, and Rafa reached down and pried Shane loose, wanting to be the one who took him over the edge. He lifted Shane's sticky hand to his mouth, sucking his fingers one by one, swallowing the familiar bitter flavor.

Shane groaned. "You like that? Like the taste of your own jizz?"

Suddenly Rafa was embarrassed, his ears going hot. He released Shane's middle finger from his mouth. "It's weird, right?"

"No." Shane grabbed Rafa's face in his hands and kissed him hard, licking into his mouth. "It's hot," he murmured. "Come on. Finish the job." He lifted his hand to Rafa's lips, sliding the next finger inside. "That's it."

Rafa licked and sucked, and when he was done, he inched back and wrapped his hand around Shane's shaft, giving himself a little more room to work as he stroked. Shane rubbed his hands up and down Rafa's thighs. Rafa wished he could take off his pants and they could be naked, but that would have to be another time.

Because there will *be another time. Has to be.*

"I can't wait to be in your bed," he murmured. "Can't wait for you to fuck me. Lick me open, like you said. And I'll do it to you.

Lick your ass. Suck your cock. God, I want to suck your cock, Shane. Want to swallow your cum."

Shane's groan ended on a sharp intake of breath as Rafa scooted his ass back and bent over, blindly guiding Shane's cock to his mouth. Holding the base of the shaft, Rafa sucked on the head.

It tasted musky and salty—so much like what he'd imagined sex would be. It was sweaty and dirty and made him feel like an animal in the best possible way. Shane's cock was cut, and Rafa loved that it was different from his own. It made it even more real that this was actually happening. He licked around the tip before taking him in.

Shane throbbed in his mouth, hard and straining, and Rafa couldn't remember any of the tips and tricks he'd read about online on Ashleigh's laptop, but as he slurped and licked Shane's dick, Shane didn't seem to mind that Rafa didn't know what he was doing. Shane's hands threaded into Rafa's hair, not pushing or prodding, but just touching him—grounding him in the blackness.

The little gasps Shane made sent shivers through Rafa. *He* was doing that—*he* was making Shane feel good. The sensation of power swept through him, giving him confidence to take Shane deeper. His nostrils flared as he choked and tried to breathe, spit dripping from the sides of his mouth as he sucked, the wet, smacking noises loud in the darkness.

"Easy." Shane petted Rafa's head, his voice shaky.

But Rafa didn't want to go easy. He wanted to make Shane tip over the edge so he could swallow every drop. And maybe he should have been concerned about safe sex, but he'd fantasized about sucking a man's dick for years, and he wasn't going to back down now.

His jaw was getting a little sore, his lips stretched wide over Shane's thick shaft, and his knees were jammed against the stone floor where he straddled Shane's legs. But he didn't care. He was actually giving a blowjob, and he was going to make a man come. Make *Shane* come.

Moaning around Shane's cock, he reached down blindly with his other hand to fondle Shane's heavy balls, the hair wiry against his skin.

"Rafa, I'm going to…" Shane tugged on Rafa's hair.

But he stayed put, sucking hard on the head as Shane shuddered and gasped. Warm, salty fluid flooded Rafa's mouth, and he wished he could see Shane shooting. But he could taste it, and he swallowed as much as he could until he had to pull off and take a deep breath.

Shane pulled Rafa's head up and leaned their foreheads together. The little puffs of Shane's exhales were warm on Rafa's skin, and he reached for Shane's cock, milking out all he could until Shane twitched and stilled his hand, pressing little kisses to Rafa's face.

"So good, baby," Shane murmured.

Rafa tried to fight it, swallowing hard and blinking as fast as he could, but tears filled his eyes as incredible warmth spread through him. Shuddering, he thought of being locked in that metal box. But it was over, and he was still alive, and Shane was there. They were alive, and they were together, and it was all that mattered.

Don't cry. Get a grip. It's okay. He can't see. Just breathe, and—

Shane froze. "Rafa?" He brushed his fingers over Rafa's face. "What is it?"

"Nothing," he whispered.

"Tell me. Please." And Shane sounded so pained that Rafa fell in love with him even more.

Sniffling, Rafa laughed at himself as tears spilled out of his eyes. "I'm just so happy. I'm so happy I'm alive, and that I'm with you. I've wanted this for so long. And when I met you, *fuck* how I wanted it to be with you. I never thought it would happen. Not in a million years."

With gentle fingers, Shane brushed Rafa's tears away. "I won't let anyone hurt you ever again. God help me, I want you so much." He sighed. "Rafa…"

"I know. I know. Can we just…let's not talk about it yet. Not yet."

Kissing him tenderly, Shane nuzzled his cheek. "Okay. Get some rest now."

"I must be heavy. I can—"

"No." Shane wrapped his arms around Rafa. "Not yet."

Sighing, Rafa rested his head on Shane's shoulder, safe in his arms for a little while longer.

Chapter Sixteen

"**W**HAT IF THEY don't come?"

Sliding his fingers through Rafa's hair where Rafa rested his head in Shane's lap, Shane answered, "They will. It's been three hours since contact was lost. They'll be crawling all over these backwoods." He'd checked the time and his phone signal—still nonexistent—and now they were settled back down in the inky black of the cave for more waiting.

Rafa had stretched out on his back and pillowed his head on Shane's thigh. They'd straightened their clothing, and they were probably so dusty and dirty that no new stains would stand out.

When the light had briefly shone so they could dress, Rafa hadn't been able to meet Shane's gaze, a skittish smile playing on his lips. Shane had tilted his chin up and kissed him softly until Rafa had looked at him with bright eyes and kissed him back.

It was true that Shane hadn't been with a man so inexperienced since he was a teenager. Over the years, sex had been a lot of things: fun, hot, crappy, so-so, and occasionally great.

But it had never been like this.

It had always been about getting off—scratching an itch on his skin with a few well-placed swipes. It had never tunneled below the surface. Never made him feel clogged with a gluey affection he couldn't explain. Never made him come so hard just because of *who* he was with.

After getting soaked, Rafa's hair had dried curly, and Shane rubbed the strands between his fingers. "I like your hair like this."

Rafa snorted. "You wouldn't if it wasn't pitch-black."

Shane continued petting Rafa with his left hand, his right palm resting lightly on Rafa's chest. Rafa tentatively drew little patterns on the back of Shane's hand with his fingertips. "I like the way it looks. Saw it that first night up in the kitchen." The night he should have known he was getting himself into deep trouble.

"But no one likes it like that."

"Says who?"

"Like...everyone. The internet. The world."

"What do *you* say?"

"I don't know. I feel like...if I don't slick it down, people will stare more. Talk more. Make memes about me."

"Screw those assholes. But I know it's easy to say." He caressed Rafa's head. Shane knew he should stop touching him, but here in the black they were in their own world, and no one could see. Which didn't make it right, but he'd already detonated the line and crossed it miles back.

He'd surrendered to his weakness—to his desire—and he couldn't push Rafa away now. Every instinct had him holding on. They still might not make it out. If they survived, he could be sorry then.

"Feels good to stretch my legs," Rafa said. "I don't know how long I was in there. An hour, maybe? What do you think their plan was?"

"I don't know. Take you somewhere. Ransom, maybe. Or political demands." *Torture you and send you back to your father piece by piece until they got what they wanted.* He shuddered internally.

"Did they sound Russian or something?"

"Yeah. If not Russian, from that region, I think. Definitely European."

Rafa was quiet for a few breaths. "Do you think Alan's okay?"

Grief flared, searing Shane from the inside out. Although he couldn't see, he squeezed his eyes shut against the image of Alan on the ground, his face pale as he bled out. How would Jules and Dylan cope? She was going to lose them all. His throat felt full of rocks. How could he have let himself get swept up in Rafa while his friend died? "I don't know," he managed. "I hope so, but…"

Clasping Shane's hand against his chest, Rafa squeezed. "I'm sorry. I'm so sorry."

"It's not your fault."

"But it is. I'm the one who came out here to the middle of nowhere. How did they find me?"

"I don't know. You didn't tell anyone where you were going?"

"No. I swear. I only talked to you when you called my cell. I didn't even know where I was going. I was just driving. It could have been anywhere. I don't know why I picked that exit off the highway. It was a whim. Driving along these back roads, stopping up at that lookout—I didn't have a reason for any of it."

The terrible suspicion brewing in Shane's gut grew stronger. "It had to be an inside job."

"What do you mean? One of you guys?"

"There's no other explanation. I know we weren't followed off the highway. I mean…it's possible. But we would have noticed. There was no one behind us for miles."

The possibilities clicked through Shane's mind. Any number of agents at Joint Ops and the White House knew the locations Alan had reported in as they followed Rafa. The signal had still worked when Shane had left the Suburban for the washroom building. They'd checked in with Harris. They'd followed procedure. Who would betray them? Betray Rafa?

"Shane? Are you okay?" Rafa rubbed the back of Shane's hand.

He blew out a long breath. "Yeah. Fuck, I can't think about this right now. No point in it. They'll find out what happened."

He caressed Rafa's hair again. "You should sleep."

"Not tired."

Shane smiled. "Liar."

"Okay, okay. But I don't think I can sleep. I... Can I ask you something?"

"Anything."

"Have you ever killed people before?" Rafa quickly added, "Not that I'm judging. Believe me, I'm glad you killed them. Which might make me a bad person, but...I guess I'm okay with that."

"You're not a bad person. I'm glad I killed them too." The memories flashed through Shane's mind—shooting the van's tire to disable the vehicle and the men streaming out with guns blazing, red figures through his night-vision goggles. He'd taken them down with kill shots, one after the other the way he'd practiced a million times. The Service demanded their skills stay razor sharp with regular training exercises, and tonight had shown why.

But along with his training and automatic responses, tonight Shane had wanted to *destroy* those men. He'd wanted it with every piece of him. He turned up his palm and caught Rafa's hand, squeezing. "I'd kill anyone who tried to hurt you."

"I know. I mean, it's your job. Not just to kill, but to die. How do you deal with that? And what if you didn't even like me? What if I was a total bag of dicks?"

"I've never had to like anyone I've protected. It's irrelevant. Liking them or not has nothing to do with my duty. It's like..." Shane huffed out a laugh. "I've always thought of it as taking a bullet for America. Not for the specific person."

Rafa laughed softly. "They should use that in their recruiting brochures. 'Take a bullet for America!' But that makes sense. That it's about the bigger picture and not the actual person."

"Yeah. It was, at least." Shane's voice was barely a murmur.

"But now…" *Just shut up. Stop talking.* But the words came anyway. "It would be for you." He brushed Rafa's hair off his forehead. "I'd take a hundred bullets. Kill a hundred men. Keep you safe no matter what."

With a shaky exhale, Rafa lifted Shane's hand and kissed his palm. His lips were dry against Shane's skin, breath hot. "I know you would. God, Shane. I was sure you were dead," he whispered. "I know we can't do this. But…" His hands grasped at Shane's head, pulling him down. As their lips met, they kissed softly.

When Shane sat up again to lean against the rock wall, he sighed in the darkness. His ass was numb and his head throbbed where the bullet had grazed him. But Rafa was safe and alive and warm beneath his touch, and that was all that mattered. Because there wasn't a damn thing he could do about anything outside the cave for the time being. Still, he wanted to know.

"What happened yesterday? Why did you want to run away?"

Rafa muttered, "I found out I'm an idiot. So dumb."

"That's not true, but tell me why."

Rafa was silent for a few moments before pushing himself up. Feeling his way in the dark, he sat next to Shane against the wall. Before he started talking, he put his hand on Shane's thigh, almost like he was holding on. Shane wrapped his arm around Rafa's shoulders, and Rafa fit against him so perfectly. Like he belonged there.

"They know I'm gay. My family. Well, apparently Matthew didn't really, but he's never been the most observant. But Chris, and Adriana, and…" He exhaled loudly. "My parents. My mother and father know. They've apparently suspected for years. My mom said…"

When the seconds ticked by, Shane caressed Rafa's shoulder and prompted, "What?"

His voice was so small in the darkness. "She said she thought we were on the same page. That I'd keep on hiding. Being with

Ash in public. That I'd keep being gay 'private.' Forever, I guess. So they didn't think we even needed to talk about it. It was like...like it's something I can just keep in a box, and it has nothing to do with my life. Like it's not *who I am*."

Fucking goddamn it. Shane's nostrils flared as he forced down the surge of fury and stayed calm. He rubbed Rafa's arm gently. "I'm sorry."

"And I realized—remember that bill a few years ago, about 'constitutional marriage'? My dad supported it. They waited until he'd gotten reelected, and I guess they figured they had nothing to lose. They trotted us all out for the announcement. It was a few days before Thanksgiving. I was so caught up in my first semester at school that I hadn't even been paying attention to what was happening in Washington. So there I was, with lights and cameras and so many people, and I had to smile while Dad talked about taking away civil rights from gay people."

As Rafa took a shuddering breath, Shane rubbed his arm. "I'm sorry," he repeated. He didn't know what else to say other than Ramon Castillo was a selfish, closed-minded bastard.

"I'd been building up to it. Coming out, I mean. I was finally in college, and he was reelected, and I was getting my nerve up to do it. But after that night, I just...I wanted to disappear. Vanish into thin air. That's when Ash and I came up with our plan. And I told myself he didn't know. My father didn't know he was talking about me. That I was one of *those* people. I told myself he would never have backed the bill if he'd known." He whispered, "But he did, Shane. Even if it wasn't for sure, deep down he knew."

He kissed Rafa's temple. "I'm glad you didn't disappear."

"But I did. I haven't really been me. Not until this summer. Until I started cooking for you. When I'm with you, I don't have to hide."

"I like watching you cook."

"Yeah?" His voice had a hopeful lilt that grabbed at Shane's heart.

"Yep. Food tastes amazing too. You're going to be an excellent chef."

"I hope so. I just wish my parents understood it."

"Maybe after this, they'll try harder."

"Maybe." He leaned his head on Shane's shoulder. "I know they love me," he murmured. "They do. But it's been so hard pretending to be someone else."

"I know." Shane stroked his curls.

After an easy silence, Rafa said, "You said your parents were good about it from the start?"

The familiar wave of guilt and sorrow washed through him. "Yes. I was very lucky. They were surprised at first, but not for long."

"How old were you?"

"Seventeen. They just listened and nodded, and my mom cried a bit. She said it was because she didn't want my life to be hard. But then she said everyone's life was hard, and it was nothing to cry about." He smiled at the memory. "She did that a lot. She'd have these conversations or arguments with herself. Me and my dad would just listen and wait to see which side won. The next day, he drove me to Brooks Street to surf and have a slushee."

"Watermelon and pistachio?"

"Yep."

"Did he surf too?"

Shane laughed softly. "No. He was okay in pools, but wasn't a fan of the ocean. Too many variables, he said. He was a math teacher, and he liked everything in order. Neat and binary."

Rafa squeezed Shane's thigh. "Sounds like they were really great."

"Yeah." His chest was too tight, but he managed to inhale.

"I'm so sorry you lost them."

Eyes stinging, Shane cleared his throat. "Me too. I should have been there. I would have gotten them out. They were on the second floor sleeping. It spread through the walls. Faulty electrical. The smoke was too thick. They only made it to the top of the stairs. Battery in the smoke detector was dead. Such a little thing. Made all the difference."

"It's not your fault."

The lead in his chest pressed on his sternum. "I was supposed to visit. Mom's birthday." He still held Rafa around the shoulders, and now Rafa snaked his arm around Shane's waist, grounding him even more in the void of the cave. "But they wanted me to work a standing post in DC. Special assignment for one of your father's state dinners. If I'd said no, I might not have had another chance. So I went. Mom was excited for me. Said we'd have another cake when I could make it out. That it was a good excuse for cake." His eyes burned. "I don't know why I'm telling you this. I never talk about them."

"I'm glad you are." Rafa nuzzled Shane's cheek. "It wasn't your fault."

"If I'd been there…"

"You might be dead too. Shane, *it wasn't your fault.*"

He'd heard it plenty of times before. Tried to believe it. Yet somehow when Rafa said it with such conviction, pressed against Shane's side and kissing his cheek so sweetly, the long-hollow places hidden inside started to fill. The warmth spreading through him loosened the weight in his chest, and his lungs expanded.

Fumbling for Rafa's mouth, he kissed him again. He memorized the bow of his lips and the slide of his tongue—tentative and eager at the same time. He tried to burn the sound of Rafa's little sighs and gasps into his memory, wishing he could see his face to kiss his freckles and the tiny dimple from his smile.

Rafa's breath ghosted over Shane's lips as they parted. "Do you really think they're going to find us? Or did you just tell me that so I won't spend our last hours freaking out?"

Shane chuckled, although low, constant worry still tugged at him, of course. "They're going to find us. The president's son missing? That's a national emergency. Every boot will be on the ground. Trust me. And if they're not here by morning, we'll dig our way out. But the protocol is always to ensure safety. There are still unknown variables out there. In here, you're safe for now. We wait for backup."

"Out there's the ocean, and in here's the pool?"

Shane smiled. "That's a good way to look at it."

"I wish we had water. Cum makes me thirsty."

Shane couldn't hold in the burst of laughter. "Such a dirty boy."

Rafa laughed too. "I can't believe I said all that stuff out loud."

"I like it." Imagining Rafa's blush, Shane ran his hand over Rafa's thigh, stroking through his chinos.

"Yeah?" Rafa swallowed audibly, and his voice got low. "What else do you like?"

"Hmm. Let's see. Pizza's pretty great. Beer. Old episodes of *The X-Files* on Netflix."

Laughing, Rafa smacked his chest. "Shut up."

"Oh, you mean what do I like about you?" Shane skirted over Rafa's leather belt with his fingers.

"Uh-huh. No, wait. Forget it. It's stupid."

"What's stupid about it?" He dragged his hand against Rafa's cock through the cotton, teasing before stroking over his thigh again. "You try to hide, but I see you."

"But you're so…and I'm…"

Shane frowned. "What?"

"I'm a skinny kid, and you're what Hollywood thinks Secret Service agents look like."

"You might have been a skinny kid once upon a time. Not now. You're long and lean, and mmm, that ass. Wish I could see you so I could lick your freckles."

Rafa sputtered out a laugh. "But—but my freckles are so *ugly*."

"Not one thing about you is ugly."

Kissing him messily in response, Rafa moaned into Shane's mouth. "Shane, will you—"

He grasped Rafa's cock through his pants. Rafa arched up, panting, and Shane broke their kiss to whisper hotly in his ear, "Do you want me to suck you?"

A sharp new noise split the darkness, and they froze. It came again—closer now—an angry blast. Shane forced in a breath. "Dogs." He was still cupping Rafa's cock, and he snatched his hand away and put some inches between them. "They'd give them your scent. Standard retrieval in a wooded area." He could picture the Malinois sniffing their way down the hillside and into the gully.

"Are you sure it's the good guys?" Rafa whispered.

"We'll know in a minute."

Sure enough, he heard the familiar sounds of tactical commands as the team reached the cave, the dogs barking with clipped determination. The point man shouted back that he'd found the bodies of more hostiles.

Shane cleared his throat and called, "This is Agent Kendrick. Valor is secure. What took you so long?"

There was a flurry of voices, and then Brent Harris shouted, "Kendrick? Repeat, is Valor secure?"

"Affirmative. Valor is secure and unharmed. You just need to dig us out. Carefully."

"Thank fucking Christ, Kendrick."

"What about Pearce?" He knew the answer, but he had to ask.

"Critical."

Shane's heart skipped, joy swooping through him. "He's still alive?"

"Passersby found him. He's in rough shape. Look, hold tight and we'll get you out."

"Thank God," Rafa said. "Maybe he'll be okay." He grasped for Shane, whispering urgently, "When will I get to see you again?"

"I don't know." Going up on his knees, Shane quickly hugged Rafa tightly. "But you know we can't do this. This was only tonight."

Rafa dug his fingers into Shane's flesh. "I know. I…thank you. For not dying, and for saving me. And for…" Drawing back, Rafa kissed him hard. "For all of it," he whispered.

"Okay, we've got some demolition guys here to examine the stability." Harris's voice boomed through the rocks blocking the cave entrance. "How much wiggle room do you have?"

Shane turned on his phone flashlight and relayed all the information he could. He urged Rafa behind him as far as they could go. Their eyes met as the first rocks were shifted, and Shane reached back to brush a smudge of dirt from Rafa's cheek. He kissed him one last time for the space of a heartbeat before he took his position, shielding Rafa from harm as they rejoined the world.

Chapter Seventeen

T HE SKY WAS brightening with the dawn as Brent and a swarm of agents led Rafa along the ravine.

"Watch your step. Can you make it up the hill? We can—"

"I'm fine!" Rafa knew they were only concerned, but he felt even more claustrophobic than he had in the cave. He took another grateful chug of the cold water a medic had given him, then craned his neck over his shoulder. "Wait, where's Shane? Isn't he coming?"

"There are a lot of blanks we need him to fill in," Brent answered. "We're going to get you to the hospital and reunite you with your family."

"Hospital? I don't need the hospital. I just need a shower." Rafa stared as they passed one of the bodies of the kidnappers, which had been covered in black plastic. Flies buzzed around it, and his stomach lurched.

Up by the smoldering remains of the Suburban where dozens of agents milled around, an ambulance waited. "I really don't need this," he insisted, but Brent and the others just nodded and whisked him into the back.

Sighing, Rafa stretched out on the gurney, and he had to admit it felt good to lie down on something that wasn't rock. Although he missed Shane's thigh as a pillow. He flushed and glanced guiltily at Brent, who cocked his head. His graying dark hair was mussed, and the lines on his face stood out starkly.

"Okay?" To the medic who climbed in after them, Brent added, "Check his vitals again."

The ambulance rumbled along the dirt road, and Rafa submitted, wincing at the cold of the stethoscope on his chest. The medic hooked him up to a bunch of little machines, and Rafa closed his eyes. "Is my family okay?"

"Aside from being out of their minds with worry, yes," Brent said. "We're all relieved to have you back safely, Rafa."

He opened his eyes and smiled. "Thanks. Nice to be back. Shane saved me."

"Seems that he did indeed. We're so glad you're okay."

"Do you think Alan will be all right?"

Brent sighed. "We don't know yet. But don't worry about any of that."

"Of course I'm worried about it. He got shot because of me."

"No. He got shot doing his job." Brent patted Rafa's arm. "You rest up."

Rafa closed his eyes again, and soon enough the swaying of the vehicle had him dozing off, even with the sirens and the poking and prodding from the medic. He thought of Shane, and when he'd see him again.

The cave already seemed like a dream. But no, it had happened. Shane had held him and kissed him and *wanted* him. Touched him and made him feel so good. There were so many more things Rafa wanted to say. Things he longed to do…

When they arrived at the hospital in DC a couple of hours later, a cacophony of shouts and noise filled the air, but he could only see black draping that had been set up to block the media and agents in suits lining the corridor as they wheeled him inside. The ER had apparently been shut down, and behind another wall of agents, Rafa glimpsed his family. He sat up, and the medic tried to ease him back down.

"I'm fine, I told you. Let me up."

"Rafa?" His mother rushed toward him, and he swung his legs over the gurney. Then he was in her arms, smelling faded lavender and pressing his face against her neck.

"Mom, I'm okay. I swear." He rubbed her back and looked at his father, standing a few feet away.

Standing there *crying*.

Rafa's heart thumped. "Dad? I'm okay. See?"

His chin wobbling, Ramon closed the distance between them and yanked Rafa and Camila into his arms. "*Dios mio.* My boy."

Aside from his family, the room was filled with at least twenty agents, who all stared into the distance as if they weren't there hearing and seeing everything. Over his father's shoulder, Rafa blinked at Chris, Hadley, Adriana, and Matthew, who all wiped their eyes.

None of them looked as if they'd slept, and Rafa realized they were still wearing the same clothes as they'd been for the aborted photoshoot. When Rafa stepped back from his parents, he smoothed down the wrinkled skirt of his mother's purple dress.

"You guys, I'm fine. See?"

Adriana and his brothers streamed forward and took turns hugging him. Hadley pressed a kiss to Rafa's cheek and smiled tremulously as she rubbed Chris's back.

Ramon was still crying, and he took Rafa's face in his hands. "There are so many things we should have done differently."

His mother nodded. "We'll talk about it all once you're rested. Oh, sweetheart." Her eyes were dry, but they shone with concern. "We were so afraid we'd lost you. Our dear boy. Did they hurt you?" Her gaze roved over him. "Are you hurt?"

"Shane saved me. I'm okay."

A woman in scrubs approached. "Rafael, I'm Doctor Kadikar. We should get you checked out, and then you can head on home."

"Okay." He followed her to an exam room, Brent and other agents in tow. At the door he turned back to his family. "I love you guys too. You know that, right?"

They nodded, and his father cleared his throat. "We know, Rafalito."

He hadn't heard that nickname in so many years, and tears stung Rafa's eyes. There was so much he wanted to say, but he supposed it would have to wait.

RAFA STARED AT the framed poster of Kelly Slater emerging from the curl of a wave, the sun glistening on the water. It had only been twenty-four hours since he'd last been in his room, but it felt like a hundred years. He wasn't sure a hot shower had ever felt so good, or his terrycloth bathrobe so soft and soothing. His hair was getting the pillow wet, but he didn't care. Moving would take too much energy.

His phone was long gone—probably tossed out the van window thanks to his kidnappers. But he checked iMessage again on his tablet. Still nothing from Ashleigh, which worried him. There was so much he needed to tell her, and he just wanted to hear her voice again. Closing his eyes, he let a wave of nausea and fear pass over him.

I'm safe now. I'm okay.

More than anything, he needed to see Shane again. Touch him and kiss him, and burrow into his arms. But Rafa knew he couldn't, and the loss already made him ache.

There was a soft knock at his door. "Yeah?" he called.

Chris stuck his head in. His hair was damp, and he was freshly shaven. "Doing okay?"

"Yeah. I just need to chill. Mom and Dad practically followed me into the shower."

Chris smiled as he closed the door behind him and came through the little entry hall to lean a shoulder against the wall. "You're lucky we're all not in here with you. Don't want to let you out of our sight."

Warmth flowed through him. "I'm fine. I really am."

"I know, but I think you'll have to put up with some extra hovering from all of us. Not to mention the agents. This rattled the hell out of them. Understandably."

"Is there any word on Alan?"

"I'm not sure. I'll find out. Oh, and Ashleigh should be here this afternoon. Agent Nguyen's sending a team to pick her up at Dulles."

"She's coming back from Paris?" Rafa pushed himself up to sitting. "But I'm fine. What about her internship?"

"Are you kidding? Raf, you got kidnapped. Of course she's coming back. She caught the first flight she could. I talked to her from the airport and she was a mess."

Tender affection for her swelled in his chest. "She's my best friend. Ugh, it shouldn't make me feel good to have people worried about me, but it kind of does."

"Course it does." Chris stuffed his hands in his pockets. "Raf, we've all been caught up in our own lives. Our own shit. We have to be better at talking. At being brothers. You should come to New York and visit me and Hadley more often. Matty too, and Ade. We need to stick together. And you know Mom and Dad love you, right? They're not perfect, but who is?"

Rafa nodded. "It's my fault. I kept so much inside, and I should have been honest."

"It's all of our faults. We should all have been honest."

"I guess so."

Chris said, "Look, they're sending up a tray for you with one of your favorites, and you should sleep for a few hours."

"I don't think I can sleep. I can definitely eat, though."

But after he scarfed down a plate of French toast, sausage, and eggs, Rafa's eyes drooped uncontrollably and he curled under his duvet. *Just for twenty minutes…*

"Raf?"

He blinked to find Ashleigh sitting beside him on the bed. Her eyes were red and puffy, and her blonde hair was yanked back in a ponytail. "Ash. You made it. What time is it?"

"Just after four."

"You didn't have to come." He sat up and hugged her close.

"Sure, I was just going to stay in Paris drinking lattes and schlepping pantyhose and shoes to photoshoots while you died a horrible death at the hands of terrorists." She clung to him, sniffling.

"Hey, hey. I'm okay." He pulled back and cupped her cheek. "No crying."

She rolled her eyes. "I know, but I can't stop. Jesus, that flight was the longest eight and a half hours of my life. The stupid in-flight wireless wouldn't work, and I had no idea what was happening. I snotted all over those poor agents who picked me up when they told me you were okay. And there were cameras everywhere, so I'm sure my awesome crying face has been captured for posterity."

He gave her a kiss and hugged her again. "I'm sorry you were so worried. I love you too."

"Are you really okay?" Her voice was muffled in his bathrobe. "Fuck, Raf. That must have been terrifying."

He sat back. "Yeah. It was bad." His breath caught as he remembered the box, but his heart slowed when he thought of Shane lifting him out. "But Shane saved me. One of the agents on my detail."

Her gaze narrowed. "Wait…is he?"

"What?" Rafa realized he was smiling, but he couldn't stop himself.

After her jaw dropped, Ashleigh hissed, "He's the Harley, isn't he?"

Biting his lip, Rafa nodded.

"Holy shit!" she exclaimed, and then slapped her hand over her mouth. She lowered her voice. "Your family is circling out there like sharks. Well, worried, well-intentioned sharks. That wasn't a criticism. What I'm trying to say is they're right outside. Okay, tell me everything. *Everything*." She whispered, "This is the guy you kissed?"

"Uh-huh. Shane."

"And after you kissed him, everything went back to Secret Service business as usual?"

"Yeah. It was the worst."

"I bet. But he saved you? That's pretty awesome."

"They fired at his head, but they missed and it only grazed him."

She gasped. "Whoa. And then what?"

"He followed us. I was in the back of a van. They put me in this box." He swallowed thickly. "It was awful."

"Oh God." She took his hand, holding it tight. "I'm so glad you're okay."

"Me too. So Shane killed them and got me out of the box." Rafa lowered his voice even more. "And he kissed me."

"Shut up! Holy crap. Keep going!"

"But then more of them came, and we had to run through the woods. There was a little cave, and we hid inside. Shane had a machine gun, and he waited for them. I guess he killed them all, but there was a rockslide, and we got stuck in the cave. The entrance was blocked."

Nodding, Ashleigh listened, her puffy eyes wide.

Rafa leaned closer, keeping his voice low. "And I figured, fuck it. If I was going to die, I was going to kiss him again. Shit, Ash. It was amazing. I was on his lap, and it was completely black, so we could only feel each other, and hear, and…" He tingled just thinking about it, his groin tightening.

"Oh. My. God," she breathed. "You had sex with your agent."

Rafa couldn't stop his grin. "Yeah," he whispered. "Well, he gave me a hand job, and I blew him. I actually sucked his cock. It was amazing. Just *kissing* him was amazing. I like him so much. Talking to him is just…it's so easy."

She grinned back. "You're totally in love with him."

"I am." He breathed deeply, and the certainty filled him completely. "I really am. Is it weird that getting kidnapped was simultaneously the worst and best night of my life? I'm a terrible person. My other agent might die, and everyone was so worried."

"You're not a terrible person. You're allowed to be happy about a good thing even when other stuff sucks." She hugged him. "Just don't ever get kidnapped again, okay?"

"Deal." His heart dropped, and he sat back. "Oh, and there's one other thing. I kind of came out to my family, but they'd already figured it out."

She nodded. "Chris warned me. That's rough—to say the least—about your dad and that fucking bill. But I think it's a good thing they know for sure now."

"But we had a plan. What about your parents?"

"I'll go see them tomorrow." Her smile faltered. "They're going to react how they'll react. Whether it's tomorrow or January. It is what it is. Maybe I should get kidnapped afterward so they realize they love me even if I'm a big ol' dyke." She laughed weakly. "I guess it's good to find out now if I'm still going to have a family after they know the truth." She rolled off the bed to her feet. "Let me grab a shower."

Rafa snagged her hand. "You'll still have a family, Ash. We're family forever."

Swallowing hard, she nodded. "Shit, don't make me cry again." She swiped at her puffy eyes. "Does the White House stock Visine?"

"Go have a shower and I'll ask Henry to dig some up."

"Thanks, babe. And hey...when are you going to see him again? Harley?"

He shrugged. "I guess I have to be patient. I mean, it's not like...we can't."

"One night's better than nothing, right?" She smiled sadly.

Rafa tried to smile back. "I hope so."

THEY MET IN the Yellow Oval Room on the second floor, which was decorated in—wait for it—various shades of yellow that probably had names like "buttercream," "sunflower," "lemon," and "apricot." Rafa settled on one of the couches with Ashleigh on one side of him and Adriana the other. His parents took the other couch across the pink marble coffee table, with Matthew, Chris, and Hadley in chairs.

Platters of finger sandwiches and cookies sat on the table, and the butler served them tea and coffee before quietly leaving the room. Everyone was showered and changed, but they were all clearly exhausted. When Rafa had looked in the mirror, his freckles had stood out even more on his paler skin. But he'd smiled and thought about Shane wanting to lick them. He'd left his hair curly and put on jeans and a Yankees tee. Fuck his chinos.

Rafa cleared his throat. "I just wanted to say how good it is to be back here with you all." He felt like he was having a peace treaty with his own family. All that was missing was a line of photographers. "I'm sorry for taking off like that. If I hadn't..."

"Don't be sorry." Ramon shook his head. "Your agents failed to keep you safe."

"No!" Rafa could feel his blood pressure rise already, and the conversation had just started. "It wasn't their fault. Alan could die, and Shane saved me. He—" Rafa cleared his throat. "They did everything they could."

Ashleigh frowned. "How did the kidnappers even know you'd be there? No one could have foreseen you running off like that."

The rest of the family shot each other glances and shifted uncomfortably. Camila sighed. "Well, that's the question, isn't it? A full investigation has already begun. But it seems someone in the Service had to be involved, as difficult and painful as that is to believe."

"An inside job," Rafa said. They all looked at him. "That's what Shane told me. He didn't know who, though."

"Yes, well, they'll find out." Ramon's nostrils flared. "By God, they'll find out." He took a deep breath. "But let's not focus on that today. We're just thankful we have our Rafa back. And…" He paused. "And there are important things we need to discuss."

"Are you sure you're up for this, Raf?" Matthew asked, his brow furrowed. "Dude, I'd want to sleep for a week after that."

"I'm sure. I don't want to wait. So, as you know, I'm gay." He motioned to Ashleigh. "We're gay. And we realize now that you suspected, but you didn't think we were going to come out. You thought we'd just live our lives in secret."

Camila clasped her hands together tightly, the material of her pantsuit swishing as she crossed her legs. "You never breathed a word. We assumed things were as you wanted them."

"Well, we tried, but they really weren't." Rafa rubbed his face. "I mean, it was our choice to pretend. It was. I'm not saying it's all your fault. Or even any of your fault. Not really. But if this is the part where you try to convince us to stay together and have a 'respectable' marriage…"

"No, Rafael. Your choices will be your own." His father tugged at his tie, a nervous gesture Rafa hadn't seen in years. "But why? Why didn't you talk to us?"

"You're kind of busy, Dad." Rafa shook his head. "Wait. No,

it's not fair to put it all on you. If I'd tried to talk to you guys, you would have listened. I don't know how you would have reacted, but I can't use your job as an excuse. I…" His feelings spun together in a tangle, and he struggled to find the right words. "I really wanted to tell you. I was going to."

Ramon frowned. "When?"

Rafa blew out a long breath, and could feel everyone's eyes on him. Ashleigh gave his hand a quick squeeze. "After the reelection. When I went to college, I realized it was time."

"When did you first think you were…" Camila waved her hand.

"*Gay*, Mom." Adriana rolled her eyes. "*Gay*. Not saying the word won't make it less true. See, this? This is why he didn't talk to you. This is why none of us talk to you. Not about anything that matters."

Their mother flinched, picking up her coffee cup and stirring the contents with little rattles of her spoon.

Chris spoke up. "Ade, come on. This isn't about ganging up on Mom."

"Easy for you to say—you're perfect," Adriana snapped.

Chris sat back. "What's that supposed to mean?"

"Oh, come *on*." She shook her head. "You're their perfect firstborn son who can do no wrong."

As Chris gestured defensively and opened his mouth, Hadley quieted him with a hand on his arm. "I think we should keep this discussion about Rafa."

"Yes. Well said." Camila squared her shoulders, and she didn't hesitate this time. "When did you first think you were gay, Rafa?"

He fidgeted as all eyes swung back to him. "I don't remember not knowing. It was like…I just knew it deep down. I didn't really understand it, but I knew. And by sixth grade, I knew what it meant. And I knew it was me." He watched his parents. "When did you first think I was gay?"

They glanced at each other. Ramon shifted uneasily on the couch. "From the time you were in junior high, I suppose. You had that friend. Bradley."

Rafa frowned. "Brad? Nothing ever happened with him."

"Yes, but the way you looked at him…" Camila said. "You never looked at girls that way. You were different than your brothers."

"Oh." It was true that he'd had a huge crush on Brad Newton. The thought that his parents had noticed all those years ago made his stomach acidy.

"And you were going to tell us," Ramon said. "After you started college?"

"I was building up to it." Rafa glanced at Ashleigh. "Ash and I talked about it a lot. I was thinking Christmas holidays, but when I came home for Thanksgiving, you made that announcement about the bill. Constitutional marriage. Because *my* marriage wouldn't be right in the eyes of the constitution. It wouldn't be worthy. After that, I couldn't tell you. Ash and I decided we'd fake it. At first it was just to avoid questions about why we weren't dating anyone. Then we came up with our plan to wait until we graduated. It was easier to go under the radar as a couple. That's…that's what I tried to do pretty much all the time. Stay unnoticed."

The silence in the room was thick and cloying in the air. "Under the radar," Ramon repeated hollowly.

"Um, yeah." Rafa kept his gaze on the table and the little delicate sandwiches without crusts. "Chris was one of the sexiest men alive and marrying Hadley. Matty was going for the Olympics, and Ade was…doing her thing. Making her own headlines. And Mom and Dad, you've obviously had a lot on your plate. I just…kept my head down. I tried to be good. To do everything right. That way…"

"What?" Camila asked tightly.

His throat felt raw. "That way none of you really noticed me. Thought much about me. That way you didn't really see me."

"I guess we didn't," Matthew said quietly. "And even if we did, we let you pretend nothing was wrong."

"But Raf, like you said, you made that choice." Chris motioned to Adriana. "We didn't want to push you. It wasn't because we didn't care. Or because we wouldn't have accepted that you were gay. We thought we were giving you the space you needed. The time."

"I know. I made those choices to stay in the closet. I can't blame any of you. But Dad..." Rafa closed his eyes, the remembered pain and humiliation washing over him. "Standing on that stage that night while you talked about taking away my rights, it just..." He forced himself to look at his parents. "It broke something in me. I've always been the awkward ugly one." As a flurry of protests filled the air, he raised his hand. "Please let me say this."

His heart pounded, and sweat gathered on his brow, but as he took a deep breath, Rafa felt strong enough to say the words for the first time. "That's always how I felt. I was the zit-faced, too-skinny Chia Pet with braces. And when I went to college, I started to feel like maybe I could be someone else. But that night..." His breath was stuck in his lungs as he remembered curling up in bed in the dark. "I wanted to die."

His mother gasped softly. "No, Rafael."

"Don't worry, I wouldn't have actually killed myself or anything. But for the first time, I knew what it felt like to really want to give up." He looked down at his hands, clasping his fingers together so tightly they were going numb. "Standing there smiling, with everyone watching, I've never felt so worthless. Like I wasn't good enough to be your son. I wasn't as good as Chris, and Ade, and Matty. I was different. And I'd never be who you wanted." He sucked in a shuddering breath. "So I guess I did give up. I decided to hide, at least until college was done. Until the White House was done. Until I could run away. And in Australia I could be the real me, but I'd be so far away that if you didn't love me, it wouldn't hurt so badly."

With a deep breath, Rafa made himself look up. His heart skipped as he saw the tears shining in his family's eyes. In his *mother's* eyes.

"But we argued with Dad about it," Adriana said, sniffling. "Didn't you know we would have had your back?"

"You guys were hardly ever here. I should have talked to you, but I was still afraid."

Ramon was silent for a few long moments. "There have been many occasions when I've wished I could go back in time and change a decision I made, but none as much as I wish it now, Rafalito. I'm sorry." He raised his hands. "I know that sounds hollow. Paltry. But I'm so sorry. I let the party pull my strings. I didn't even believe a word I was saying. You know what I really think? The Bible is a storybook created by men, and used by men to further their selfish goals."

"Ramon," Camila murmured.

"Haven't I bitten my tongue all these years? If I can't be honest here with my family, then where?" He gazed at Rafa again. "I'm so very, very sorry." He stood and circled the coffee table, pulling Rafa to his feet and into a rib-crushing hug. "You're exactly who we want. Who you were meant to be." He kissed Rafa's head, and Rafa sniffled as his father held him.

"Anything to add, Mom?" Adriana asked sharply.

"Rafa knows I'm sorry." Camila blinked, and a tear slipped down her cheek. "Of course I am."

"Mom, we don't always know," Chris said quietly. "Sometimes it's really nice to hear it."

Camila stood, and Ashleigh did as well, scooting off to the side of the couch, saying, "I'll just…"

Rafa turned from his father and into his mother's arms.

"I'm sorry, Rafael. I wanted what I thought was the best for you. It blinded me." Camila leaned back and kissed his forehead. "When I thought I might have lost you... Rafa, nothing else matters as long as you're healthy and happy. Nothing."

"Even if I want to move to Australia and be a chef?"

She sighed and brushed back his loose curls. "If you must, my darling."

"That's as good a blessing as you'll get, bro. Take the money and run," Matthew said, popping a cookie into his mouth.

The thick tension broke, and it felt good to laugh. Even their mother smiled wryly. "You know I only want what's best for you all." Her smile faded. "I do realize I'm not the easiest person at times. But I love my family."

"Of course we know," Ramon murmured, kissing her cheek and sliding his arm around her shoulders. "Rafa, if cooking is your passion, then that is what you'll do." He cleared his throat. "But you will finish your degree at UVA first. No ifs, ands, or buts."

"Absolutely. I promise." Rafa realized he was grinning. "Thank you."

A quiet knock came from the door, and when Ramon called out to enter, his top aide stepped inside. "I'm sorry to interrupt. Sir, the media is growing extremely restless without a direct statement from you."

"Yes, yes." Ramon nodded.

"Is Rafael up to being on camera?"

The comforting warmth that had filled Rafa evaporated. "They want *me* to go on TV?"

"Are you kidding?" Adriana asked. "You're the top news story around the world. President's son kidnapped by apparent terrorists? The media's losing its collective mind."

He remembered what Ashleigh had said about cameras at the airport when she arrived, and his stomach twisted. "Oh. I really don't…do I have to?"

"No," his parents answered in unison.

Camila addressed the aide. "The president and I will make a statement in the Rose Garden. We'll be down in two minutes for a briefing."

With final hugs, his parents left, and Rafa flopped back down on the couch with Ashleigh beside him again. For a moment, he just sat there. "Wow. So that happened. God. I think I need a drink."

"*Hell yes* you do." Chris clapped his hands together while Hadley and Matthew laughed. "Baby brother, it is high time you got drunk at the White House. We'll show you how it's done. We've got your back."

Laughing, Rafa nodded. "Let's do it."

"And ohhh, we need to talk about boys," Adriana exclaimed. To Ashleigh, she added, "And girls. There is so much to catch up on!"

Rafa thought of Shane and blushed furiously. He couldn't breathe a word of it yet, and he wouldn't. But one day Shane wouldn't be his agent, and he let himself imagine that he'd be so much more.

Chapter Eighteen

AS THE KNOCK came again, Shane sighed and pulled a T-shirt over his head. His flannel pajama bottoms had a hole worn through in the ass, but whoever wanted to talk to him now could damn well deal with it. With his hand on the knob, he checked the peephole in case a reporter had gotten his address, which was only a matter of time.

"It's me. Open sesame."

With a chuckle, Shane let Darnell inside and they hugged. "I'm fine."

Darnell slapped his back. "You look like you rolled around in a tube of rocks."

"Thanks. Feel like it too."

Darnell stepped back and kissed him lightly. "You slept at all?"

"Nope." Shane rolled his neck, wincing as the bones cracked. "Just got home and showered. Fuck, it's been a long day. Long night before it."

"I bet. I won't stay long. Just wanted to make sure you're okay."

"Thanks, man." Shane went to the kitchen and twisted the cap off a bottle of beer, passing it to Darnell before getting his own. He seemed unendingly thirsty and should probably have more water, but screw it. He'd earned a beer. It was getting dark, and he flipped on a few lights and made sure to close his blinds up tight.

Darnell sat on the couch and patted the cushion beside him. "Let's talk about you."

"Do we have to?"

"Afraid so. Doctor Darnell is in session. Start spilling."

Shane dropped down beside him and stretched his legs onto the coffee table, crossing his ankles. "Hell. I can't believe it happened. We train so much for it, but part of you never thinks it'll really happen, you know? That someone will actually make a move on your protectee. I've never felt so damn scared."

Darnell pointed at the shallow wound on the side of Shane's head where the bullet had grazed him. "Close call."

"Yeah. They bandaged it up, but it came off in the shower. Eh, it's fine."

"Still makes you think about life, doesn't it? Remember when I took that hit in my leg a few years back? Flesh wound, but the what-ifs got pretty loud for a while."

"Yeah. I guess I haven't really had time to think about it. Spent most of the morning at the site taking them through it. Then at HQ. And it doesn't matter about me. Rafa's okay. That's what counts. And thank Christ Alan made it through surgery. Can't see him yet. Wanted to go anyway to be with his wife, but they sent her home with some Valium. Tomorrow, I hope."

"He's tough, right? He'll make it. And it *does* matter about you, but I hear what you're saying. Any idea how the fuckers got to you? Rumor in the news is that it's Karelian radicals. Pissed about Castillo's involvement in the treaty with Russia."

"Could be. They sounded Eastern European. Or more Scandinavian. Karelian is similar to Finnish, right?" Shane blinked, images of dead men swimming before his eyes.

"I think so. This is the first time you've shot anyone on the job, right? Or off it."

"Yeah. It was...I don't know. Loud. Dark. I guess I should be upset that I killed people."

"You did your job. You did what needed to be done to get Rafa back. Those men made a choice, and they suffered the consequences. This is what we train for. Not that it isn't hard. I'm sure the Service will send you to a shrink to talk all about your feelings."

Shane grimaced. "I'm sure they will. It was strange, you know? I've practiced so many times over the years. We go to the training center regularly and run through protocols and act out scenarios. The natural instinct when a person hears a gunshot is to drop to the ground. We have to train to stay on our feet and block our protectee. Take the bullet if need be. We've trained over and over to stay calm and use deadly force when it's called for. So I did it. And it wasn't like training, but it still doesn't feel quite real."

"I'm sure it'll sink in. But you know, you don't have to be upset about it. There's no rule. Like I said, those men made their choice."

"I'd kill them again in a heartbeat. When I think about what they would probably have done to him…" Shane gripped his beer bottle and forced himself to breathe. "I don't know how they could have followed us. How they'd even have known we were leaving Castle. It was a pop-up. Rafa had a fight with his parents and we barely managed to follow him ourselves. Never seen him like that. So upset." Shane shook his head, shoving away the thoughts of Rafa. "I think it was an inside job. Told them it had to be."

"Any idea who?"

"Not a fucking clue. I don't want to think it was someone I work with. We all have each other's backs. We have to. If we don't…well, I guess this is what happens."

"Anyone else getting those updates while you were on the road?"

"Sure. The team at Castle, and any number of people at Joint Ops at HQ. There's regular communication, and since the kidnappers managed to block our sat phones after they moved in, it stands to reason they could hack them earlier. It could have been anyone. For any number of reasons. Money. Revenge. Who knows."

"Yeah. I don't envy the investigators on this one. The Service is going to take a lot of heat."

Shane sipped his beer. "At the end of the day it was our fault. *My* fault."

"Hey, you're human. And you got him back. Saw Castillo and his wife on TV just before I came over. They said the kid's resting. First time I can remember ever seeing her look...I don't know. Shaken, I guess. I'm glad he's okay. Details were scarce, but it sounds like you were a one-man army out there, 'Unnamed Agent.' That has a ring to it."

He shrugged. "Had to get him back. It's my job."

"It is. But your feelings go deeper than that. It must have been tough. Trying to keep your cool when someone you care about is in danger."

Shane rested his head back on the sofa and stared at the ceiling. "I've never felt like that. That kind of worry. I...fuck, D. I've never felt like this about anyone. I'm in too deep." He closed his eyes. "Let myself go way too far."

"How far are we talking?"

He pressed his lips together and opened his eyes. "Orgasms were involved."

Darnell whistled softly. "Well, shit. When?"

"Last night."

His eyebrows shot up. "How'd you find time to squeeze that in?" He held up his hands. "So to speak."

Shane had to laugh, just a little. "After the threat was eliminated, we were stuck in a cave. The gunfire set off a rock slide. Too risky to try and dig out. I knew they would find us before long, and I had Rafa safe and contained. So we sat back and waited."

"And got busy."

He sighed. "It was wrong. I know. But in that moment...I didn't care. He was *alive*, and he was kissing me. And I might have kissed him first, when I found him. Seeing him again, all in one piece, it was...powerful." Shane's heart sped up just thinking about it, his stomach flipping with remembered anxiety and relief. "I didn't know if we'd actually make it. Figured what the hell." He rubbed his face. "It was incredibly irresponsible."

"Yeah, but it was also an incredibly fucked-up and scary situation. You were pumping with adrenaline. Wanting to have sex is a pretty common response. Reaffirms that you're alive. Besides, it's more than sex. Shane, if you just wanted to bang Rafael Castillo, I'd tell you to suck it up, go pick up some hot young Latino hunk at a club, and get it out of your system."

"Maybe that's what I should do."

"Nope. Because it's not just sex."

Shane gulped his beer, his palm wet from the condensation where he gripped the bottle. "How do you know?"

"Because I know you. And you've been sleepwalking for a long time now. But this boy woke you up."

"I haven't been sleepwalking," Shane scoffed. "I've been busy. The Service asks for a lot. It's a demanding job."

"Bitch, you think I don't know from demanding jobs catching murderers and rapists?"

Shane relented. "True. So you should understand why I haven't had time for dating and all that stuff."

"All that stuff," Darnell echoed. "Like friends, for example."

"I have friends."

"You have a couple guys from work, and you have me. And do you know why you have me? Because I'm a stubborn son of a bitch, and I stayed in touch with your sorry ass while you were transferring all around the damn country. I didn't hold it against you when you took two months to answer an email."

"Yes, I can tell," Shane replied dryly. "It didn't bother you at all." He took another sip from his bottle. "I know I've never been the best at that stuff."

"And when your folks died, you shut down completely." Darnell raised his hand as Shane opened his mouth. "And I understand why. I do. I understand why you became even more of a workaholic, and the Service was only too happy to bleed you dry. But sometimes life smacks us upside the head when we least expect it. You've been smacked but good, Shane. Admit it."

As Darnell waited, Shane struggled for the words. "I don't understand why I feel this way. I do want to fuck him. God, do I. But it's more than that. I like talking to him. He's funny and smart. I want to keep him safe. Not because it's my job. But because I hate to think of him unhappy or hurt. I want to see him smile. There's this...when he smiles for real, I can tell the difference. I want him to smile like that all the time."

"You wanna see that face when you wake up every morning?"

Shane rolled the question around in his mind, his heart beating loudly in his ears. He exhaled. "I do. I really fucking do. This is crazy. I'm out of my mind."

"It happens to the best of us, Shane." Darnell patted his arm. "Hoo boy, I tell you I knew this was different. Could see it in your eyes when you told me about that first kiss. If I offered to take your mind off your worries right now, what would you say?"

Sex with Darnell had always been fun and casual. No strings. No stress. But not anymore. "I'd say no. I'd say it would feel like cheating. Like a betrayal. Christ, this doesn't make any sense. I'm way too old for him. Eighteen years. That's...a whole other person. Jesus, I could practically be his father."

"Since when does love make sense?" Darnell sipped his beer. "And sure, you're technically old enough to be his daddy—just— but you're not. Nothing wrong with someone younger or older bringing a different perspective to a person's life. A new energy.

Isn't that what it's all about? Finding people who make our lives better? Friends, lovers, whatever. People who wake us the fuck up."

"Yeah." Shane fiddled with the label on his beer bottle, tearing off a long strip. "I'm thinking about surfing again because of him. Thinking about home. Mom and Dad." His eyes stung, and he shook his head. "Shit. I'm gonna start blubbering. I'm a wreck."

"What you are is exhausted. Not to mention emotionally repressed. Hey, you can blubber any time, my friend. And if this kid's getting under your skin and loosening up that shit-ton of guilt and grief you've got built up? That's a damn good thing in my book."

Breathing deeply, Shane got himself together. "I guess it is. But it doesn't really matter. It's impossible. Even if I moved off his detail, it's not like we could start...*dating*." He barked out a laugh. "I'm just imagining the faces at HQ. It can't happen. I can't even call him. Had his number in my work phone, but they took it at the scene as evidence. Routine procedure. He might as well be on the moon."

"But come the new year, Castillo's out of office. Rafael will be just an ordinary citizen."

Shane quickly smothered the flare of hope. "He's moving to Australia to go to the Cordon Bleu school there. It's just not going to happen. It's not feasible for a million reasons."

"Hmm. Maybe not. But stranger things have happened, my friend."

"Doubtful." As Shane finished his beer he knew it was impossible. There were fantasies, and there was reality. He and Rafa didn't have a future. They couldn't.

But a little part of him still whispered, *maybe*.

IT FELT LIKE his head had barely hit the pillow, but when Shane squinted at the clock, it was five a.m. He fumbled for his personal cell phone on the bedside table. "Kendrick."

"It's Nguyen. We need you at HQ for an official depo. Zero-seven-hundred."

"Right. Any word on Pearce?"

"He's stable. Surgery was a success. It won't be quick, but they expect him to recover."

Thank God. Shane breathed a little easier. "Glad to hear it. See you soon."

He hauled himself out of bed and into the bathroom. After splashing his face with cold water, he stared at his bleary reflection in the mirror. He wanted to sleep for days, but it wasn't an option. His gut simmered with acid as he rushed through his morning routine and put on a clean suit. His pistol had been bagged as evidence, along with the M-16. He felt naked without his weapon, but quickly snapped his badge and handcuffs to his belt.

In the unmarked headquarters building, they wound up in a windowless boardroom with an oval table. Harris, Nguyen and five other agents he didn't know sat along one side. Shane took one of the empty chairs on the other, facing them. He doubted they'd slept.

"Morning," Nguyen said. "Sorry to get you back in so early, but you know the routine."

He'd actually never been involved in a protectee incident, but Shane could imagine he was in for endless questions. "No problem." He breathed and kept his tone even. "How's Valor?" To not be able to even talk to him was more torturous by the minute. Let alone the ache to take Rafa in his arms again.

"He's good," she answered. "Shaken up, but handling it well. There will be counseling, of course. But he's a tough kid."

"Glad to hear it." It was on the tip of his tongue to ask to see him, but Shane resisted. It wasn't how they operated. He wasn't supposed to care. "So, questions? Shoot." He grimaced. "Probably a bad choice of words."

Nguyen smiled—a momentary flick up of her closed lips, before indicating the man on her right. "This is Agent Blonsky. He has a few preliminary questions."

Blonsky nodded briskly and referred to a piece of paper in an open folder. "Your parents are deceased?"

"Yes. A house fire six years ago." *But you know that already.*

"You don't have any siblings?"

"No."

Blonsky still looked at the paper. "Are you in close contact with any other family members?"

"No. My mother was an only child, and my father wasn't close with his brothers. I haven't spoken to my uncles or cousins since before I joined the Service." Resentment simmered in his gut. *No, I don't have any family ties. Yes, that makes me a better mark to be turned by the enemy. Whoever the fuck the enemy is this week.*

"And you're homosexual and don't have any children. Correct?"

"Correct." Shane knew he should bite his tongue, but couldn't seem to. "That's never been an issue before. Is it now?"

Blonsky glanced up, speaking calmly. "Not at all. We're simply gathering facts to aid our investigation."

Nguyen jumped in. "Here's the thing, Kendrick. This had to be an inside job. Nothing else makes sense."

"I agree. I told you that yesterday morning at the scene."

"Yes, you did. And we just need to go over a few things involving your actions, and the actions of Agent Pearce."

A hot rush of anger slammed through him. "Alan didn't have anything to do with this."

"Why do you say that?" she asked evenly.

"What do you mean? Because I know him. Because he would

never do this. Jesus, they nearly killed him."

"Yes, they did," Nguyen said. "Pearce would have surely died if he hadn't been discovered when he was. You, however, weren't seriously injured."

Shane ran his fingers over the wound on his skull. "Because I got stupidly lucky. I almost got dead."

"Very lucky," she agreed.

Harris and the rest of the agents watched with grim expressions, and Shane wished he had water. *I'm innocent. Why the fuck am I so nervous?* "It would be a hell of a shot to pull off if it was on purpose."

"It would." She glanced at Harris and back at Shane. "Here's the thing. We don't want to think you had anything to do with this. But there was a major breach of protocol. And that breach led to Valor being in an unsecure location where he could be grabbed."

"What breach?" Shane ran back the hours after leaving Castle in his mind. "We followed pop-up protocols to the letter." He looked to Harris. "Alan relayed our locations to you every thirty."

"Every location but the last," Harris said.

"What? No. That isn't right." Shane's mind spun. What the fuck was Harris talking about?

Harris continued. "Once we determined that contact had been lost and Valor's location was unknown, we were scrambling. You followed protocol except at the crucial moment."

"No. You're wrong. Pearce called in the last location. I heard him as I left the vehicle to follow Valor inside the rest stop."

"Why were you the one to go inside?" Nguyen asked.

"No reason in particular." *Stay calm. Breathe.* "Valor was more accustomed to me. We knew he was agitated and upset. It made sense for me to try and talk him down. Talk him into returning to Castle." No one took notes, but Shane knew he was undoubtedly being recorded.

Harris and Nguyen shared a look. "We received no communication from Pearce at the rest stop," Harris said.

"He called it in. I know he did." Shane watched Harris across the table. "I heard him say your name."

Harris shook his head. "Kendrick, I did not receive the call." His voice was calm, but there was steel beneath it. Something else Harris had said echoed in Shane's mind.

"I'm just about done with this whole damn place. All of it."

No.

Shane's heart thumped. Not possible. As disillusioned as Harris had seemed to become, he wouldn't do this. Wouldn't sacrifice Rafa and set up two agents to be killed. He was a good man. It had to be someone else. *Fuck. Fuck, fuck, fuck.* Shane shifted in his seat. Nguyen, Harris, Blonsky, and the others watched him intently.

Suddenly this interview felt a lot like an interrogation.

"Then I don't know what to tell you." It was on the tip of Shane's tongue to hurl an accusation across the table, but he bit it down. *Harris was bitter, but was he* that *bitter?* He looked at Harris across the table. Was the man lying now? How well did he really know him? Shane cleared his throat. "Have you checked the recordings of incoming communication?"

Harris's jaw tightened. "I would remember receiving the call."

"Perhaps it was misdirected, or—"

"You and Pearce have a direct line to me. I'd remember if the call had come through. It did not." Harris didn't raise his voice, but he folded his hands tightly on the table.

"We'll check the data to eliminate the possibility that the call was somehow rerouted," Nguyen said. "Good suggestion, Kendrick. As soon as the doctors allow it, Pearce will be interviewed. We're hoping that's later today, but it will likely be tomorrow. I'm sure you understand that the brass is extremely alarmed by this incident, and the potential security breaches that might have taken place if an agent has been compromised. Since you and Pearce were the agents at the scene, the investigation must start with you."

Nodding, Shane took a deep breath. "Of course."

"Let's table this for now," Nguyen said. "We're going to go back to the site and have you take us through the events in real time, starting at the rest stop."

Take them through the events. Like when Rafa jerked off and I listened. Maybe I should come clean now.

But he couldn't find the words. It felt too much like a betrayal of Rafa's trust to share such an intimate moment. And maybe it was simply an excuse for his own weakness, but Shane would keep their secrets for as long as he could.

STANDING INSIDE THE rest stop again, this time with a group of investigators in tow, Shane recited the litany of events—of course leaving out the masturbation and his own unprofessional reaction to it. His head pounded, and the dank concrete building felt claustrophobic.

"Valor was upset about an argument with his parents. We discussed it briefly. I convinced him to return to Castle. When we walked out the door, I was hit." He indicated the side of his head. "I was briefly stunned by the shot. My vision and hearing were temporarily impaired. Valor was taken. I discovered our radios and phones were being jammed. Agent Pearce was seriously wounded." He mentally shook free the memory of Alan's pale, frightened face. "I immediately pursued Valor."

An investigator frowned. "You didn't hear the van approach?" he asked.

"No."

"And Agent Pearce didn't alert you to its presence?"

"The radios were jammed."

The investigator glanced at the door. "It's a matter of feet. Surely Agent Pearce could have shouted?"

"I…yes, he could have." *Why didn't Al shout?*

"And you didn't hear Agent Pearce get shot?"

"Not when I was inside the building," Shane answered. "I assume it happened at the same time they shot me. There was a lot of noise. Or I suppose they had a silencer."

Another man asked, "And you say it was Agent Pearce who was tasked with communicating this location to the detail leader?"

"Yes. He was calling Harris when I left the vehicle and entered the building."

They scribbled some notes, then led him outside. As Shane took them through the next moments, his mind whirled.

Harris insisted he didn't get the call.

Why didn't Al shout?

Why didn't I hear the van?

Why the hell didn't Harris get that call?

Dread in the pit of Shane's stomach unfurled, slithering through him.

If they were scrambling the signal when Shane went inside, Alan would have called out and alerted him. And the signal had definitely still been working, since Alan had checked in with him some minutes later—seven or so. Yes, the radio had definitely still worked.

At that point, he'd been talking to Rafa by the sinks. As occupied as he'd been, he would have heard an approaching engine. After the years on the job, it was second nature. He didn't even have to think about noting potential trouble spots; potential danger. It was rote.

There had been no engine. The van had to have rolled in silently. It had been dark and rainy, but Alan would have seen it. Even without lights, he would have noticed the movement. He'd been out of the Suburban when they'd shot him. Some feet away from it. He should have honked or shouted when they'd approached.

Why didn't he shout?

Shane finished talking and stood in the rest stop parking lot, which was cordoned off with yellow tape. The investigators made more notes as he waited. As he desperately tried to find answers to his questions that didn't result in the same terrible conclusion.

"We're moving on," one of the investigators said. "Ready?"

Shane nodded, but his stomach roiled as the terrible pieces of the puzzle began to slide inexorably into place.

He wasn't ready at all.

Chapter Nineteen

"**B**ACK IN UNIFORM, huh?"

As Rafa came out of his room, he blinked at Matthew in the hall before looking down at his slacks and button-down shirt. He ran a hand over his tamed hair. "I guess."

"Sorry, that was a dick thing to say. There's nothing wrong with how you look. How are you feeling?"

"Good," Rafa lied. "A little banged up, I guess. But I'm fine." *Except for the fact that I need to see Shane again like I need air.*

Matthew's cheeks puffed out as he exhaled and shuffled from one foot to the other, scuffing his sneakers on the carpet. "I'm heading to the airport. Have to get back to training. But I just wanted to say I'm sorry. I should have paid more attention. You know I couldn't wait to get away when I went to college. And I was doing my thing out there, and you were doing your thing here, and I figured you were fine. I shouldn't have assumed."

"It's not your fault. I could have talked to you. It's two ways. Communication, I mean. I made my choices."

"I still feel like a bag of dicks. You're my little brother." Matthew swallowed thickly and tucked a lock of his shaggy hair behind his ear. "You know I love you and all that shit, right? That I don't care about the gay thing? I think it's great. So I just want to make sure you know."

"I do, Matty." Rafa blinked rapidly. "But thanks for saying it.

I love you too. And all that shit."

"Cool. I'd better go." He closed the few feet between them and yanked Rafa into a hug. "Just be yourself, and everyone else can fuck off." He slapped Rafa's back.

When he was gone, Rafa wandered into the Solarium, waiting for his parents. They'd asked to speak with him, and even though he understood why they had to arrange a time and place, it always made their conversations feel so official and fraught with tension.

He thought about his father arranging a time to talk about Rafa's mid-term grades not long after they'd moved into the White House. Rafa had worried about it for two days, sure that his mostly As weren't good enough, and that he'd be punished for the two B-pluses on ninth grade math and science. But his dad had only congratulated him on his hard work and taken him down to the kitchen for surprise milkshakes.

As he paced by the curved wall of windows, Rafa stared out at the sunny day. The Washington Monument soared against a blue sky, and cars and people went about their business.

He wondered where Shane was. There were new agents on his detail, and he'd nodded politely to them when he'd gone down to the kitchen to ask Magda for some cilantro and avocado. He'd asked if Alan was okay and when Shane would be back, but they hadn't had the answer to the latter. At least Alan was apparently recovering. That was something, at least.

His new phone buzzed in his pocket, and he grimaced at the text from Ashleigh.

They're at work until tonight. Tell me it's a bad idea to get drunk this afternoon before telling them.

He quickly tapped in: *It's a bad idea. You sure you don't want me to be there?*

The three dots appeared, followed by her message.

I'm sure. You've got your own shit. I can do this. I'm not promising I won't get drunk after. Have you talked to the media yet? They keep calling me. I'm going to have to change this number. People are gagging for an interview with you.

Ugh. He'd briefly looked at the news coverage on TV and online, but it was too surreal. All the years of flying under the radar, and suddenly he was the most famous first kid in decades. He tapped the keyboard.

The PR people are writing a statement for me. I'm hoping it'll all blow over in a couple days and someone from a reality show does something dumb and/or offensive.

She replied: *We can live in hope. Later, babe.*

Rafa pocketed his phone. He'd Googled Shane, and tried 411 and every way he could think of to find Shane's phone number. No luck, and it wasn't as though he could just go over to Shane's house with his detail in tow. That was assuming he could even find out where Shane's house was. Maybe it was an apartment, or a condo, or who the hell knew.

The reality that he might very well never see Shane again was a constant fear, jagged and sharp. He had to find a way. He just needed to talk to Shane and hear the rumble of his voice. Hell, he'd settle for a text, or a freaking Snapchat. But Shane was just...gone. And it wasn't as if he could call Rafa either, or drop by to say hi.

But does he miss me the way I miss him? Does he want to see me again? Does he still care?

It had really felt like Shane cared. When Rafa closed his eyes, he could imagine he was back in the cave, his head on Shane's thigh, and Shane's fingers combing rhythmically through his hair. It had felt so good to just be together and talk—to actually be able to touch Shane and hold him. It had all been so...*intimate.* Now Rafa felt like he really knew what that word meant in reality and not just theory.

And having sex for the first time had been pretty spectacular. Even if they hadn't gone all the way, he was pretty sure orgasms counted.

At one of the windows, he pressed his forehead against the

glass. The need to be with Shane again was a hunger, and it was more than physical. So much more.

"Rafa?"

He jolted back from the window, whirling around to find his parents watching him with matching frowns.

"Are you all right? Did you have lunch?" Camila asked. "We can have something brought up." She pivoted in her heels, her black skirt flowing around her knees.

"It's okay, Mom, I ate. I'm fine, just a little spaced out, I guess."

"Let's sit." His father motioned to the couch, taking off his suit jacket and carefully hanging it from a nearby wooden chair.

Rafa tried to relax on the couch, sitting between his parents. "So," Rafa said.

"Well, we obviously have a lot to discuss." Ramon templed his fingers. "First off, a therapist will be coming tomorrow to meet with you."

"I'm fine. Really!" He looked between his parents. "I am."

"Darling, you suffered a traumatic event," Camila said. "It can't hurt to discuss it with a professional. We'll all be meeting with her separately. Not just you."

"Oh. Okay, I guess."

"Okay," Ramon agreed. He hesitated. "Then there's the matter of your sexuality."

Rafa tensed. "I thought we already talked about that."

"Yes, but we need to discuss your plans for going public."

His heart dropping, Rafa picked at the jagged edge of a fingernail, his gaze zeroed in on it. "Don't worry. I'll keep it private until you're out of the White House. That was always the plan. I don't want to screw things up for you."

"Rafa." His father's tone was stern. "Will you look at me, please?" When Rafa raised his head, Ramon went on. "I'm only worried about you. I have less than six months left in the White

House, and I don't want you living in secret a day longer if that's not what *you* want. I don't care what the party thinks. I've done their bidding long enough. We've been reading about this…" He waved his hand. "Coming out. The experts say it should always be on your terms."

Rafa smiled tentatively. "Oh. You really wouldn't mind if I told everyone I'm gay? I thought… I mean, you wanted me to stay in the closet. You assumed I would."

Camila's face pinched. "We did. And we realize now it was quite a mistake to make that assumption. To assume that because you hadn't said otherwise, you were happy with the status quo. If you want to come out publicly, we'll support you completely."

As his father nodded, Rafa considered it. "Would you be saying this if I hadn't been kidnapped?"

His parents shared a glance, and Ramon answered sadly. "I don't know, Rafa. Maybe not. Maybe it would have taken more time to reach this point. I'd like to think we'd have arrived here either way. But to come so close to losing you…it puts life in perspective. That was the darkest night of our lives. It was like an eternity waiting to hear if our son was alive or dead. To know if we'd ever see you again." He shuddered. "Perhaps one day you'll have a child of your own, and you'll be able to imagine this terror."

His mother sat rigid beside Rafa. He reached for her hand. "Mom…"

Her smile was brittle as she squeezed his fingers. "I made a bargain with God. I swore that if you were returned to us whole, nothing else mattered. Not my ambitions for you, or my expectations, or wants. Only your happiness. And I always keep my promises, Rafa."

"I know." He kissed her cheek. "Thank you."

"So, it's up to you, Rafalito," his father said. "We can arrange for an interview with one of the news programs, or a magazine. Or you can simply begin living openly and see other boys. The rumors will fly, and we can simply say yes, our son is gay. And that will be that. Or you can do nothing at all. The choice is yours."

"I don't really want to give an interview, but it would be nice not to pretend anymore. Can I think about it?"

"Of course," Camila answered. "There's no rush. We just wanted you to know you have our support."

"That means more to me than I can say. Thank you." Rafa swiped at his eyes. "Ugh. I think I've cried more in the past few days than I have in my entire life."

Ramon laughed softly. "Yes. I think that's true for all of us."

"And if you guys are supporting my choices, you're still on board for Australia and the Cordon Bleu after I graduate UVA?"

"We are. Right, my dear?" Ramon looked to Camila.

Fingering her pearls, she nodded. "If that's truly what you want."

"It is. The next intake for the Grand Diploma is in July—their winter session. I'm thinking I'll move down there at the end of January after the inauguration. Get a job in a restaurant. Settle in and get used to normal life before school starts."

"And how long is this course?" Ramon asked.

"Two and a half years."

Camila frowned. "But surely there are cooking schools closer to home?"

"Mom, I really want to go to Australia. It doesn't mean I'm going forever. But I've been dreaming of this for years."

She looked down at her hands, fiddling with her diamond ring. "Truly? For years?"

"Uh-huh."

"I wish you'd said something."

"I wanted to." Rafa hitched his shoulders. "But you always hated the idea of me cooking. Even when it was a hobby."

She pressed her red lips together. "Yes."

"But why? There are a million male chefs who aren't gay, Mom."

"Of course there are. It wasn't that." She shook her head. "You were always different in your own way, and I admit that scared me." She glanced at Ramon. "We worked so hard to erase the parts of us that were different. To assimilate."

"Republicans can be chefs, Mom."

Camila sighed and re-crossed her legs. "Do you know what your grandfather did for a living?"

Puzzled, Rafa nodded. "He was a businessman. An entrepreneur."

"That's what we tell people. He was a cook. Not a chef. Nothing close to that. He cooked at a diner. And his business was cleaning grease. He had a little machine on wheels that he towed around. After a day at the grill making burgers and French fries, he cleaned the vats. Then he went to the other restaurants in the neighborhood, and he cleaned their vats too. We could never quite get rid of the smell of grease in our little apartment. Even after he died, it was like the grease hung on, a film over everything. The thought of you cooking...it made me ashamed. Like we were going backwards when we'd come so far."

Rafa stared at his mother. "I... I don't know what to say."

"You don't have to say anything." She patted his knee. "As Adriana would say, it's my issue. I'm sorry I let it affect you so much. It's silly now that I say it out loud."

"I guess we all have issues." Rafa tried to imagine his mother as a little girl, but couldn't quite.

"Rafa, we were wondering..." Camila paused. "Well, we wanted to know...is there anyone special? A young man you've managed to keep hidden?"

His heart skipped. "No," he said too quickly. "Not yet. I was so busy with school."

"Well. Yes, plenty of time for…that." She shifted uncomfortably.

Rafa tried to imagine what they'd say if they found out about Shane, and nausea rolled through him. No, better to cross that bridge later. Much, much later. *Unless Shane tells the truth to the Secret Service.* Rafa couldn't see why he would, but the longer he went without being able to talk to Shane, the more his imagination went into overdrive. Surely Shane wouldn't tell a soul. He had more to lose than Rafa did.

"There's one more thing, son." Ramon put his hand on Rafa's arm. "We know it won't be pleasant, but you'll have to answer some questions for the Secret Service."

Rafa's pulse thundered. "About what?"

Ramon's brows drew together. "The abduction, of course. We've put them off this long, but you'll have to meet with them tomorrow morning. It's necessary, I'm afraid. You might have seen something, or heard something that could help."

"I don't think so." Rafa went back to his nail, peeling off a strip. "I was pretty much just in the metal box until Shane rescued me."

Camila shuddered. "Oh, darling. I can't imagine." She ran her hand over his head.

"It was…bad." He shuddered as he remembered the sensation of being blind, squashed in the box with his muscles cramping. "Why would they do that to me? I mean, what was their plan?"

His father squeezed Rafa's shoulder. "Terrorists want to disrupt our lives. Instill fear in us. They're cowards. When all is said and done, the why doesn't even matter. These people aren't worth another moment of our thoughts." He grimaced. "Of course that's easier said than done. If they'd succeeded…taken you away…"

"It's okay. Shane saved me. I'm fine, Dad. I am."

Ramon kissed the side of Rafa's head. "You're a brave boy."

"Um, thanks." Rafa's palms were sweaty, but he managed to

keep his tone casual. "Hey, can you get Shane's number? I really want to thank him again."

"Oh, I'm sure you'll be able to once the investigation is over," Ramon replied, tugging on his tie.

Rafa sat up straighter. "Why can't I thank him now?"

"Darling, I'm sure he's very busy." Camila rubbed his arm. "Now, let's talk about—"

"What aren't you telling me?" He looked between his parents.

His father sighed. "Rafa, we don't know yet how this happened. Or who was involved."

"I thought they were Karelian."

"Yes, the kidnappers were. But to get to you the way they did, they had help."

"Yeah, but…" Rafa's mouth went dry. "Wait. Not from Shane. Is that what the Secret Service thinks?" He jumped to his feet. "He didn't help them. They almost killed him! I saw the bullet hit his head! The blood. And he *saved* me. He killed them all!"

"All right, all right." Ramon stood as well and put his hands on Rafa's shoulders. "We're not accusing Agent Kendrick of anything. They're investigating, and I'm sure they'll discover the truth very soon."

Rafa forced himself to inhale and exhale slowly. "Okay." *Calm down. Don't let them see. Shane's innocent. He's fine.*

"Let's go down to the kitchen and get a snack." Camila led Rafa away from the couch. "Don't worry about any of that now, all right? You have a future to plan. You can tell us more about Australia. We were there what, five years ago, Ramon? We held a koala. I think it was as stoned as a hippie."

As his mother talked, Rafa followed his parents downstairs and told himself not to worry. And as he thought of planning his future, he knew without a doubt he didn't want one without Shane.

Chapter Twenty

"J ULES." SHANE FORCED a smile as he opened his arms. It was getting late, and the hospital was quiet. Nguyen and Harris had driven him over, and now they hung back at the end of the hall. "How is he?" Shane asked, holding Jules close, her dark head just reaching his shoulder.

She stepped back and nodded. "Much better than yesterday. He's been able to talk. He can't remember anything." She rubbed her red, puffy eyes. "But he's going to make it."

"Thank God." The relief warred with the horrible suspicion growing stronger and stronger. Shane's throat was dry. "How's Dylan?"

"As well as can be expected. I'm keeping him away from the hospital." She pressed her lips together. "He's had enough of hospitals already, and there'll be so much more to come."

"And how are you?" He squeezed her shoulder.

Jules shrugged. "One day at a time and all that crap." She nodded to an older man at the other end of the hall. "My dad's going to take me home to sleep. You can go in and see Alan for a minute. He was asking about you." She smiled tremulously. "I'm so glad you're okay and that you got that poor boy back. When I think about how it could have gone, I just—" She shuddered. "Thank God it turned out the way it did."

"I know." *But the worst might still be coming.* "Rest up. I'll see you soon." He hugged her again, and Jules kissed his cheek before walking away. Shane took a few deep breaths. Nguyen and Harris were still in conversation at the end of the long hall. Feeling like he was outside his body, Shane moved his feet.

At the threshold to hospital room 21C, he stopped. The steady *beep-beep-beep* of Alan's heartbeat pinged in the stillness.

Bile rose in Shane's throat. It couldn't be true. There had to be another explanation. There was no way Alan was involved. It was impossible. Utterly impossible. Could he really have done it? Christ, not Al.

Please let me be wrong.

Alan's eyes were shut, but he must have sensed someone, and he blinked blearily, a smile trying to lift his lips. But then something flickered across his expression, his eyes widening.

It was fear and shame, and it was unmistakable.

The air whooshed out of Shane, and he shook his head as he shuffled his feet forward, closing the door behind him. "Tell me it isn't true." His voice cracked, and the words cut like shattered glass. "Please, Al."

Swallowing thickly, Alan licked his lips. His skin was almost as pale as the clear tube in his nose. "What?" he croaked.

Shane stopped beside the bed. There were flowers on every surface, and an old picture of the Pearce family before they'd lost Jessica sat in a frame on the closest table. They had wide smiles and arms around each other. "You know exactly what I'm talking about, don't you?"

"Kenny…"

"How did they get to you? You know, it doesn't even matter. Was it money? How much was Rafa worth? And how much for my life? It was just dumb luck that bullet missed. Did they turn on you, or was your bullet supposed to be the one that grazed?"

Alan shook his head, his lips trembling. Days of beard growth darkened his face, making his skin even paler.

"Yeah, guess they double-crossed you. HQ thinks it was me. And I've been racking my brain trying to figure out who could have done it. But now I see. It had to be you. When we reached that rest stop and I went inside, you didn't call Harris. I thought maybe he was the one. That he was lying. Because I knew you'd called. I heard you on the phone as I left. But you weren't calling him at all. You were giving them the all-clear to approach. How did they follow?"

Lips parted, Alan breathed hard with wide eyes.

Shane's own voice sounded distant. "Was it a tracker hidden on you somewhere? Or did you just call them? Did you have another phone that HQ couldn't trace? I was so focused on Rafa that I didn't notice. That way they could follow and stay a few miles behind. Far enough that I wouldn't see them. Were they on standby, waiting for your call and the right opportunity? Bet they were. These fuckers are nothing if not patient, huh?"

Alan just stared at him, and the rapid beeping of his monitor filled the room with staccato sound.

"Were you going to let me go down for it too?"

"No!" Alan coughed violently before settling. His voice scratched roughly. "It wasn't supposed to be like this."

"Right. Because I was supposed to be dead."

"*No.* Don't you see?"

"See what?" Shane shouted. "What the fuck did you do, Al?"

"It was only supposed to be me who died. That was the deal."

An older nurse opened the door and strode into the room. "Alan? Is everything all right?" She circled the bed and leaned over him. "Okay, that's enough excitement. Sir, visiting hours are over. You have to leave."

"No." Shane barely looked at her.

"Excuse me? Don't make me call security. I don't care who you are or what badge you carry. I won't have you agitating my patient."

Shane breathed deeply through the urge to scream and throw one of the vases of flowers through the window.

"It's all right," Alan rasped. "Please. He has to stay."

The nurse frowned, her hands on her hips. "A few more minutes, but you have to calm yourself." She helped him drink some water and then eyed the IV bag attached to his arm. "Maybe it's time for another dose of morphine."

Alan shook his head. "I need to think."

"We'll be fine," Shane said, surprised by how calm he sounded to his own ears. The nurse didn't look convinced, but left as Shane turned back to this stranger who wore his friend's face.

Clenching his hands into fists, Shane kept his voice even. "Tell me about the deal."

Alan was quiet for several moments. Then, his gaze on the ceiling, he whispered, "Ten million offshore. Untraceable. Half up front." He breathed in and out, in and out, his chest rising and falling with effort. "Jules would get the rest as an anonymous donation in a month. Even if the other half wasn't delivered, what I have is enough for her and Dylan to go to Sweden for the experimental treatment. And with my death benefits as well, she wouldn't have to worry. I could take care of them."

"By *dying*? By leaving them alone?" Shane wished to God he was sleeping and this was a nightmare.

"What good have I done them?" Tears slipped down Alan's cheeks. "I killed Jessica, and Dylan won't be too long behind her. I had to make it right. It was the only way I could save Dylan and leave them secure. The government's slashed benefits to the living, but a dead Secret Service agent is still worth a lot."

"And if I died too, that was okay?"

"No!" Alan shook his head violently, finally meeting Shane's gaze again. "It was only supposed to be me. I swear. They were just going to knock you out. We had a deal!"

"And if you can't trust terrorist scum to keep their word, who can you trust these days, huh?" Shane's skin crawled, and he dug his nails into his palms. "They came a millimeter from splashing my brains over that rest stop."

"It wasn't supposed to be like that. It wasn't!"

Shane had to take a breath and swallow down his shout so he could calmly ask, "And how was it supposed to be for Rafa?"

Alan squeezed his eyes shut, more tears escaping. "They promised not to kill him," he whispered. "They were going to trade him for war prisoners in Russia. Get Castillo to arrange a deal."

"And we know what their fucking promises are worth!" Shane slammed his fist into the mattress, looming over Alan. "You gave him up to those bastards. They crammed him into a little metal box. God knows where they were taking him, and what they'd do. How many body parts they'd cut off to FedEx to the president as they made their demands." Spit flew from his lips, and heat rushed through him. "How could you do that to him? He never hurt anyone. He's a good kid. A good man. It was our job to protect him. To *die* for him. You betrayed him. What did he do to deserve that?"

Alan's lips trembled. "It wasn't personal. I—"

"And what about me? Wasn't personal with me either? *I* trusted you." Shane angrily swiped his wet eyes. "You were my brother, Al. Even if they hadn't killed me, do you know what it was like seeing you shot? Knowing Rafa was gone? We give our lives to this job. To fail is the worst thing we can do. You betrayed me. Betrayed the Service. Everything we stand for."

"Yes, we give our lives," Alan spat, his breath coming faster and his cheeks flushing. "And what do they give us? I did my tour in the sandbox in Afghanistan. Then I signed up to protect America's leaders. To keep America safe at home. And when Jessica was diagnosed, what did they give me? A denial of benefits. They found a loophole. I tried everything. Talked to a hundred people. No one could help. Their hands were tied." He gripped the sheets. "I heard it over and over. Everyone at the insurance company and the benefits office was *sorry*. They were so fucking *sorry*. But they didn't do a damn thing."

Fury and sorrow and compassion scraped Shane raw and hollow. "It doesn't make this right."

"What's right in this world anymore? We mortgaged our house as many times as we could. Racked up every penny of our credit. I watched my little girl die, and my country stood by and did nothing. *Nothing!* That bastard Castillo approved the cuts in our benefits. He slashed healthcare across the board for government employees. Oh, but not the senators or the congresspeople. No, they still get their packages and their vacation time and their big, fat salaries for bleeding the rest of us dry." He gritted his teeth. "I couldn't watch Dylan die too. Couldn't do it. When the Karelians approached me, it...it felt like a sign. Like fate."

"This wasn't the way, Al. How could you ever think it was?" The anger had drained out of him. Shane wanted to curl up and sleep, and wake to find the world the way it had been that morning, before he knew this terrible truth. "I know it isn't fair that Jessica died. That Dylan has the same disease. It isn't fucking fair. And it isn't fair that the insurance company wouldn't pay. But this wasn't the way. This was never the way."

"It was only supposed to be me who died," Alan insisted, fresh tears staining his face. "It was supposed to be me."

The nurse marched in. "That's enough. Sir, you're leaving. *Now*. Do I need to call security?"

Shane could only shake his head.

Alan reached out. "Please."

Despite it all, Shane found himself taking Alan's grasping hand.

"I'll tell them everything." He looked to the nurse anxiously. "It was me. It wasn't Shane. He had no idea."

Frowning, she pressed a button on the IV. "All right. Time to rest."

"Tell Valor I'm sorry." Alan's eyes were already glassy as the morphine spread through his system, but he clutched Shane's hand with surprising strength and drew him right down to his face, whispering, "And be careful when you're with him. Or everyone will see."

Shane lowered Alan's hand to the mattress, and his eyes drifted to the framed picture. It had been Christmas, with the glowing tree behind them and wrapping paper strewn at their feet. Jules and her bright smile, tucked under Alan's arm, and a Santa hat on his head. The kids stood in front of them, Jessica in footie pajamas, proudly showing off the gap between her teeth, and little Dylan clapping, his cheeks red from the excitement.

"I'm sorry, but you really have to leave now." The nurse motioned to the door.

Alan was sleeping already, his chest rising and falling steadily, lips parted. Part of Shane wanted to dig in his heels and wait until Alan woke, because there should have been so much more to say—more hurt and fury to vent. But Shane found he'd said enough after all.

He shuffled down the hallway to where Nguyen and Harris waited. As he neared and opened his mouth, Nguyen spoke first.

"We got it all, Kendrick." She nodded grimly. "Good work."

Harris clapped a hand on his shoulder, his face drawn and sorrowful. "It's a hell of a thing, Shane."

Shane stood there blinking, utterly drained. He wasn't sure where they'd hidden the camera, but he should have known. Of course they'd suspected. At least it was done.

Harris squeezed his shoulder. "Go home and get some rest."

"Are you going to tell Valor before he finds out in the news?"

"Of course," Harris answered. "And he's extremely eager to see you again—wants to thank you. Maybe later tomorrow, okay? He's been like a dog with a bone, telling everyone that you saved him and had nothing to do with the kidnapping." He chuckled. "Never seen the mouse so forceful. But he sure wants to see you. Nice to have a grateful protectee, huh?"

Not trusting his voice, Shane nodded. As he took the elevator down to meet a waiting G-ride, he leaned back against the wall. Despite it all, he couldn't stop the glimmer of a smile.

WALKING BACK INTO Castle, Shane felt like it had been weeks instead of what—four days since he and Alan had raced out after Rafa? When he'd woken in the morning, for a moment he hadn't remembered. Then the sick sensation—dread and grief—had settled in again as what Alan had done returned to him.

Now he walked the same path he'd taken that first day with his friend at his side, past the West Wing, and through the Palm Room into the main residence. He wasn't on duty, so he wore his suit without his badge, handcuffs, or replacement pistol. Other agents nodded sympathetically, and staff whispered and stared. Harris and Nguyen stood outside the Secret Service office in the residence basement.

Nguyen asked, "How are you doing, Kendrick?"

"Okay, I guess. Still hard to believe any of this is real."

She nodded. "I hear you. At least Pearce is cooperating. They've put him on suicide watch, and the charges will be filed later this week. He's telling us what he knows about the Karelians. Seems it was a small splinter group that approached him. The FBI is taking over that part of the investigation." She sighed. "I suppose a dying kid makes for a desperate father. He told us he had a two-week window for the kidnapping. If the pop-up hadn't happened, there would have been an ambush next week."

"What will happen to his wife and son?" Shane asked. "The medical bills?"

Her expression regretful, Nguyen shook her head. "I don't know. Pearce's employment is obviously terminated, effective immediately. He's left his family in a bad situation, to say the least."

Shane had tried calling Jules, but there had been no answer at the house. He'd called a few times and finally left a message simply saying he was sorry and that he wanted to help. She and Dylan didn't deserve to suffer because of Alan's desperate choices, but they undoubtedly would, and it didn't feel like there was anything Shane could do about it.

Harris sighed. "I still can't wrap my head around it. What the hell he could have been thinking."

"He wasn't," Shane said. "I think he went down a tunnel of grief and rage and smacked right into hopelessness. And he couldn't see his way out. Couldn't see right from wrong in that dark place." He quickly added, "Not that it's an excuse."

"No," Nguyen agreed. "There is no excuse. We're just glad that shot missed and you were able to recover Valor. Speaking of whom…"

Shane turned to find Rafa approaching down the corridor with his parents and agents in tow. Shane's belly actually somer-saulted like he was a kid picking up his date, all nervous excitement and eager affection.

Act normal. Be normal.

Rafa wore his standard type of preppy outfit, and had combed back his hair as usual. His gaze was on the polished floor, and when he reached Shane and looked up, smiling, his nose wrinkled. Shane nodded, keeping his expression placid.

The president stepped forward with his hand extended. "Mr. Kendrick. I wanted to personally thank you for saving my son's life."

Shane shook his hand. "I was only doing my job."

Castillo chuckled. "Well, Rafael was very intent on making

sure we all knew you had nothing to do with that unfortunate business."

The first lady shook his hand as well. "Yes, Rafa has been extremely insistent that you went above and beyond to ensure his safety. So thank you. You have our eternal gratitude."

Shane kept his gaze away from Rafa. "You're welcome. Like I said, I was only doing my job."

An aide appeared. "Mr. President, the meeting is beginning shortly."

"Well, duty calls." Castillo shook Shane's hand again and gave Rafa's shoulder a squeeze. "I'll see you tonight."

As the president left for the West Wing with his detail in tow, Rafa spoke up, his voice studiedly casual. "I've got to go check the sauce. Shane, want to come up with me? I just wanted to say a couple things. I know you were doing your job, but it still means a lot to me."

"Sure," Shane said, his pulse zooming.

"Yes, Rafa's cooking for us." Camila smiled tightly. "Thank you again, Mr. Kendrick." To Rafa she added, "Darling, I'll see you in a couple hours for dinner. I look forward to it."

"Thanks, Mom." Rafa nodded to Harris, Nguyen, and his detail. "See you guys later." He turned for the stairs, and Shane followed a few steps behind.

As they passed the second floor on the way to the third, Shane looked at his feet and not Rafa's ass in front of him. They were in the private part of the residence now, but household staff could still be around.

Stay professional. Steady.

They passed the Linen Room and went down the little corridor to the kitchen. Rafa motioned Shane ahead of him, not meeting his gaze. As Shane stepped inside, he heard the *click* of the door closing. When he turned, Rafa was standing close, his lips parted, and chest rising and falling rapidly.

"Shane..."

Their arms snaked around each other like they were meant to, fitting so naturally together. Rafa bent his head, pressing his face against Shane's neck, and the wet sensation of his breath was warm and sweet and *good*. Shane hugged him closely and never wanted to let go. He knew he would—that he had to—but for a minute, he let himself hold on.

"I was afraid I wouldn't see you again," Rafa mumbled. "I've missed you so much."

"Missed you too."

Lifting his head, Rafa edged back, his hopeful eyes bright. "Really?"

Shane smiled, running his fingers up and down Rafa's spine. "Really."

Rafa kissed him, sweet and gentle at first, and then deeper. Shane drank him in, memorizing every sigh and gasp, and the raspy slide of Rafa's tongue against his. He tasted like tomatoes and oregano, and the air was thick with it.

Shane wanted to stay, but he had to be strong. He gently broke the kiss. "You're cooking dinner for your parents?"

Rafa beamed. "Chris, Hadley, and Adriana too. I'm nervous. I'm just doing spaghetti, but I want it to be good."

"Smells great." Shane couldn't resist licking into Rafa's mouth again. "Tastes great."

Laughing, Rafa murmured, "Wish you could stay for dinner."

"But we both know I can't." Exhaling, Shane stepped back, resting his hands on Rafa's shoulders, unwilling to break contact just yet.

Rafa's smile faded. "I know." His worried gaze searched Shane's face as he squeezed his waist. "Are you okay? They told me about Alan. I can't believe it. I never thought even for a second..."

"I didn't either. I should have. I've known him for years. I should have realized something was off."

"No! Don't you dare blame yourself. You're not a mind reader, Shane. It wasn't your fault."

He cupped Rafa's cheek. "You know if I'd suspected anything, I would have stopped him. I'd never have let them take you. Never let you get hurt."

"I know." Rafa rubbed his smooth cheek against Shane's palm, his hands warm on Shane's back as he inched closer. "I told them it wasn't you. I was dying not being able to see you. Can we text? Or I could call you from Ash's phone if you give me your number. That way it won't be so bad waiting to see you again."

"Raf…we can't do that. You know I can't." Shane dropped his hands and stepped back, keeping Rafa at bay with a hand on his chest. "It's not possible."

"We'll find a way!" Rafa glanced at the closed door and lowered his voice. "I need to see you. Need to be with you."

Shane dropped his hand, because the longer he touched him, the harder this was. "You're young, and—"

"Don't! Don't use that bullshit excuse." His eyes flashed. "I may be younger than you, but I know what I want. I know what I feel. Don't dismiss me like I'm a dumb kid."

"You're right. But you'll feel it again. Right now it's new and exciting, and forbidden. But that will fade. You're just starting out. You're going to Australia, right?" A selfish part of him wanted Rafa to say no, even though it wouldn't change anything. He could never stay in the Service and date a former protectee.

So quit the damn job.

Shane gave his head a mental shake, shocked at the thought. He'd worked almost seventeen years as an agent. He'd get his pension after twenty-five. This was his career. His *life*.

Wasn't it?

"But even if I go to Australia, we could still… There's Skype and phones, and all that stuff."

"You have the whole world to explore. There are so many

experiences waiting. Even if we could, you don't want to be tied down to an old man."

Rafa's nostrils flared. "You're not old. So, you think I should go fuck a bunch of other guys? That I won't want you anymore? That this is just…what? A crush?"

Shane forced the lie out. "Yes."

"You're wrong. You're so wrong."

"Even if we were just two people who were free to be together, I'm too old for you. We both know it."

Rafa shook his head. "Bullshit. I don't accept that."

He'd never heard Rafa so forceful, and it sent fire through Shane's blood. God, he wanted to throw him against the door and rut together. But Shane forced himself to say what needed to be said. "I can't see you again. It doesn't matter how much I want to. I was wrong to cross the line. You know that."

"But…" Rafa's shoulders sagged.

"I'm putting in for a transfer," Shane said quietly.

"You're leaving?" Rafa's eyes shone.

"It's for the best. It would only make it harder if I stayed in DC."

"In January I'll be out of here. No one will be watching me anymore."

"If they ever found out what happened while you were my protectee…"

Rafa jammed his hands in his pockets. "Yeah. I know. I just wish…" His Adam's apple bobbed. "But I guess if wishes were horses we'd all have a horse, or whatever."

Shane smiled softly. "Yeah, something like that."

Rafa breathed in and out for a few moments. His voice was barely a whisper. "Where will you go?"

"I'm thinking the Santa Ana field office. It's in Orange County, where I grew up. It's time I went home for a little while. Thanks to you, I've been thinking about it more and more. When my parents died—" He inhaled sharply, forcing himself to keep going. "When they died, I didn't want to ever think about home again. Not surfing, or beaches—none of it. Because then I'd think about them, and that I wasn't there to save them."

"You can't save everyone," Rafa said quietly. He took Shane's hand. "I know you think you should because of what you do, but there was nothing you could do."

Shane gripped his fingers, wanting so much to pull him close again. "Logically, I know you're right. But I still need to work on accepting it." He tried to smile. "Need to wade through my bullshit."

"So it's all decided."

It was so tempting to let Rafa talk him out of it, but Shane nodded. "Transferring is usually a bitch, but after what happened, I think they'll be accommodating. I just need to get away from DC. It'll be good for me to go back. Get my head on straight. Figure out my priorities." *Try to forget about you.*

Rafa stared at their feet. "I don't want you to go, but I understand why you have to. I guess it's easy for me to say that we'd be able to work something out. It's not my career on the line." He met Shane's gaze with big brown eyes, his dark eyelashes glittering with unshed tears. "But I hate it."

Giving in and tugging him close, Shane wrapped Rafa in his arms one last time. "Me too," he whispered. He kissed the side of Rafa's head. "You'd better check that sauce. I'm glad your mother's coming around. You're going to do just fine."

But Rafa ignored Shane's words, kissing him fiercely. The aching pressure in Shane's chest threatened to explode as he kissed him back, wishing they were in the dark of the cave again, where the rest of the world had seemed so far away. He breathed Rafa in, their bodies driving together and wanting more. Needing more as they gasped and gripped each other.

With every ounce of self-control he had left, Shane ripped

himself away. At the door he turned back a last time. Rafa stood in the middle of the little kitchen, his chest rising and falling as red sauce simmered on the stove behind him.

Shane cleared his throat. "Remember that with some waves...you can't catch them. Better to dive through and wait for another one. There's always another one."

Rafa stood forlorn, hugging himself.

With a shuddering breath, Shane managed to walk away, nodding to people downstairs who said things to him he didn't hear over the rush of blood in his ears. He didn't stop for anyone as he hurried to the parking lot. Just kept moving until he sped down Pennsylvania Avenue, leaving his heart behind.

Chapter Twenty-One

Five months, seventeen days, and twenty hours later

RAFA INHALED DEEPLY, the salt in the air complementing the lingering flavor of watermelon and pistachio on his tongue. The January sun was surprisingly strong over a quiet Brooks Street Beach late on this Saturday morning, and the four-foot waves carried loyal riders clad in black wetsuits. Rafa watched them paddle out and wait for their turns, popping up gracefully on their boards as the waves broke.

He'd forgotten his sunglasses on Adriana's coffee table, and Rafa held his hand over his eyes as he watched Shane ride a wave into the shore. This was the third one he'd caught since Rafa had arrived, and Rafa could have happily stood on the sand watching for hours with his sneakers off and duffel at his feet, the sand gritty between his toes. Just seeing Shane again was enough for the moment.

But with his board under his arm, now Shane picked over some rocks at the shore and headed across the sand. Not many people were on the beach. Lightheaded and tingling, Rafa was about to call out when Shane jolted to a stop, staring at him.

At a distance, Rafa couldn't quite make out his expression, and his mouth went dry. Would Shane even want to see him? He'd probably moved on, and this would be awkward and weird and a huge mistake. His heart went into triple time as Shane changed course straight for him, walking steadily with his board still attached to his ankle by its leash. Too late to run away now, and Rafa waited.

When they were a few feet apart, Shane thrust his board into the sand on its end and peeled open the Velcro leash around his ankle. His dark hair was still shorn close to his glistening head, and water dripped off the end of his nose. Rafa could see he hadn't shaved for a few days, and thought of how Shane's stubble had felt on his skin that night in the cave.

He's actually standing here. This is actually happening. This is real life.

"Come to catch a wave?" Shane asked nonchalantly, the low rumble of his voice so wonderful to hear.

"I...uh..." They stood there staring at each other, and suddenly all of his carefully rehearsed words evaporated in Rafa's mind. He thrust out the slushee. "I stopped by Maddie's for you. It really is good. I hope you don't mind that I had a sip."

"Course not." Shane took the cup, their fingers brushing. He had a sip through the straw. "Thanks."

Stay cool. Don't spaz. "You looked great out there. Glad you're surfing again."

"Thanks. It's been really good getting back into it. I don't know how I managed so many years without it now." He took another sip. "I saw a bit of Livingston's inauguration the other day. You're officially done, huh?"

"Yeah." Grinning, Rafa glanced around. "No detail. It's weird, just walking around by myself. But awesome too. So far people don't seem to recognize me much."

Shane's lips lifted. "It's the hair." He dropped his gaze to Rafa's jeans and purple Ripcurl hoodie. "And the clothes. Looks good on you. You'll fit right in with the other surf rats."

Rafa ran a hand through the loose curls that spilled over his forehead. "Thanks."

"Saw the interview you did with your parents a few months ago. You were really good."

He shrugged, blushing a little. "Figured I owed it to those little gay kids out there. And I realized it was easier to just say what I wanted to say so people could deal with it and move on. That way there wasn't the whole is he or isn't he thing."

"Makes sense." Shane took another sip of the slushee. "So. You just stopping by on your way down under?" he asked casually.

Rafa's palms were sweaty, and he jammed his hands in his pockets. "No. I mean, yes. I am on my way to Australia."

"Packing light." Shane nodded to the duffel.

"The rest of my stuff's at Adriana's in LA. I just…I needed to find you. I have to say this, and I don't expect anything from you." He'd planned it all so perfectly, but now his mind was buzzing, and Shane was right there in front of him, waiting and watching with an unreadable expression.

Fuck it.

"I wanted to say that I'm totally in love with you. And that might be crazy, and I know I'm young and that you're older than me and you have a life here, but I want to be with you." The words tumbled out, and Rafa figured he might as well say them all now that he'd started.

He forced himself to keep Shane's gaze and went on. "What I really want more than anything is for you to come to Australia with me. And I'm sure that's not possible with your job, and you probably wouldn't even want to anyway, but I can't stop thinking about you. Missing you. And you're probably so over me anyway, and—"

Shane's wet lips were salty, and his scruff rasped against Rafa's skin as he held Rafa's face and kissed him deeply, the slushee abandoned and splattered at their feet. Rafa opened his mouth under Shane's, moaning into the kiss as he yanked Shane against him, not caring if he got wet. His fingers dug into the thick neoprene wetsuit as their tongues met.

Breathing hard when he broke away, Shane pressed his fore-head against Rafa's. "Are you sure?"

"About which part? Yes. All of it. Are you…? Do you…?" Rafa could hardly breathe.

With a smile that creased his cheeks and lit up his face, Shane leaned back to look at him. "I love you, Rafa. I knew it then, but when I moved back here, it became clearer and clearer. I want to be with you. In Australia, or Timbuktu. I don't care. Anywhere. I want to surf with you and eat everything you want to cook. Want to wake up with you every morning."

"You do?" Rafa thought he might have floated away, rocketing right up into the California sky if not for Shane's hands on his shoulders. He wanted to laugh and shout and sing. "But what about your job?"

"My last day was a week ago. Working in the field office here was fine. Pretty much nine to five, investigating local counterfeit-ing. All the treasury department stuff the Secret Service does that no one really pays attention to. I was going to finish my twenty-five years and get my pension, and then do private contracting. Security consulting; that kind of thing. But I'd have to wait six and a half years, and I decided that's too damn long. Not when I could have that time with you."

Rafa was pretty sure his heart was going to explode in a spray of red goo. "You want that? You really want me?"

Shane cupped his cheek with one hand, his blue eyes steely. "Yes. I want you, Rafa. Maybe we're nuts, but I've been miserable without you." He shook his head, laughing softly. "I quit my job and lined up a security contract with a firm in Sydney. I was going to find you down there. Go knock on the door of the Cordon Bleu if I had to. Hope you still wanted me." He exhaled. "I was afraid you wouldn't, but I had to try. My friend said I was sleepwalking through my life, and he was right. You woke me up.

I'm all in, Rafa."

Grinning, Rafa hugged him tightly, burying his face against Shane's damp neck. *He wants me. We love each other. It's real.*

"I'm getting you wet," Shane murmured.

Rafa pulled back. "Then you'd better get me out of these clothes. Your house isn't far, right?"

"How did you know? I'm subletting from an old friend."

"I got your address from Brent Harris. Told him I really wanted to thank you again in person for saving my life." His happiness dimmed. "I heard Alan pleaded guilty."

Shane nodded. "Let's talk about that later." He smiled softly. "We've got time, right?"

Excitement rippled through Rafa, and he licked his lips. "As long as we want. No one to tell us we can't."

Shane's gaze flicked between Rafa's mouth and his eyes. "Then what are we waiting for?"

"WOW. THIS HOUSE is great. Right on the water." Rafa kicked off his sandy sneakers and walked through the bungalow's little living room to the sliding glass doors leading to a deck on the beach.

He peered at the waves glittering in the sunshine. It hadn't been a long drive from Brooks Street, and Shane had just thrown down a towel on the seat and driven the truck in his wetsuit. Rafa had asked meaningless questions about the area to fill the thick silence and calm his nerves.

"It must be nice to—" As Rafa turned, the words shriveled and died in his dry throat. Shane had unzipped the wetsuit, and now he peeled it down his arms, then his legs, and then he was naked.

And he was *amazing.*

Dark hair grew on his chest—not too much, not too little. The perfect manly amount, at least in Rafa's estimation. Then there was the hair below his belly button, which led down to a trimmed thatch at his groin. His cock was thick and long as it swelled beneath Rafa's avid gaze. Shane's balls were big and heavy, hanging down between his powerful thighs, which were dusted with dark hair.

Rafa opened his mouth to say something—what did people usually say at moments like these? Something seductive or sexy? He should say something like that. "Uh…"

A smile tugged on Shane's lips, and he held out his hand. "I've got sand in small places. Let's have a rinse and warm up."

Crossing to where Shane stood at the juncture to the hallway, Rafa nodded, not trusting his voice. Gripping Shane's hand, he followed to the bathroom. While Shane fiddled with the taps in the glass shower stall—providing an incredible view of his firm ass—Rafa took a deep breath and yanked off his damp clothes.

He wished it was dark again, but he forced his arms to his sides so he didn't look like a nervous kid. His cock was already rock hard without even a tug.

Shane stepped under the water, and Rafa followed, squeezing in and pulling the door shut. The stall was fairly big, and Rafa had an excellent view of Shane's body as Shane lathered a bar of green soap and rubbed himself with soapy hands. Then Shane was washing him. They were actually naked together, and Shane was touching him all over. Rafa hoped he could get through the shower without jizzing.

Running his soapy hands over Rafa's back, Shane pulled him close. "We don't have to do anything. We can go slowly," he murmured.

Rafa rubbed against him, quivering as their cocks met. "I don't want to go slow. I want to do it all." He eyed the scar on Shane's neck and ran his finger over it, making Shane shudder.

Shane smiled slyly. "We will, don't worry. But I can hear you thinking. Worrying."

"I'm not worrying about that." Rafa bit back a gasp as Shane ran his slick hands down over his ass.

"Then what?" Shane frowned. "I don't want you worrying about anything."

"It's just that…" Rafa tried to find the words. "You're…*you*, and I'm like…"

His frown deepened. "Like what?"

"Um, like this. You know." Rafa shrugged and tried to laugh. "It was easier in the dark."

"Uh-uh." Shane shook his head while he caressed Rafa's body, steam rising around them. "I want to see you. See how beautiful you are."

Rafa scoffed. "I'm not—"

His words were swallowed as Shane kissed him deeply, licking into his mouth and pressing him back against the cool tile. When Shane leaned away, his blue eyes were dark. "I want to see how your lips get swollen and wet." He rubbed his thumb over them, and then down to Rafa's chest. "Want to see how your skin flushes when I touch you. When I look at you."

He dragged his thumb over a nipple, and Rafa gasped. "Want to see how hard your nipples get when I tease them." He bent his head and latched on to Rafa's throat, sucking forcefully, gripping Rafa's hips with his hands. Breaking the suction, he bit the tender skin. "I want to see my marks on you."

Panting, Rafa was on fire. "Well, when you put it like that."

Shane laughed, a throaty, *glorious* sound. But then his smile faded. "But I don't want to go too fast for you. Tell me if I am, okay?" He leaned in and kissed Rafa softly, running his hands down Rafa's back. "Because I'd be happy just holding you. You feel so good. Could do this all day."

Leaning into his touch, Rafa shuddered with pleasure, stroking Shane's broad back. "I know. But it's not too fast. I want it. Want you." Rafa kissed him again, and Shane's tongue met his, teasing and tasting. Rafa's head spun, and he was surprised he was still able to stand. But he remembered he had something important to say, so he broke away.

"I brought condoms and lube, but I really want… I don't know if you've been tested lately? I've only ever done things with you. I got tested just in case. You know, so it's official, and everything's negative."

"You didn't hook up with anyone at school after you came out?" Shane sounded pleasantly surprised.

"Uh-uh. I've only been with you." He laughed awkwardly. "I know—it's lame."

Shane shook his head, his gaze intense as he took Rafa's head in his hands and kissed him hard. "Not lame," he mumbled against Rafa's mouth.

Rafa found himself rambling as Shane's hands roamed his body. "I went out to some bars and parties and stuff. I was, like, the celebrity gay of Charlottesville. Guys hit on me, but it was just…none of them were you. I wanted you. But I'm sure you've been with plenty of guys since then, right? Which is fine. Of course it's fine. And if you aren't sure, then we'll totally use condoms. Safety first and all that stuff. Important stuff."

Shane circled his fingers lightly on Rafa's hips. "But if I've got a clean bill of health, you want me to fuck you raw?"

His breath catching, Rafa jerked his head in a nod, his cock swelling even more to hear it.

"I've been tested, and I haven't been with anyone since you."

Rafa's heart skipped. "You haven't? Why not?"

Shane pressed against him, his hard cock nudging Rafa's. "Because they weren't you." He leaned in, his breath hot on Rafa's ear. "Because I wanted to make sure it would be safe. Because I want to come inside you."

A shiver raced down Rafa's spine, and his balls tingled. "Oh God."

"You still want that?" Shane slipped his soapy fingers into the crease of Rafa's ass. "You want me to fill up your tight hole with my cum?"

"Yes, yes, yes," Rafa panted. "Now. Please. Do it, Shane."

Shane circled a finger around Rafa's hole. "Not yet. First I want to suck you." Trailing his lips down Rafa's chest and belly, he sank to his knees and nuzzled Rafa's cock.

Seeing his straining dick slap against Shane's cheek was almost enough to send him over. Shane teased Rafa's ass with his fingers, and took Rafa's cock with his free hand, rubbing his thumb over the tip and pulling down the foreskin. Looking up at him, Shane licked the shaft, his tongue teasing the ridge along the bottom.

When he took Rafa into his mouth, swallowing the whole head, Rafa's thighs trembled. "Fuck, Shane. I can't…"

With a wet *pop*, Shane let him go. "It's okay. Don't hold back. I want you to come for me." Then he swallowed Rafa almost to the root, his cheeks hollowing and his hand sliding down to play with Rafa's balls.

The hot suction was even better than Rafa had imagined a blowjob would be. So wet and tight and *good*, and he ran a hand over Shane's head, needing to touch him as he came already, spurting into his mouth with bursts of pleasure so intense he smacked his head on the tile wall as he cried out.

Shane's mouth was gentle on him as he milked out another few drops, and Rafa's legs shook. "Oh, fuck me."

Pushing to his feet, Shane grinned. "That's the plan, Raf."

They dried off quickly, both breathing hard and stealing kisses as they went, making their way into the bedroom. Big windows faced the water, and the sheets were warm beneath Rafa as he stretched out. Shane tossed the duvet on the floor and stood at the foot of the bed watching him. His cock was red and straining, and he stroked it once, twice.

"Jesus, you're beautiful. And before you say something self-deprecating, just listen to me. You're beautiful and I love you. I want you." He stroked his cock again. "See how hard you make me?"

Lips parted, Rafa nodded. He pushed himself up and flipped over onto his hands and knees. Lowering his head, he turned his face on the mattress and reached back for his ass cheeks. His pulse thundered as he waited.

Shane took an audible breath. "Look how pretty you are. Spreading yourself open for me like I said I wanted. You want me to lick you?" The mattress dipped with his weight. "You want my mouth? My tongue?" He ran his fingers up and down Rafa's spine.

"Yes." Rafa's voice was hoarse. He looked out to the distant waves beyond the windows, his cheek pressed against the warm sheets and his ass up in the air. He dug his fingers into his flesh as he spread himself open, and he'd never felt so exposed. Twisting his neck to look back, he could see Shane kneeling behind him, and he wished Shane would say something else as the seconds ticked by. Maybe he didn't want to? Was this the wrong thing to do?

"I can hear you thinking again," Shane said. His breath ghosted over Rafa's hole, and he covered Rafa's hands with his own, easing them down to the mattress. "I've got you."

Then Shane spread Rafa again, and when he licked Rafa's crease from his sac to the dimples in his ass, Rafa made a noise that was part shout, scream, and moan. Shane's scruff rasped against Rafa's inner thighs and his ass, and the contrast between the wet of his tongue and dry of his stubble sent sparks shooting through Rafa to the tips of his toes. He grasped at the sheets as Shane licked around his opening.

With Rafa whimpering and shaking, Shane leaned back and spit on his hole. For some reason spitting seemed so *dirty*, and Rafa's dick twitched as Shane did it again and he felt the wet splat of saliva and heard the sound. Then Shane licked into him, burying his face in Rafa's ass, spreading him with strong hands. Rafa's mouth was open as he groaned, rubbing his cheek against the sheets and closing his eyes.

When Shane backed off, Rafa couldn't hold in a whine. Shane chuckled softly. "Don't worry. There's more. You want more?"

"Yes. Everything. All of it. All of you. Now."

"Patience, Grasshopper."

With gentle hands, Shane urged him over onto his back, sliding a pillow beneath Rafa's hips and spreading his legs wide, his hands on Rafa's knees. Splayed out like that, maybe Rafa should have felt silly, but as he watched Shane's hungry gaze travel over him, he felt *good*. Powerful. Wanted. And not just for sex. Wanted for so much more. Shane had planned to move to the other side of the world for the *chance* to be with him.

"You really want me." It wasn't a question this time.

Shane's gaze snapped up to meet Rafa's, and he stroked his palms over Rafa's parted thighs. "More than I've ever wanted anyone."

He reached over to the bedside table and fished out a bottle of lube from the drawer. He squeezed a dollop onto his fingers and pushed the tip of one into Rafa's ass. "Want to see your face while I stretch you." He pushed more. "Want to see you open for me." He thrust with that finger, and Rafa gasped. "How does it feel?"

"Hot. Like...burning. Hurts a little. But don't stop."

"It'll get better." Shane caressed Rafa's hair with his free hand. "I'll make it good for you, baby. Just relax for me, okay?" He worked in a second finger and groaned. "You're so tight."

"Is it going to fit?" The question slipped out before Rafa could stop it, and his cheeks burned.

But Shane only smiled tenderly, his fingers still exploring Rafa's ass. "It'll fit. And when you're used to it, I'm going to pound your ass so hard. Going to make you feel it for days. You want that?"

"Yes. God, yes." Rafa's mouth was so dry, and he swallowed convulsively. "Want that now." He squeezed around Shane's fingers, and Shane groaned.

"You have no idea what you do to me." He leaned over, his fingers still in Rafa's ass, and kissed him messily.

Rafa could taste a musky bit of himself lingering on Shane's tongue, and it made his balls prickle. "Please, Shane. I'm ready."

Shane nuzzled his cheek. "Don't want to hurt you." He edged in a third finger, and Rafa tensed. Even though he'd done it to himself, it wasn't the same as having someone else do it. Shane was going deeper, and the burn merged with pain. "Breathe," Shane urged. "I've got you. Won't give you more than you can take."

Inhaling through his nose, Rafa exhaled, concentrating on relaxing his bunched muscles. "Want your cock, Shane. I've waited so long."

"Oh, don't worry." Smiling, Shane kissed his lips lightly. "You're going to get it." He slid his fingers out, and squeezed more lube into his hand.

Rafa could barely blink, his eyes glued to Shane's cock as Shane slicked it up, sitting back on his heels between Rafa's spread legs.

It was actually happening.

Nervous anticipation ricocheted through Rafa. He'd wanted this for years—since he was old enough to know it was possible. That it would be with a man he loved so damn much made it more perfect than he'd dared imagine. His breath caught, and his eyes burned.

Wiping his hand on one of the white towels they'd brought from the bathroom, Shane froze and peered at him closely. Leaning over him, he brushed his knuckles over Rafa's cheek. "What is it?"

"I'm happy. Sorry. Apparently I get choked up when I'm

really, really happy."

Shane's cheeks creased as he smiled. "Don't ever be sorry for that." He kissed Rafa's nose, and then pushed Rafa's knees up and back, hooking his legs over his shoulders. "Breathe for me."

As the blunt head of Shane's slick cock breached him, the burn was intense—way more than he'd ever felt from fingers. Rafa bit his lip, trying to breathe through the sensation of being torn in half. He clutched Shane's arms, the muscles flexing under his fingers. He squeezed his eyes shut.

"Look at me."

Rafa did as he was told, and met Shane's steady gaze.

Shane pushed in, sweat gathering on his brow. "That's it, baby. Breathe. Relax."

Maybe he shouldn't have, but Rafa loved it when Shane called him that. He felt warm and safe and cared for. He took a gulping gasp of air, and as he blew it out, Shane slid farther into him.

Inch by inch, it got easier, and Rafa's softening cock started to fill again. Looking down, he realized Shane was all the way inside him, his hips against Rafa's ass. Shane's cock was like an iron brand searing him, and Rafa tipped his head back on the pillow, his mouth open.

Shane pulled up Rafa's head, fingers tight in his hair. As he kissed him, he began rocking back and forth with little pushes of his hips. "So tight, Raf. You feel so good."

"Do I?" Rafa asked before he could stop himself.

Shane's thrusts slowed and he caressed Rafa's cheek. "Amazing. Even better than I imagined. You doing okay?"

Rafa nodded vigorously. "Don't stop."

"Oh, I won't. Gonna fill you until it's dripping out." Shane thrust a little harder, groaning. "Gonna make you mine."

"No one else's. Not ever." Rafa grabbed Shane's head and kissed him hard, their teeth clashing. "Fill me up." It still hurt, and he knew Shane was holding back, but as Shane wrapped a hand around Rafa's cock, it all became pure pleasure, white hot as Shane jerked him and fucked his ass.

Rafa's feet were in the air over Shane's broad shoulders, and he loved the feeling of Shane on top of him, bending him in half until he could hardly breathe, their damp skin sticking and rubbing together. *Taking* him, but giving so much at the same time.

Shane thrust against a spot that had to be Rafa's swollen prostate, and Rafa cried out as his cock jerked. "There," he moaned. "Please."

Shane brushed against it again, stroking Rafa's shaft faster. "That's it. Wanna see you come with my cock raw inside you. Never fucked anyone like this before. Only you."

His balls tightened, and the orgasm rushed through Rafa, breaking over him like a wave on a reef. He cried out and sprayed his chest, Shane milking him. Shane panted, grunting as he planted his hands on the mattress beside Rafa's head, his hips slapping against Rafa's ass as he fucked him.

"Come on," Rafa muttered, running his hands up to Shane's shoulders and over his back. "Need it. Need it all. I love you so much."

Lips parted, Shane came, jerking and shuddering and spilling deep inside Rafa, wet and hot. Rafa managed to get his rubbery legs down around Shane's back, and he held him there as Shane relaxed on top of him, his mouth open on Rafa's collarbone, breath puffing in short blasts as his cock softened.

"Fuck," Shane mumbled. "Rafa." He pressed kisses to Rafa's skin. "You're amazing."

His face heated with a fresh blush. "You did all the work."

Lifting his head, Shane smiled so tenderly as he brushed back Rafa's curls. "What am I going to have to do to get you to take a compliment?"

"I don't know. I guess you could fuck me again and see what

happens."

Groaning, Shane pushed himself up, gently easing his cock out of Rafa and reaching for the towel. "I'm an old man, remember? Forty now. Gotta give me a few minutes here at least."

Laughing, Rafa lifted his leg and let Shane clean him. It was strange how *not* embarrassed he felt as Shane caressed his hole with his fingers after wiping down his chest, inner thighs, and ass.

"Doesn't hurt too much?"

He shook his head. "I can feel it, but...I like it. Always wondered what it would feel like to be really fucked."

"And?" Shane raised an eyebrow, rubbing his palm over Rafa's ass.

Rafa grinned. "Feels spectacular."

Shane stretched out beside him. The sun beamed through the windows, and Rafa sighed contentedly as Shane propped his head on his hand and traced his fingers over Rafa's belly. To just be together without having to look over their shoulders was wonderful. Rafa leaned up and kissed him lightly just because he could.

A smile played on Shane's lips. "I can't believe you're really here."

"Me either." Rafa shook his head. "All these months I wished I could at least call you. But I didn't want to screw up things for you at work." He brushed his hand over the fuzz of Shane's close-cropped hair. "Are you really ready to move halfway around the world with me?"

Shane didn't hesitate. "Yes."

"You haven't liked being back here?"

"It's not that." He was quiet for a few moments as he swirled his finger around Rafa's bellybutton. "Coming back was something I had to do. Reconnect with old friends. Surf again. Just...be home, even if it's not home anymore." He went silent, and his voice was barely more than a whisper when he spoke again. "It took me a month to get up the nerve to go back to my old street. Drive up to the house. But of course it's not our house at all anymore. It has the same number—eighty-three—but the fire destroyed ours. It was just a pile of black wreckage. The newly built house there now doesn't look a thing like the place I knew." He drew circles on Rafa's skin. "I think I had to come back so it wouldn't have power over me anymore. I was so afraid of this place for a long time. But now I can move on. Find a new home."

"What does it look like now? Where your old house was?"

"Nice. Lived in. There's a split-level there. Pretty flowers at the top of the lawn. A basketball net nailed above the garage, and hopscotch drawn on the sidewalk with chalk. They would like that. My parents." He leaned over and kissed Rafa's cheek. "They'd like you too."

"I wish I could have met them." Rafa caressed Shane's chest, still marveling that he could do this now. He could lie here in bed with Shane and touch him and talk to him, and it was allowed. "You'll just have to tell me all about them."

"I'd like that."

Other thoughts inevitably returned, and Rafa sighed. There was no good time to bring it up, and he might as well get it over with. "I'm sorry about Alan. I know it must have been really hard for you. He was your friend."

Shane's jaw tightened, and he watched his fingers on Rafa's belly. "Yeah. But you're the one who got hurt because of him. Could have gotten killed. Worse." He flattened his palm on Rafa's stomach as if he could hold him there and keep him from harm.

"I'm fine. The shrink says I have a remarkable capacity to look at the glass as half full. In a weird way, I'm glad it happened. Or else I might not be here right now. *We* might not be here together."

"Maybe not." Shane sighed. "I guess good things can come out of bad. I just wish it could have been different."

"Me too." He hesitated. "Have you talked to his wife?"

"Jules is doing as well as she can, I guess. Her husband's going away for life, and it's going to take time to come to terms with what he did. But she's got enough money to take Dylan to Sweden to try the new treatment. That's something, at least."

"That's great. How did she get it? Um, I assume not from the kidnappers."

"No, the FBI tracked down that cash fast." Shane shrugged, caressing Rafa's belly and running his fingers through the trail of hair there. "I guess she raised enough money."

"How did you afford it?"

Shane's gaze shot up. "Why do you think it was me?"

Rolling his eyes, Rafa snagged Shane's hand and lifted it to kiss his palm. "You don't fool me."

A little smile tugged up Shane's lips for a moment before sadness settled over him again. "I had money from the insurance settlement for the fire. I hardly touched it. Didn't feel right. I've never been a big spender. I have plenty of savings, and now I can make good money as a consultant. Set my own hours. I don't need a million from the insurance company. And no matter how wrong Alan was, Dylan deserves a chance." His brows drew together. "Does that bother you? After what Alan did? That I helped his family?"

"Of course not." Rafa toyed with Shane's fingers. "They aren't to blame. And he was desperate. Suicidal. Maybe I'm a sucker, but I forgive him."

Shane leaned over and kissed him softly. "What you are is a good man." He snuggled closer, sliding down to lay his head on Rafa's chest, their legs tangling.

Smiling to himself, Rafa ran his palm over Shane's head. The afternoon sun warmed the room, and his eyes drooped.

He wasn't sure how long it had been when Shane said, "We need to talk to your parents."

Oh, right. *That.* His parents were definitely going to object.

Rafa pushed away the swell of anxiety. "They'll have to deal with it. They dealt with me being gay. They can handle this too. I'm an adult. I get to make my own decisions." He grinned to himself. "Besides, I'll have my own bodyguard. How can they argue with that?"

Shane flipped over and crawled up Rafa's body, covering him and returning his grin. "Well, I'm out of the protection business, but I guess I can make an exception. What's your codename going to be?"

"I dunno." A giddy whirl of happiness bubbled through him. "I always thought it should have been Virgin, but I guess that's out."

Laughing, Shane kissed him. "We'll just have to stick with Valor."

"No." Rafa snorted. "That never fit."

Shane regarded him seriously. "It did."

And as Shane kissed him again, Rafa could actually believe it.

Chapter Twenty-Two

BLINKING AS HE woke, Shane stretched his legs, his feet rubbing against warm flesh. As he focused on Rafa flopped on his back beside him, lips parted as he enjoyed a well-earned nap, warmth rushed through him. Rafa's curls stuck up and tumbled over his forehead, and Shane propped his head on his hand, barely resisting the urge to reach out and touch.

That Rafa was actually here—in Shane's bed, no less—was more than he'd dreamed possible. In the mid-afternoon sunlight, he watched Rafa's chest rise and fall. There were flakes of dried semen caught in the sparse hair on his pecs, and Shane smiled to himself as he wondered how many more times he could get Rafa to come before nightfall.

Part of him wanted to take a picture to send to Darnell, just so he could share how beautiful his…what was Rafa now? Boyfriend? Lover? Partner? He didn't care what they called it, but he wanted to share how gorgeous and perfect his Rafa was.

Of course that was a bad idea, although he trusted D explicitly. Nothing taken on a phone was private, and they'd have to be cautious to never provide the tabloids ammunition. It would be bad enough dealing with Rafa's parents without leaked post-coital pictures of their son.

The reminder of the Castillos dulled the edges of his happy glow. Rafa would obviously have to tell them, and Shane didn't want to keep secrets. But he had to admit he didn't relish talking to Rafa's parents about their relationship. In their shoes, he'd wonder what the hell was wrong with a forty-year-old man who took up with someone almost half his age.

As he watched Rafa murmur and lick his lips in his sleep, Shane wished he could put it into words. He'd told himself Rafa had surely moved on. He'd seen a few pictures of Rafa out at a bar at school with young guys panting after him. The tabloids had breathlessly speculated about who he was dating now that he and Ashleigh had come out.

It had been torture wondering who Rafa was seeing. Shane had hated the thought of Rafa with anyone else, even though he wanted him to be happy. To know now that he was still the only man to ever touch him filled Shane with a primal pride. Maybe it was something lingering from the cavemen days, but he couldn't deny the surge of possessive satisfaction it gave him.

As he leaned down to wake Rafa with kisses, a flash of movement outside the window caught his eye. He slipped out of bed and hurried to the glass on bare feet, cursing himself for not taking the time earlier to shut the blinds. He'd been sloppy at the beach as well, too wrapped up in Rafa actually being there to pay the attention he should have.

A man disappeared around the side of the house from the beach that ran up to the deck to the right of the bedroom. In that split second, Shane was calculating how long it would take to reach his lock box under the bed and load his gun. Then the man reappeared, carrying a children's ball.

"Daddy! Throw!" A little boy commanded, racing into view around the porch.

Through the glass, Shane could hear the man's muffled response. "Okay, but be careful! We have to stay away from the houses." He tossed the ball back toward the wide strip of public sand in the distance.

Exhaling, Shane tried to let go of the tension. He lowered the blinds and shut them facing up, so sunlight could still get in. Behind him, Rafa murmured and moaned, tangling his feet in the sheets as he kicked restlessly. Then he woke suddenly.

"Shane?" Groggily, he blinked.

Crawling back into bed, Shane let himself smile as he kissed Rafa. "Hey, sleepyhead. Bad dream?"

"No. Just weird. Not bad. Not like…" He shook his head and pulled Shane closer. "Never mind."

Shane slipped in beside him and pulled the sheets over them.

"No, no." Rafa kicked the cotton away with a smile. "I want to look at you." He turned on his side and ran his hand over Shane's chest, digging in lightly with his blunt nails. "I love that I get to do this now."

"Me too." He smoothed his hand over Rafa's side and hip, wanting to touch, touch, touch. "So, not like what? You were going to say something about your dreams."

Rafa lowered his gaze. "It's no big deal. I have nightmares sometimes. The therapist said it's normal."

"Nightmares about what?" Shane kept his voice even as the flickers of anger flared to life. He could very well guess.

The puff of Rafa's long exhale was warm. "The box."

Shane was torn by the dueling urges to hold Rafa against his chest or punch the wall. Calming himself, he kissed Rafa's forehead and cheeks. "I'm so sorry."

Rafa looked at him then, his gaze narrowed. "Don't be sorry. I mean, you can be sorry it happened and that it was scary and is hard to deal with sometimes, but don't be sorry like it was your fault." He touched Shane's cheek. "Okay? Because it wasn't your fault. It was Alan's fault, and it was the fucking terrorists' fault. You saved me. If I have a nightmare about it, when I wake I remember you lifting me up, and the sound of your voice, and the feel of you kissing me, and knowing that I'd be okay because you were there."

Shane swallowed hard. "But if I'd—"

Rafa gripped the back of Shane's head, his gaze unflinching. "No buts. You did everything you could. They came so close to killing you, Shane. Like, it couldn't have been closer." He ran his fingers over the side of Shane's head where the bullet had carved a faint scar. "None of it was your fault. Stop blaming yourself for things you can't control."

"I'll try. It's…" Shane shrugged a little. "It's hard. I want to protect you. The people I care about. I hated not being with you these past months. Trusting other agents to keep you safe. After Al, I kept wondering what if."

"But here I am. I worry about you too, you know." Rafa smiled. "We'll keep each other safe, okay?"

"Okay." Shane rubbed their noses together.

Still smiling, Rafa bit his lip. "Were you really going to go to Australia for me?"

"Yep. Figured even if you told me to hit the road, I could get in some surfing." He kept his tone light, but even with Rafa in his bed, he ached at the thought of how it would have felt if Rafa hadn't wanted him.

"No way." Rafa grinned and kissed him softly. "I've had a million daydreams about that happening. But then I decided to go for it. Not wait around for you to sweep me off my feet."

"I'm glad you didn't."

"I can't believe you're really coming with me." He laughed, clearly giddy. "I've waited so long, and I feel like my life is finally starting." He reached up and pressed his finger to Shane's lips. "And before you say it, yes, I want it to be with you, and no, I don't care that you're older."

Busted. "How do you know what I was going to say?"

Rafa scoffed. "You think you're all stoic and unreadable, but I've got your number. So just let it go, okay? I'm right where I want to be."

But what about tomorrow? Or the next day? In a year, or five?

Shane forced the worry away. He felt like his life was finally starting too. Time for some optimism. "Okay."

Rafa's gaze raked over Shane's body, and he caressed idly, sending shivers down Shane's spine. Shane inched closer, nudging his thigh between Rafa's.

"So...do you ever...um..."

"What?" Shane traced around Rafa's nipple. "You can ask me anything."

"Do you ever... Does anyone ever fuck you?" Rafa's cheeks flushed.

"Once in a while. Do you want to?" Shane had never had a great time bottoming, but for Rafa he'd do anything.

"I don't know. Maybe?" He laughed nervously. "I've never really thought about it. I always fantasized about being fucked. Is that weird? I know being a bottom is, like..." He waved his hand, his face getting redder.

"Like what? Effeminate?" When Rafa nodded, Shane shook his head. "That's bullshit. Anyone who thinks that has their own issues to deal with, starting with misogyny."

"So you don't think...I don't know. Less of me or whatever? For wanting it?" He ducked his head.

Shane tipped up Rafa's chin. "Do you think less of me for wanting to fuck you?"

"Of course not."

"Then why would it be okay for me to want to fuck you, but not for you to want to get fucked?"

Laughing, Rafa shook his head. "I don't know. I guess I just...I want to make sure I'm doing everything right."

"Oh, you're doing it right. Trust me." Shane ran his fingertips across Rafa's nose, brushing his freckles, which stood out even more when he blushed. "Your ass is made for being fucked." He reached behind Rafa to tease his crease, and Rafa lifted his leg over Shane's hip. "Mmm. See? Comes naturally to you, doesn't it?" He circled Rafa's tender hole, careful not to push. "Did you like having a cock up your ass?"

Nodding breathlessly, Rafa bit his lip. "Have you really never done this before? Fucked raw, I mean."

He shook his head. "You're the first." *Last. Everything.* "You have no idea how many times I jerked off imagining this."

His eyes lighting up, Rafa sucked in a breath. "Can I see?"

Shane chuckled as heat tingled through him. "Want to see me touch myself?"

Even though he blushed furiously, Rafa kept his gaze on Shane's. "Yeah. I want that."

Shane disentangled himself so he could reach the lube on the side table. He bent up his left leg, giving himself some purchase while not blocking Rafa's view on his right side. Slicking his palm, Shane stroked his cock, which had been twitching to life for the past few minutes and now swelled in his hand. He groaned, and Rafa did too.

"Oh my God, I'm going to shoot in five seconds." Rafa tugged on his dick, which was indeed straining already.

"Don't touch yourself. I'm going to make you come after."

Nodding eagerly, Rafa pushed up and sat back on his heels, keeping his hands behind him. His cock bobbed, glistening, and Shane licked his lips. Rafa watched him avidly, his lips parting as Shane twisted his own nipples and thrust up into his hand.

Shane didn't think anyone had watched him jerk off since he was a kid messing around with the other boys down at the beach, and the way Rafa looked at him like he was the sexiest, most amazing thing he'd ever seen sent another surge of possessive energy through Shane.

He wanted to show Rafa everything. Teach him how good it could be, with no shame or hang-ups or other people's bullshit. Spreading his legs more, Shane reached down to tease his balls. "This is all for you, Rafa. No one else."

As Shane worked himself, breathing hard, Rafa watched. He was so beautiful, and Shane felt like the luckiest bastard in the whole damn world.

"Don't come yet," Rafa murmured breathlessly, his eyes locked on Shane's groin. "I want you inside me again."

Shane smiled to hear Rafa give an order of his own. "Yeah?

You know what you want?"

"Uh-huh." His Adam's apple bobbed and his cock leaked.

The urge to bury himself in Rafa any way he could was building and building, but Shane forced a deep breath. "I don't want to hurt you, baby. It's only been a couple hours, and—"

"I know what I want." Rafa scrambled onto his hands and knees. "Like this. Please. I've always... I want you to take me from behind."

With a groan, Shane pushed to his knees. They both moaned as he leaned over Rafa and licked down his spine. He spread Rafa's ass and blew a stream of air over his hole. It was red and would surely be sore tomorrow, but Rafa was pushing back desperately.

Shane took his time, using so much lube it was dripping down Rafa's thighs. Rafa panted and grunted, and when Shane eased inside him as gently as he could, Rafa cried out and pushed back.

"Fuck, Shane. It's so much better than..."

He thrust deeper. "What?"

"When I would use my fingers and pretend it was you."

Shane groaned as he pushed into Rafa's body. "Did imaginary me fuck your tight ass good?"

"Uh-huh. Don't stop."

Shane didn't think he could if he tried, especially as Rafa squeezed around him. It felt so good without rubber between them, and he was so grateful that they could have this.

"I'll never let anyone hurt you again." The words spilled out. "Never," Shane muttered, running his hands over Rafa's back.

"I know, Shane." Rafa looked back at him with trust shining in his eyes. "Me either."

When Shane eased out a few inches and pushed back in, Rafa cried out so prettily, dropping his head. Fuck, he was everything Shane had imagined, but so much more. So free and generous, moaning his pleasure as sweat slicked their skin.

His hips bumped against Rafa's ass, and he watched as he thrust in and out. Shit, he wasn't going to last long at this rate. Tangling his fingers in Rafa's curls, he leaned over and lifted his head for a messy kiss.

On the next stroke, he found Rafa's prostate, rubbing over the swollen nub as Rafa called out, grunting and panting. Shane dug his fingers into Rafa's hips, wanting to empty himself so badly, but not before Rafa came.

Reaching around, he jerked Rafa's rigid cock, whispering into his ear the words he knew he wanted to hear. "Going to fill you with my cum until it's leaking out of you. You want that?"

"Yes, yes, yes." It was like a prayer as Rafa spread his knees wider and dropped to his elbows, jerking as he spurted on the tangled sheets.

He clamped down on Shane's cock, and it was Shane's turn to come, his mouth open as he emptied himself. The sensation of spilling right into him made Shane's eyes roll back and his hips snap forward, rutting against Rafa's ass.

Gasping, Shane bent forward and braced his hands on the mattress. He pressed kisses to Rafa's back and shoulders, the salt of his sweat tangy on his lips. He was still inside him, and it was wet and messy and *wonderful*.

Curls tickling his nose, he kissed the back of Rafa's damp neck. "How was that?"

Rafa's voice was raw. "It was okay, I guess."

The laughter burst out of Shane, joy and warmth shaking his limbs as he collapsed. He pulled out and stretched his legs, lifting up enough for Rafa to stretch out too before covering his body again. Tenderly, Shane touched his fingertips to Rafa's sticky hole. "I'll try to do better next time."

"Mmm. Could you?" Rafa mumbled. "That would be great."

"So you're a wiseass in bed, huh?"

Rafa turned his head. "I guess sometimes I am." He frowned. "Is that weird?"

Pressing a kiss to his cheek, Shane murmured, "That's perfect."

Chapter Twenty-Three

A SHARP WIND danced off the waves, and Rafa shivered as he stepped off the back porch of Shane's little house. The sand was cold as the sun made its way above the horizon, but he still dug his toes into it as he walked toward the Pacific's edge, his jeans rolled up past his ankles. Stopping short of where the sand was wet, he turned on his phone, laughing at the extended text from Ashleigh.

I'm going to take your silence as a positive sign that you and your man are fucking ten ways to Sunday. When you're able to climb off his undoubtedly well-endowed dick for a few minutes, send me an update. Things in New York are pretty good. My job at the modeling agency is soul-sucking, but your sister-in-law remains the sweetest and took me to a party to network with fashion types. My parents barely acknowledged my birthday, but whatever. Oh, and there's one new thing. I met a girl at a bar last night who is a DaVinci and a half. Her name is Penelope. (For real.) Babe, I'm in love.

He quickly typed out a response.

It was actually eleven ways to Tuesday. We spent practically the whole day and night in bed. My ass is sore, and I've never been this happy in my entire life. He's coming with me to Australia. It's happening, Ash. Have fun with Penelope, and I'll tell you all the details later. Love you. Breaking it to Mom and Dad now. Light a candle for me.

Taking a deep breath, he hit their number in his contacts.

While it rang, he listened to the sleepy gulls cawing over the rolling surf.

"Rafa? Hello, darling. We got your text yesterday that you're safe and sound. Is the hotel all right? You're sure it's not in a bad area?" His mother's voice went distant. "Ramon! It's Rafa." She spoke into the phone again. "He's just coming in from shoveling the driveway."

Rafa smiled. "You're really back to the real world, huh?"

"Indeed. Well, we still have a detail outside, of course. One of them helps shovel. Lovely young man."

"How's the new house?"

"We're still settling in. It's…well, it'll be just fine. A good amount of property, so we can't see the road or the neighbors. It's nice to have privacy again. Well, it's mostly private. Oh, here's your father. Let me put you on speaker."

"There's no one else there? No agents inside?"

"No, they don't come in the house. They're set up in a granny cottage out back, and they patrol the property. There are cameras on the perimeter as well, of course. But most of the time I forget the agents are there." Her voice went tinny. "Can you hear us? You're on the speaker."

"Yep. Hi, Dad."

"Hello, Rafa." His father's rich baritone echoed down the line. "How was the flight? I see it's eighty-five in Sydney today. I hope you're appreciating it, because New Jersey is cold as a…cold thing."

Rafa laughed, imagining his mother's glare. Then his smile faded, and he swallowed down a swell of nerves as butterflies went to town in his belly. "Actually, I'm not in Australia."

Silence. Then his mother spoke. "What do you mean? Where are you?"

"In Laguna Beach. I changed my flight so I had a stopover in LA. Not just a connection."

"All right," she said. He could imagine his parents exchanging glances and having a silent conversation. "Are you visiting your sister? Neither of you mentioned this."

"I did crash with her on Friday night." Digging his toes into the cold sand, he inhaled and exhaled deeply, his shoulders almost brushing his ears before dropping back down. "Now I'm with Shane Kendrick."

More silence. This time it continued.

Rafa went on. "Uh, he was the Secret Service agent who—"

"We know who he is," Ramon said tightly. "What are you doing there with him?"

With his free hand, Rafa tugged on the strings of his hoodie. "We're...well, I came to see him. He transferred out here after the kidnapping. I...I have feelings for him, and I wanted to see if he felt the same." It was true enough. Minus the fact that anything had happened in DC.

"Feelings," Camila echoed.

"Um, yeah. I know this must be surprising to you. It surprised us too."

"Us. There's an 'us'?" Ramon asked. "He returns your...feelings?"

Rafa gripped the strings, pulling them tight. "He does. And I know he's older than me—"

"Yes, he certainly is!" Camila's voice rose. "Exactly how old is this man?"

"Forty, but it doesn't matter. We really care about each other."

Camila sputtered. "It most certainly matters!"

"Rafael, I want an honest answer," Ramon commanded. "Did this man do anything to take advantage of you while he was on your detail?"

"No! I swear, he didn't." It was the truth—Shane had never taken advantage. "Look, I understand why you'd think that, but it's not like that. I'm not a child. I'm twenty-two now. You guys were practically married at my age. I know what I want. And I want to be with him."

His mother exhaled sharply. "So you're abandoning your plans for Australia? The Cordon Bleu? Throwing away your dreams?"

"No! Of course not. Shane's coming with me. He quit his job. He's going to do security work down there."

After another silence, his father asked, "How long has this been going on? How long did you plan this without saying a word to us?"

"We didn't plan anything. Honestly. I showed up yesterday, and we talked, and we realized we both want the same thing. To make a go of this. To make a go of being together. Maybe it won't work, but if we don't try, we'll never know. And I know I'd always regret it."

"So you realized these feelings for each other while he was protecting you," Ramon said.

"Well…yeah. And after the kidnapping, he transferred because he knew it was a conflict of interest. He knew we couldn't see each other anymore. He's not…I understand why you'd think he's taking advantage or whatever, but he's a good man. And he really cares about me. He…he loves me. And I love him."

His heart thumped as another silence hung between them.

"Darling." Camila sounded pained. "I think it's likely very normal for people to develop strong feelings after experiencing a life-and-death incident. But…"

"It's not that, Mom. It really isn't. I know it's weird for you— me actually dating a guy."

"A *man*, Rafa!" she exclaimed.

"But I'm a man too, Mom. I'm not a kid anymore."

She sighed. "We've tried very hard to support you and encourage you to be happy. We really have, darling. But you should be seeing boys your own age!"

"It's not what I want. Last semester I tried it. I met other guys at school. But I don't want anyone else. I love Shane. I *love* him."

After another pause, Ramon said, "Well. This was certainly not the phone call we were expecting."

"I know. I'm sorry to spring it on you. But I needed to see if he even wanted to be with me." A powerful wave washed higher on the beach, and Rafa jumped back just in time to avoid a soaking. He smiled to himself. "And he does want to be with me. I just...I can't tell you how happy I am."

His father said, "Things can be wonderful when they're brand new. But when the shine wears off..."

"Then we'll see what happens," he insisted. "We love each other, and we're going to make it work. We'll never know if we don't try. Don't you remember when you were first in love?"

"Vaguely," Camila replied dryly. "But love is hard work, Rafa."

"I know. But I'm not going to give up on something I want— something that makes me so, so happy—just because it won't always be easy. You didn't teach us to be quitters. You always said anything worth having is worth hard work."

His father's voice had a smile in it. "I suppose you've got us there." He sighed. "And I don't suppose we really have a choice but to accept this."

Grinning, Rafa danced away from another wave, not caring that his feet were like ice now. "You said you were worried about me going to Australia alone. Well, not only will I have company, but he'll keep me safe too."

"He'd damn well better," Camila snapped.

Rafa laughed. "Language, Mom."

"Yes, yes. When are you going to Sydney now?"

"Soon. Shane just has a few things to wrap up."

"Perhaps we should visit California before you go," Ramon said. "We can get to know this man better."

Rafa sucked in a breath. "Oh, uh, I don't think there's time."

He imagined sitting across from his parents in Shane's living room, the Secret Service lingering outside while they make awkward conversation. *Shit, we'll go tomorrow if we can.* "Besides, aren't you guys doing that event for the foundation?"

"We are," Camila said. "You're off the hook. For now. Australia isn't really so far away."

"That would be great if you came to visit." At least he'd have a couple months to plan awkward conversation topics. Glancing over his shoulder, Rafa saw Shane on the porch with a mug. He lifted it and nodded toward the house. "I've got to go. But I'll talk to you guys soon, okay? I'll give you my new itinerary when I have it. And thanks. For not completely freaking out and stuff."

"Oh, we're completely freaking out, dear. But you're lucky. Having Adriana as a daughter taught us roll with the punches, so we'll cope with this too. No matter what, we love you. We'll speak to you soon. This conversation isn't over." She added, "And tell Shane Kendrick we'll have him killed if he hurts you."

Rafa smiled. "I love you guys."

Turning off his phone, he slipped it into his hoodie pocket and hurried back to where Shane waited with coffee and a soft, slow morning kiss.

"THAT'S IT. PADDLE. Paddle!"

Freezing water splashed his face as Rafa moved his arms in his new wetsuit. The wave was breaking, and he needed to catch it at just the right time and pop up into a crouch. It swelled beneath him, and he pushed up, trying to use his core and get his feet under him—

Tumbling through the white water, he squeezed his eyes shut and let the wave take him in. His rented board thumped into him as he found his feet. Coughing, he watched as Shane rode in the next wave, balancing so easily and carving out a line right to him. Shane hopped off his board and scooped it up, shaking water off his head.

"Okay?" Shane squeezed Rafa's shoulder.

"Uh-huh." He shivered. The sun was already setting and it wasn't even five o'clock yet.

"Want to quit for today?"

"No. One more time."

On their bellies on their boards, they paddled out. His shoulders burned, and Rafa knew his arms would ache in the morning, but he was determined. They'd spent most of the morning on the sand while he practiced popping up from his stomach into the crouch. St. Ann's beach had smaller waves, which Shane had insisted on. Earlier there had been some local body boarders, but as the afternoon waned, they almost had the place to themselves.

When they'd paddled past the reef, they sat on their boards, straddling them as they waited for a wave. Shane squinted toward the horizon. "Might be a minute."

Rafa breathed in the salty air as he peered around, closing his eyes as he bobbed on the water. "These beaches must be packed in the summer, huh?"

"Yep. I like it in the winter. Even if the water's a little nippy."

"Just a little." Rafa rubbed his numb hands together. "Guess we won't have that problem in Sydney." Excitement zipped through him. "I've been reading about all the beaches. Maybe we can find a place near the water. Something like your friend's house here if we can afford it. Which we probably can't, I know. But it would be so amazing to be able to see the ocean and hear the waves. Don't you think?"

Shane smiled softly. "Yeah. I think that would be pretty damn great." Reaching out, he tugged on Rafa's hand and pulled him close, giving him a briny kiss. Then he glanced over his shoulder. "Here it comes. Paddle! It's yours!"

Adrenaline surging through him, Rafa got on his stomach and paddled, feeling the power of the ocean gathering below him. All around him. *In* him. With a shout, he popped up into a crouch, thrusting his arms out for balance as the wave lifted him.

For a glorious moment, he was doing it. He was up on his board, and he was *surfing*, the roar of the ocean filling his senses.

Then he wavered wildly and tipped over the front of his board, slamming down to the sandy bottom and scraping along until he was deposited in the shallows. Rolling onto his back, he laid there with his board nudging him, another little wave carrying him almost to shore. Shivering, he blinked at the streak of orange across the pale blue wash of the sky.

He heard splashing. "Rafa!" Then Shane was kneeling over him, his face pinched in concern and his hands tight on Rafa's shoulders.

He grinned. "I did it, Shane. Did you see?"

Exhaling sharply, Shane's face melted into a smile. "I saw." He brushed back Rafa's wet curls. "You're first wave, and so many more to come." He leaned over and kissed him. "Now let's get out of these wet clothes, hmm? And I believe someone promised to make me dinner. From what I understand, he's an incredible chef already." Standing with the setting sun ablaze behind him, Shane reached down his hand.

Rafa took it, and he was never letting go.

THE END

Read about Rafa and Shane's new life together in the conclusion of the *Valor* duology!

Test of Valor

They're free of the White House, but can their forbidden romance survive in the real world?

With his father no longer president, twenty-two-year-old Rafa Castillo can finally be with ex-Secret Service agent Shane Kendrick. Shane's given up his career for Rafa, a move his fellow agents question the sanity and morality of. Eager to get away from the questions and judgement, Rafa and Shane are building a new life together in Australia. Though Shane struggles with nightmares and his over-protective instincts while Rafa fights his own insecurity, they love each other more than ever.

Now they just have to get through a visit from the former president and first lady.

Rafa's parents certainly don't approve of his romance with forty-year-old Shane, and they're determined to make him see reason. They don't see how their son could possibly be happy settling down with an older man, and they question Shane's motives. Shane and Rafa just want a normal life together—but when they must suddenly battle for survival, they fight to prove their fierce love can withstand any threat.

This gay romance from Keira Andrews is the conclusion of the *Valor* duology. It features a May-December age difference, sex on the beach, and of course a happy ending.

Afterword

Thank you so much for reading *Valor on the Move*, and I hope you enjoyed the first half of Rafa and Shane's story. I'd be grateful if you could take a few minutes to leave a review on Goodreads (or wherever you'd like!). Just a couple of sentences can really help other readers discover the book. Thank you!

Join the free gay romance newsletter!

My (mostly) monthly newsletter will keep you up to date on my latest releases and news from the world of LGBTQ romance. You'll also get access to exclusive giveaways, free reads, and much more. Join the mailing list today and you're automatically entered into my monthly giveaway.

Here's where you can find me online:
Website
www.keiraandrews.com
Facebook
facebook.com/keira.andrews.author
Facebook Reader Group
bit.ly/2gpTQpc
Instagram
instagram.com/keiraandrewsauthor
Goodreads
bit.ly/2k7kMj0
Amazon Author Page
amzn.to/2jWUfCL
Twitter
twitter.com/keiraandrews
BookBub
bookbub.com/authors/keira-andrews

Read more age-difference and adventure from Keira Andrews!

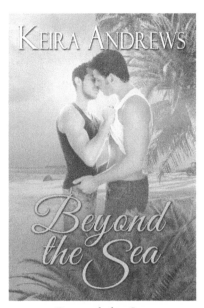

Beyond the Sea

Two straight guys. One desert island.

Even if it means quitting their boy band mid-tour, Troy Tanner isn't going to watch his little brother snort his future away after addiction destroyed their father. On a private jet taking him home from Australia, he and pilot Brian Sinclair soar above the vast South Pacific. Brian lost his passion for flying—and joy in life— after a traumatic crash, but now he and Troy must fight to survive when a cyclone strikes without warning.

Marooned a thousand miles from civilization, the turquoise water and white sand beach look like paradise. But although they can fish and make fire, the smallest infection or bacteria could be deadly. When the days turn into weeks with no sign of rescue, Troy and Brian grow closer, and friendship deepens into desire.

As they learn sexuality is about more than straight or gay and discover their true selves, the world they've built together is thrown into chaos. If Troy and Brian make it off the island, can their love endure?

This LGBT romance from Keira Andrews features bisexuality, finding love where you least expect it, eating way too many coconuts, and of course a happy ending.

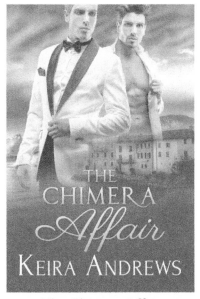

The Chimera Affair

His mission was seduction—not falling in love.

When young Sebastian Brambani meets a sexy and exciting older man, he's easily seduced. But for spy Kyle Grant, it's all business. Sebastian is simply a pawn in Kyle's mission to acquire a dangerous chemical weapon from Sebastian's criminal father. Kyle's life is his work for a shadowy international agency protecting the world from evil, and he can't worry about what will happen to Sebastian when the job is done.

Sebastian's unwitting role in Kyle's plan is the last straw for his ruthless father, who has been embarrassed by his gay son for the last time. But when Kyle discovers Sebastian could be the key to finding the deadly Chimera, he rescues him from a hired hitman and fights to keep him alive. Can a hardened spy and naïve college student take down a criminal kingpin, stay one step ahead of the killers on their trail—and fight the scorching attraction between them?

This gay romance from Keira Andrews features sexy spies, an age difference, a sheltered and passionate virgin, action and adventure, and of course a happy ending.

BONUS STORY INCLUDED: *The Argentine Seduction*, a sequel for Kyle and Sebastian featuring unexpected jealousy, protectiveness, and a dangerous mission in the simmering heat of Buenos Aires. (And of course a happy ending!)

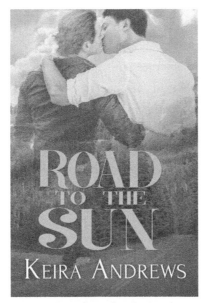

Road to the Sun

A desperate father. A lonely ranger. Unexpected love that can't be denied.

Jason Kellerman's life revolves around his eight-year-old daughter. Teenage curiosity with his best friend led to Maggie's birth, her mother tragically dying soon after. Insistent on raising his daughter himself, he was disowned by his wealthy family and has worked tirelessly to support Maggie—even bringing her west on a dream vacation. Only twenty-five, Jason hasn't had time to even think about romance. So the last thing he expects is to question his sexuality after meeting an undeniably attractive park ranger.

Ben Hettler's stuck. He loves working in the wild under Montana's big sky, but at forty-one, his love life is non-existent, his ex-boyfriend just married and adopted, and Ben's own dream of fatherhood feels impossibly out of reach. He's attracted to Jason, but what's the point? Besides the age difference and skittish Jason's lack of experience, they live thousands of miles apart. Ben wants more than a meaningless fling.

Then a hunted criminal takes Maggie hostage, throwing Jason and Ben together in a desperate and dangerous search through endless miles of mountain forest. If they rescue Maggie against all odds, can they build a new family together and find a place to call home?

Road to the Sun is a May-December gay romance from Keira Andrews featuring adventure, angst, coming out, sexual discovery, and of course a happy ending.

About the Author

After writing for years yet never really finding the right inspiration, Keira discovered her voice in gay romance, which has become a passion. She writes contemporary, historical, paranormal, and fantasy fiction, and—although she loves delicious angst along the way—Keira firmly believes in happy endings. For as Oscar Wilde once said, "The good ended happily, and the bad unhappily. That is what fiction means."

Find out more about Keira's books and sign up for her (mostly) monthly gay romance e-newsletter:

keiraandrews.com

Made in the USA
Coppell, TX
01 February 2022

72812856R00166